The Bay Street Boys and Girls Sporting Club

The Bay Street Boys and Girls Sporting Club

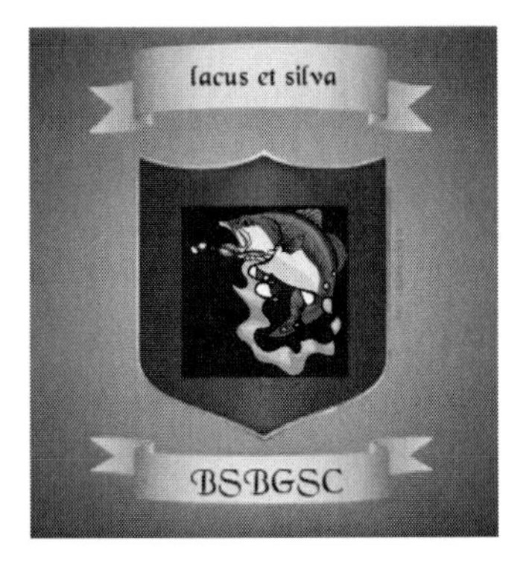

The Bay Street Boys and Girls Sporting Club

by

W W Walton

This is a work of fiction

William Warren Walton
277 Hearst St
North Bay, ON P1B 8Z2
Canada

Billwalton38@gmail.com

ISBN: 978-1-71674-505-1

Cover and photos: Bill

The Bay Street Boys and Girls Sporting Club Formerly the BSBSC

Introduction

Six men who worked in the Bay/Queen Street area of Toronto founded the Bay Street Boys Sporting Club in 2001. They met at least once a week at the Disraeli Club tavern after work to plan a sports outing, most often fishing and occasionally hunting, or in winter, to watch the Maple Leafs endeavour to play NHL calibre hockey. Those of the men who were married seemed to have understanding wives. The wives sometimes planned their own outings, but seldom fished with the men. The men were open-minded about most things but the thought of having women join the BSBSC never crossed their minds until Amelia and Geraldine won the Lake Simcoe Bass Tournament in 2005. By coincidence, they were the new owners of the *Bites and Bucks* sporting goods store just off Yonge Street south of Bloor. Alexander, the lawyer who at that time was involved in work relating to Pay Equity, suggested that the Club ought to expand and become the Bay Street Boys and Girls Sporting Club. The motion to adopt the change passed unanimously. *Bites and Bucks* immediately offered a 10% discount for all Club members. The Bay Street Boys spend considerable discretionary sums on tackle and outdoor gear.

These stories are supposedly in chronological order; however because my filing system evolved from paper to digital, from my desk draw to my computer, from windows 2.0 to Windows 8 (some stories may even reside on a Cloud somewhere) I may have incorrectly entered the dates on some of the older files. Some of the stories may have appeared in published collections when I entered them in writing contests, or passed them around to members of the Club for their reading entertainment. Please take their veracity with a grain of salt.

BSBGSC Index page

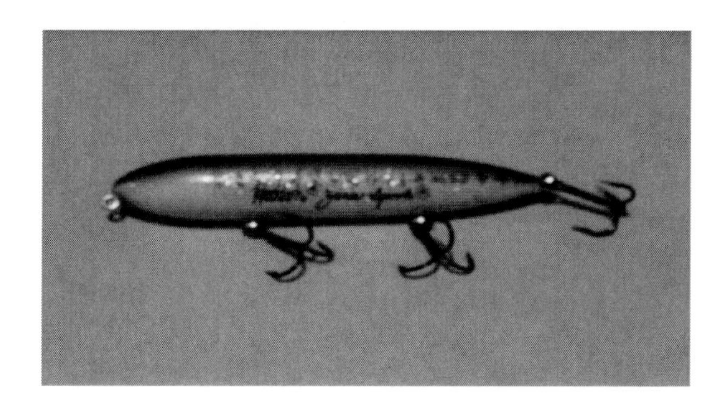

Muskie Bites Woman
(2001 & 2015)

"Hi, Bill," Katherine said when I answered my cell phone. I have a special ring tone for members of the Club – a few notes from the William Tell overture. Isn't technology great?

"Hi, Kate, How was your week up north?"

"It was wonderful. Amanda and I had a fantastic time. We'll tell you all about it on Friday at the Disraeli. I just wanted to tell you I met Ervin Peltier and he said to say hello to you and the other men."

"Ervin Peltier – that name sounds familiar . . ." I said.

"He's the part owner and head guide at the Lodge on the French River where we were last week."

The memory connections clicked even though it had been some 15 years since we met Ervin. "Oh, yeah. How is he? How was the Lodge?" I said.

"He's doing well, but they are closing the Lodge."

"Oh. That's too bad – I liked the place. Great fall fishing in the West Arm. I often thought we should have gone back . . ."

"Is that story true – about the Muskie biting Alice – whoever she was?"

"How did you hear about that?" I asked.

"I was reading an old newspaper clipping on their notice board when Ervin came by so I asked him about it. Ervin said he wanted to call the North Bay Nugget to set the paper right about the muskellunge biting their tourist. It took some persuading, however his partner finally prevailed and they kept the story alive. He said to Ervin that they could live off the headline for years."

"I never saw the newspaper story, Kate. Tell me about it," I said.

"Well, the story mentioned a group from Toronto called the Bay Street Boys so I explained to Ervin that Amanda and I were part of the old Club now called the Bay Street Boys and Girls Sporting Club. We would be most interested in hearing anything about the old Club members."

The past can come back to haunt you, I thought.

"Ervin said they were closing the Lodge for the last time this fall. He said I might be interested in learning what happened on August 28, 2001. The fishing is still good, down in the West Arm area of Lake Nipissing, but the camp relied on the American Plan system and the new rules by the Health Ministry simply made it impossible for them to turn a profit as the Government forced them to meet the new food service and lodging regulations.

"Over the years, they upgraded the cottages, even put in private washrooms in each unit; they kept the communal showers since the health people allowed them to drain the grey water into a holding pond, not the septic bed. Three years ago, they put in satellite TV and the internet connection tower. However, installing a $40,000 walk-in freezer and fire-proofing the cooking area simply did not fit the bottom line of an old seasonal fishing camp. It was bad enough keeping sales tax records on chocolate bars, playing cards, jointed-pikies, and Rapalas but the new HST on video rentals was just another straw they did not need. So they were closing the Lodge. They were selling the island where the Lodge stood for almost 80 years and they can both retire on the proceeds.

"If you do not remember, Ms Westcott," Ervin said to me, "the last week of August in 2001 was a scorcher. Folks talk about the dog days of summer and this was a prime example. A large high system had settled over all of Northern Ontario. The sky was the same dusky blue every day, the winds calm. The temperature hovered in the 80-degree range during the daytime and only dropped into the 60's at night. It was hot and sticky in daytime, and not much better at night.

"The fish stopped biting. I could not find the muskellunge and I was using the old standby tale about the Muskie losing their teeth at this time of year as an explanation for the lack of action on the lake. The perch were still biting but the Bay Street Boys were looking for Muskie, not perch. Not even the promise of a catch of walleye would do for them. Despite the searing heat, they cast, they trolled and even bobber fished for that one big muskellunge.

"The Bay Street Boys, as I remember them, were a group of middle-aged hotshots who fished hard, drank hard, played hard and left great tips for the women who cleaned the cottages and served the meals. Young Perry, who hustled the boats and bait, did very well the last week in August.

For reasons that slowly became clear, a woman came with the six men in 2001. She was the new girl of one of the men and she certainly did not belong in a fish camp. I think she was worried that her boyfriend, I think his name was Jason and he worked in Television, was heading up north for a week of debauchery, not Muskie fishing, and she insisted that she accompany him.

"As I recall, the thought of touching a slimy fish was too much for her. She thought our dining room was boorish because the cedar tables did not have tablecloths, only oilcloths. Heaven knows what she thought of our flatware that was made in China. Our food was too plain, the mattresses too soft and the water in the Lake too cold for swimming. The men played poker too late into the night and the one late-season mosquito in the camp bit her. Her name was Alice and she was quite pretty, in a blonde sort of way, especially sunbathing on our dock when the men were out throwing nylon line around underwater stumps, lily pad roots, and tree limbs growing too close to shore.

"Despite her attractive looks, she finally ticked off everyone in the Lodge. She even lost all sympathy from me, on the evening of August 27, when I warned her about dangling her feet off the dock in the evening. She might attract a big Muskie that could bite her. When she told me to "piss off" even I was offended. I have a little native blood in me and I held my tongue when I normally might not have. But my native blood loves a good joke too.

"August 28 was really hot. The still air was heavy with the taste of wood smoke from faraway forest fires. The sun took on an orange glow as it lowered in the evening sky, bronzing the ripples around the dock. The Bay Street Boys, tired from another hot frustrating day in the boats, decided to sit out on the long porch of the lodge after dinner, sipping cognac, smoking cigars and talking of years gone by when the Muskie were biting. Alice, as was now her habit, went to the dock to escape the cigar smoke and dangled her feet in the cool water. Unseen, sixty feet away, I pulled the snorkel over my mouth and slipped into the water. Young Perry, on cue, wandered down to the dock and repeated the story about the Muskie biting people.

"Even the men on the porch were telling Alice to watch out. In defiance, she splashed her feet more vigorously. Waiting under the dock, I took a deep breath, dove and then grabbed her ankle with the rough leather glove I wore. I pulled her off the dock, tugged firmly enough to scratch her foot and then released her. Young Perry jumped in to save her and the fact that he was fully clothed added veracity to the story reported by Alice's boyfriend to the North Bay Nugget newspaper the next day. I guess that Jason fellow just could not resist a good story – him being in the TV business. Alice insisted on bandages for the little scratches but that made for a better photograph in the newspaper."

"Yes, Ms Westcott, we lived off that story for many years. "Muskie Bites Woman" is a good headline. It has been on our notice board at the Lodge for 15 years," Ervin told me.

"I wish I had a copy of that story for my files," I said to Catherine. "I wonder if the newspaper has it in their archives."

"Yes, that would be interesting," Kate said. "I must ask Jason about the story of the fish biting his girlfriend. I gather she and Jason are no longer an item?"

"No, the next day she dragged Jason back to Toronto – she wanted her doctor to look at the bite even though I think Ervin did an excellent job of disinfecting it and bandaging it. Jason had been

John's fishing partner so the last day young Perry fished with John. They caught a 44-inch muskellunge. Did you and Amanda have any luck?"

"Amanda caught a 20 pound pike and I caught a muskie – 45 inches long! I caught it casting off the dock, just at dusk when Ervin said I should try a floating Zara Spook."

The Moose Hunt

(2002)

Stepladder Bill

I was sitting in my office on a bright warm Wednesday afternoon early in October, trying to work out a computer program that would print out more of the useless data that Statistics Canada requires every month, when the phone rang.

"Bill, it's Alex."

"Hi, Big Al. What's up?" I asked.

"There are a couple of guys I work with here at the office who are looking for 3 or 4 guys to make up a moose-hunting party. Are you interested?"

Alex knows that I only hunt with a camera but that I do enjoy the stalking of game and the camaraderie of the hunt camp. An evening of poker or Liar's Dice is a pleasant way to pass the hours after a good dinner. Unless you are losing your shirt.

"Yeah, maybe. When?"

"This weekend - I know it is short notice but let's meet after work and I'll give you the details."

That meant a meeting of the BSBSC at the Disraeli Tavern. I rang my wife and said I'd be a little late for dinner and got clearance for the weekend. The Mother-in-law was supposed to visit this weekend so my absence would not be noticed. Maybe it would even be appreciated.

Pierre, John and Alex were already at the Disraeli when I arrived. It turned out that these fellows from the Ministry of Housing had a nice camp that we could drive to, right on the edge of the moose hunting zone west of Algonquin Park. There were three men from Alex's work plus the four of us. That made six hunters since Pete does not hunt but would be our cabin man and chef.

Well, five hunters with rifles, me with my 35mm camera that was mounted on the stock of an old Mossberg .410 shotgun. Where the others had 2 and 4 power scopes, I had a Nikon 55 x 300 zoom lens. It was becoming difficult to find 400 ASA 35mm film as most amateur photographers were moving to digital cameras. My cell phone had a camera but the quality was poor. I would be embarrassed to take a picture of a moose with it. The moose would likely be embarrassed also.

Alex said these men were all experienced hunters and were very careful in the bush. He did mention that one of them, Tony, was known as Mr. Clean, a nick name that he had picked up from his meticulous ways around the office. He was also pretty tight with a dollar, but generally a good chap once you got to know him.

We divided up the pre-camp chores and I drew the grocery shopping. Pierre would call me tomorrow with the detailed list of all the things he needed to feed seven men from Friday evening until Sunday noon. Pete is a gourmet cook so I was prepared for some unusual items.

My moose hunting days ended right after I shot my first moose back in 1995. It was a good bull, with a handsome rack that measured 72 inches from tip to tip. I got him one misty morning just as he came down to the lake to drink. He was a magnificent beast and as soon as I had pulled the trigger on my old Lee Enfield, I wished that I hadn't. Now I had my Nikon on a mount that Alex had made for me. The telephoto lens can be focused from a little rubber wheel on the fore stock; the trigger, using a fine cable, activates the shutter release. It's the kind of delicate work that Alex is known for. I have taken some very interesting shots with this set up and have not killed a creature with it yet.

Pierre's shopping list ranged from New York cut steaks with fresh Cremini mushrooms for Friday night, Tilsit cheese, capers, apples (a dozen McIntosh for eating and a dozen Spy apples for the pie), and bay leaves. He would use the frozen pie crusts as it was not worth the effort of bringing pie-baking ingredients for such a short visit. I was a little rushed that Friday morning at work so I hurried through the shopping list hoping that I had not missed anything.

The camp was the only cottage on a small lake that we reached after bumping over the last few miles of road in Alex's Suburban truck. We had to walk the last 500 yards because a beaver had flooded part of the road. There was plenty of room in the cabin, with bunks for ten, a large dining table, two card tables and several large stuffed chairs. There was a propane refrigerator and stove and a hand pump for water on the counter by a sink. There were Coleman lanterns for light and air-tight stove for warmth. It was a very cozy place for the weekend. After a dose of Mistovan the outdoor Biffy did not smell too bad.

And there were fresh moose tracks on the beach!

Breakfast, ham and eggs with pancakes on the side, was ordered for 6 a.m. with hunters ready to go to their watches at 6:30. We were split into two groups, with Jean and Tony, Alex's friends, being the guides. They gave me the moose horn. It was a genuine birch bark horn and my practice the night before met with approval of the hunters.

In the morning Tony took me to a point on the lake and left me with instructions to start calling at 7:30, right after sunrise. The men would have all been in their places by then for half an hour, long enough for the bush to settle down after them tramping out to the watches in the cool frosty, morning air.

I found an old pine log to sit on, got my camera ready and pulled my wool jacket up around my ears to keep warm. A blue jay spotted me and squawked a few times but when I refused to acknowledge it or offer it a peȧnut, it flew off to bother someone else. At the prescribed time I started calling moose. After several minutes an answer came echoing back across the lake. I replied a couple of times but after listening carefully to the sound coming from the far shore I decided that it must be another hunter calling to me. He did not sound very realistic. In the next hour I called again a couple of times, but by this late in the morning, the call was not likely to work. Moose like to get their mating finished early in the morning so they can spend the rest of the day munching on twigs and lily pad roots.

The plan was to stay at our watches until around eleven o'clock when the guides would pick us up. Tim, the camp owner, was going to 'dog' around to see if he could get some action in the swampy area to the west of us, perhaps chasing a moose out to one of the watches. The sun broke through the morning mist about ten a.m. and the fall warmth was very relaxing after the chilly early hours. I ate my peanut butter sandwich, took off my heavy jacket with the Hunter's Orange covering, and made myself comfortable, keeping a good watch along the lakeshore.

I must have dozed off because I was suddenly aware of the water sloshing a few feet away. I opened my eyes to see the grand-daddy of all moose standing about twenty feet from me. It was looking at me.

Bull moose tend to be a little unpredictable in the rutting season. My Nikon, even at 20 feet and set on action mode was not going to stop him. There was a tall birch tree about three jumps away-with handy branches.

The moose must have read my mind because he gave a snort and started towards me. I was faster than a red squirrel with a cat after it. In two jumps I was at the tree, scrambling up through the branches until I was about 15 feet from the ground. The moose paused and then decided to scare me to death by butting against the tree, standing on his back legs, thrashing about with his huge antlers. I did the only thing I could. I hung on and yelled for help.

Tony heard me and from a few hundred yards away, fired two shots into the air, yelling that he was coming. The moose headed in the other direction, but not until he trampled my jacket and the moose horn. He finished them off by deftly hooking his antlers under them and depositing them in the lake. I was just climbing down from the tree when Tony arrived, all out of breath from running to my rescue.

"What's wrong . . . what happened?" He panted.

"Bull Moose," I said, fishing my torn jacket out of the water. The birch-bark horn was ruined.

"You mean . . .?" Tony started to ask.

"Yeah - put me right up the tree!" I said, examining the rip in my pants and new shirt.

When he stopped laughing and caught his breath he said, "I got to hand it to you - it takes guts to hunt with only a camera, but maybe you should bring a stepladder the next time . . . it'd be a lot easier on the clothes!"

The Bay Leaves

We were back at the camp by noon without a shot having been fired by any of the other hunters. "Stepladder Bill", as Tony was now calling me, was the butt of a number of what I thought were rather harsh comments. I was tempted to destroy the film in my camera lest it accidentally fall into the hands of some unscrupulous member of the BSBSC, but I did want to see for myself what those shots from the tree were like. Still, I could picture in my mind Nick the bartender at the Disraeli showing some candid shots of a birch tree and the south end of that north-bound moose. Ah well, that's part of the thrill of hunting - living down your mistakes.

Pierre had prepared a large platter of sandwiches with cheese and dill pickles with freshly baked apple pie and cheddar cheese slices for dessert. It was a real treat to have a gourmet cook at a hunt camp. Pierre had already befriended a chipmunk and a pair of whiskey jacks. He seemed to be enjoying his weekend.

"What will we do without a moose call for tomorrow morning?" asked Alex as we drank our camp tea.

The remains of the old call were examined and pronounced beyond repair. The pieces of birch bark were hung on the wall with a note explaining the event as a reminder.

"Why don't we try the water trick?" suggested John, "We know there is a bull moose in the area."

"Yeah," Tony agreed, "that's probably our best bet."

"What's with the water?" Pierre asked from the kitchen. John explained, "You get a bucket of water and slowly pour it into the lake. It sounds as if it is a female moose peeing and this attracts the male moose."

Pierre thought they were pulling his leg. "Com'on guys, that doesn't make sense."

"Sure it does. The cow moose will only urinate in the water when she's replying to a bull in rut - when she's in heat. The bull hears this - you know how sound travels across the water - and he comes over, all full of romance, if you know what I mean."

I was going to join in Pierre's defense when I recalled that I had answered a call of nature just before getting comfortable that morning. I did not mention that I had peed in the lake.

The afternoon hunt was organized and we got ready to go out into the woods again. "Hey, Bill, did you get those bay leaves I asked for?" asked Peter.

I had probably forgotten them in my rushed shopping but I had long ago learned to make excuses for my shopping. Martha gives me a written list with a pencil and I can still forget something. "Maybe they fell out in the truck. I'll take a look for them," I offered.

"Okay. I need them for the spaghetti sauce. Just pick them up on your way back. I'd get them myself, but I'm afraid of being treed by a moose!"

On that happy note we left camp for the afternoon hunt. I knew darn well that I had forgotten those bay leaves. Oh well. We hunted all afternoon, walking around the south part of the lake, just poking along, nobody was too serious about seeing a moose. I got a couple of good shots of a ruffed grouse and one of a rabbit as it bounded away.

We arrived back at camp at about 3:30 having had enough hunting for that day. Tony collected all the ammunition and checked all the guns to make sure they were empty. Once the bar was declared open, the gunpowder/alcohol rule was enforced. All the ammo was locked in a small chest.

"Hey, Stepladder, you've got to unload yours too," Pierre called from the sink where he was preparing some snacks.

"Yeah," put in Alex. "We wouldn't want to lose any of those shots you took while you were perched in the birch tree."

It sounded like blackmail in the making but popular demand had its way. I took the film out of the camera and Tony locked it in the chest.

"Did you look for those bay leaves, Stepladder?"

"No, I forgot. I'll go look right now," I said. "What do they do, anyway?"

"Ah, my spaghetti sauce de Pietro is not the same without them. All true Italian sauces have bay leaves in them. It's just not the same without it!"

I checked in my duffle bag to get one of the small plastic bags I always carry to pack my film in when I travel. I tried to picture what a bay leaf looked like and just as I reached the truck, I remembered that they were the leaves my wife puts in the cupboards to keep the flour beetles and their ilk out of the perishables.

Now a willow leaf is a little narrower than your standard bay leaf, but the shape is close. Those on the ground were about the same olive green colour. I found a spot where nothing but a rabbit had walked and I rummaged around until I had my little plastic bag full. I tasted one to make sure it was not nauseous. Really, it was not that bad. Now all I had to do was find a way to get them into the pot without Pierre being able to inspect them.

"Hey, Pierre I found them," I said, holding up the bag. He was working on his pork cutlets and did not look up. The tomato sauce was already on the stove. "Do you want me to wash them for you?" I was thinking that Tony would not be comfortable with unwashed bay leaves.

"Wash them!" He yelped and muttered a few expletives that properly assessed my abilities as a gourmet cook. "Sacrament! - You don't wash bay leaves! You use them just as they are."

"Oh," I said, trying to sound repentant and as if I was willing to mend my ways, "Can I put them in the sauce for you?"

His hands were still sticky from handling the cutlets so he said, "Sure. Put in seven. Use the ones that are whole, not the broken ones. Give the sauce a good stir after you add the bay leaves."

"Okay," I said as I quickly added seven willow leaves to what may have been a great sauce. I stuffed the remaining evidence into my jacket pocket. "Anyone want a drink?" I asked, needing a bracer or two in case that sauce did not tum out the way the gourmet chef had planned. There's nothing worse-humored than a hunt camp cook whose reputed piece de resistance fails the grade.

How was I to know that willow leaves are a diuretic?

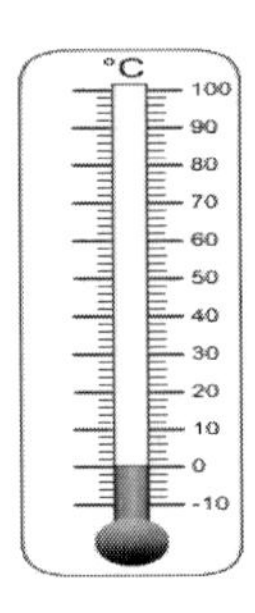

CELSIUS

(2002)

The unfortunate thing about watching American television's sporting shows is that some people believe what they see and hear. To me, they place too much emphasis on technology. If one was to believe those sports shows and their instructions on how to catch a fish, there would not be any fish left. Anywhere. Besides, they give all of their instructions in Imperial measure, something I find annoying now that I have almost conquered the Metric system. Yet I must admit that they occasionally do offer a valid tip on how to catch a striped bass in the Florida backwaters and perhaps the method shown for snagging an over-weight catfish in the Mississippi delta would yield results but when Jason and John started talking about how important the water temperature was to finding fish, I had to object.

"The only important thing about the temperature and fishing," I said, "Is whether it is warm enough to sit in a boat and fish."

"I agree with Bill," Big Al took up the debate. "Sure, fish like warmer water in the spring and cooler water in the summer, but that's only natural - they are trying to keep their body temperature at its most efficient level. As well as following their food - which is doing the same thing."

"Yes, I agree," Jason admitted, "but the trick is to find

where that warmer water is - whether it's twenty or fifteen feet down. If you're fishing at fifteen feet and the fish are all above that, you'll never catch them."

"That's right," John said. "This fellow on TV has charts to prove where the fish are at certain times of the year. He based them on his findings by recording the water temperature when he caught a fish. Now he has patented a Thermal Fish Spotter."

"And I suppose you guys have ordered one?" asked Pierre who is very unscientific about his fishing but generally catches more fish than the rest of us.

"Jason and I are going half each on one. It was $79.49 US dollars. It should be here before we go into THE LAKE," John replied.

THE LAKE is our secret fishing lake that we pretend no one else knows about. It's just a short portage off an old logging road where no one else seems to fish. We never say the name of the lake at the Disraeli tavern because there are potentially other fishermen at nearby tables.

I motioned to Nick the bartender to bring us another round of Upper Canada Pale Ale, our latest beverage of choice. If we had to get all the details on thermal layers and temperature charts, we had to have more beer. "Just how does this Thermal Fish Spotter work?" I asked as soon as our glasses were replenished.

"Well," Jason began, "fish prefer to feed in warming water, especially bass. They will swim around until they find a layer of warmer water, and then follow that thermal layer until they find food. Pike do the same but they aren't as particular as bass or walleye."

"Hey, I don't mind all this hi-tech garbage, but please do not refer to pickerel as 'walleyes'," Alex interrupted.

"Sorry, Alex," Jason continued, "What you do is take some water readings with the Spotter to get the general inversion layers chart of the lake, and then you fish in the warmest layer. If you don't have luck in that layer, you drop down to a colder layer and so on until you find where the fish are feeding."

"Does this thing take the temperature, or what?" Pierre asked.

"As I understand it," John said, "It reads the differences in temperature by a sonic refracting beam."

"Something like looking for submarines," Alex commented. I had a brief vision of Sean Connery and the Hunt for Red October, and nodded when Alex said, "Ping, ping."

"That's right! Exactly what it does! It finds all the big fish, too, I'll bet," Jason said.

"What if the fish moves from layer to layer, like a sub, trying to conceal itself in an inversion." Pierre asked just a little facetiously.

Jason, who was drinking a B-52 because he was on a girl-friend imposed diet, poked his straw down into his drink, saying that he was testing the temperature of his colourful, layered drink. He was at the strawberry pink layer.

"Let me see that," Pierre said. He took the glass and carefully placed the straw down to the first layer. He sipped. "Eh bien! Grand Mariner," he said. With great care he then immersed the tip of the straw down the inside of the glass so we could all see that he was in the second layer. He sipped again. "Ah ha! Bailey's!" Now he went right to the bottom of the glass and sipped again. "Yes," he proclaimed, "It's the specific gravity of the Kahlua – this drink is all the same temperature - about 12 degrees, I'd say. However it is the only the density of the Kahlua that has sent it to the bottom."

"Aw, come on, Pierre!" John said. "Those liqueurs are all different temperatures - no wonder they don't mix. Let me show you." He took the drink and rapidly stirred the mess with the straw. Sure enough, it became a disgusting colour, all the effect of layering destroyed. "See, I told you it was the temperature!" Before anyone could argue, he drank the evidence. "Just watch the real demonstration when we get to THE LAKE. We'll show you how to catch fish!"

As it turned out, John needed to change his days-off unexpectedly and had to miss the trip to THE LAKE. A rich prospect wanted to see a residential listing up on the Bridle Path. The commissions are great, but it does occasionally put a crimp in John's fishing plans. Jason conscripted Freddie to be his partner the weekend we headed out to fish at Deception Lake. Oops, gave the name away! (it is near Novar in case you want to try it).

Freddie is a little more practical when it comes to gadgets than John and Jason but he does tend to get carried away with his computerization of things. I am certain that he could have written a program to co-ordinate the Hummingbird fish finder and the Spotter. All he would need was a power-pack. As it was, he and Jason had to carry in a big 12 volt battery to run the Thermal Fish Spotter.

Freddie had missed the night at the Watering Hole when we discussed the thermal layers and the theory behind the Spotter, so on the way into the lake, Alex and I tried to give him all the advice he did not need. Jason had his instruction book and a graph pad, everything he needed to operate the Spotter. Actually, there were a few add-ons that the Spotter people sent with the kit. Things like a thermometer on a 20 pound test line that was to be lowered to the desired level, given a quick snap to set the mercury, and then retrieved to record the reading on a chart. The line attaching the thermometer was marked off in fathoms so the fisherman could get the exact depth of the water where the fish would be caught. The theory being that there had to be more than one fish in every deep hole in the lake bottom. There was also a 'sampler', a glass tube to collect water from the lake that could be used to test the PH factor. Alex kept snooping in the box to see what they had to measure the specific gravity of the water but I think Jason had forgotten that part of the kit at home.

It took Freddie and Jason a little while to get their gear stowed in the canoe, hook up the battery to the Spotter and get their charts organized in a handy place that did not interfere with paddling and casting. Alex and I waited just off shore for them, Alex taking a few practice casts and calling out the results . . . "Mark one", "3 degrees Celsius", "Mark Twain", "PH 6." "Whoa, fish on!" A smallmouth bass about ten inches long danced across the water and finally threw Alex's bait.

"Where did you catch him?" Jason called out from shore.

"Right about here," Alex replied, pointing to his lower lip.

"Okay, you smart-asses, you'll soon see how to catch fish," Jason said.

Arranging to meet at the little island for lunch, we headed out to work the lake, one canoe with high technology equipment, the other with plain ordinary tackle. Alex and I had caught and released a couple of small bass and had kept one pike, about a six pounder. By noon time, Jason and Freddie had the lake pretty well figured out. They had superb charts of thermals layers, accurate records of water temperatures at various points and depths, the PH factor of the lake well established at approximately 5.5 and no fish. But they were confident of the afternoon. I made a note of the warmest place they had found and intended to try that area before we left for the day. Freddie and Jason were deciding what lures were best, according to this Florida inventor's ideas. All indications were for flatfish, the same thing that Alex and I were trying, just from habit. It was about three in the afternoon when we had worked our way back to the warm spot I had seen on their chart. Jason and Freddie were already there, jig-fishing. "Any luck?" I asked.

"Yes, we just got a nice pickerel" Freddie said, pulling up the stringer for us to see a respectable blue pickerel about 50 cm long.

"What are you using?"

"Worm harness with a little red spinner." Jason said.

"How deep is it?" Alex asked,

"Two fathoms," Jason replied.

Alex looked at me.

"About three and half metres, Alex," I translated.

We fished for a couple of minutes without any action. "They must be hiding under a thermal layer," Alex muttered, just loud enough for Jason to hear.

"Yes, I'm going to let out another half fathom of line," Jason said.

"I wonder what the temperature is," Alex said. "Hey, Freddie, what's the temp at two fathoms?"

Freddie looked at his chart and answered before Jason could stop him from giving away the secret, "Forty two degrees."

Alex looked at me again.

"That's about 6 Celsius, Alex," 1 said.

"Yeah, I thought so. You would think they would know enough to send their instructions to Canada in our official language, wouldn't you?" Alex said. "Hey, Jason, did they send you a calculator to do the conversions into Celsius or are the fish still using Fahrenheit?"

Before he could reply, Jason had a strike. His line went zinging off the reel and the battle was joined. Freddie retrieved his line and got the net ready. After a few minutes, Jason brought a big pike to the surface. The great northern flashed away at the sight of the canoe and it was another couple of minutes before he was exhausted enough for Jason to bring him alongside. "Must be ten or twelve pounds," Freddie called to us.

"Looks about five kilos to me," I said to Alex.

Freddie had the netted fish into the canoe and was trying to get the hook free. "Are you going to keep him?" I asked Jason.

"No, I'll let him go. It's too big to eat." That was a line any of us seldom used.

"Hey, Freddie, before you throw him back, take his temperature, will you?" Big Al laughed.

"Go ahead and scoff," Jason said, "But I'll bet you there is another one, just at the same depth and temperature as that one!"

They released the big pike and Jason instructed Freddie to lower the thermometer to get an accurate reading for his next cast that was guaranteed to bring an even bigger pike.

Freddie was tiring of this constant temperature assessing.

"Jeez, Jason, it's said 52° all day. It'll be the same this time."

"Maybe not. That big pike might have been down deeper." Freddie cast out the temperature kit to the spot where Jason had caught the pike. He read off the line markings, "Two fathoms, three fathoms . . ."

"Five metres," I said.

The line was still going down. "Five fathoms . . ."

"There's something wrong," Jason said, "It can't be that deep . . ."

Freddie pulled back the cord. "Snagged," he said. Then, "Holy smokes!" The line went flying off the wooden spool.

"Hang onto it!" Jason yelled.

Freddie grabbed at the braided cord, yelped as the rough nylon cut his hand. He finally got the line stopped. Out of the water came that Great Northern Pike. I am sure it was the same one they had just released. The thermometer kit firmly in its mouth, it gave a couple of vicious shakes of its head to set the thermometer reading while dancing on its tail across the water, then threw the kit. It seemed to us that the pike threw the thermometer right at Jason and Freddie.

Nobody said a word as Freddie pulled the line back to the boat. The bleeding cut on his hand, while hardly bad enough to draw sharks, was dripping a watery red. He held up the device: “It says,” He used his finest stentorian voice, “52 degrees. The same at it has said all day! 52 bloody degrees!”

“Eleven Celsius” I whispered to Alex.

Turn Off the Lights
(2002)

It was a wet and windy stormy Tuesday last week when we met at the Disraeli, a tavern we claim as the BSBSC headquarters. As Pierre shook the rain from his overcoat he asked, “Did you guys see the notice that was with your last hydro bill?” We call our electricity bill the ‘hydro’ bill because for many years falling water generated the electric power in Ontario. It is a Canadian cultural thing since we generate most of our electricity by water. Some day we will get a ‘Wind’ bill or a ‘Solar’ bill or a ‘Atomic’ bill, but for now we all knew what a hydro bill was.

“No, I didn’t,” Alex said. “What was it?”

“Oh, just the new rates. Only a 5% hike in the cost of heating and lighting your house!”

“Five per cent!” Jason exclaimed. “They can’t do that to me. How, in heaven’s name, can anyone justify that kind of an increase?” The Ontario Government was privatizing Hydro Electricity in the province – supposedly in an effort to reduce costs. This did not auger well for citizens.

“Well, I suppose part of it is taxes, but that still leaves a hefty increase,” I said, wondering again why I had voted Conservative last election.

"Yes, and if I know our local Hydro Commission, they will blame it all on Ontario Hydro - or whatever they are calling themselves today," Freddie said. The recent restructuring of the old Ontario Hydro into generation and distribution companies had not changed the public perception of that old monopoly. "I haven't received any notice yet, but I guess it will be coming."

Freddie lives in the rural area just northeast of the City and gets his electricity directly from Ontario Hydro. "At least I will only have to pay for the power I use, not for the power you guys in the city waste," he said with a glint in his eye that I recognized as an opening gambit for today's discussion. I had wanted to arrange a weekend to fix up the ice-fishing hut, but I could see we were not going to get anywhere on that topic tonight. The hut needed a new stove to keep the small building on skids warm enough to play poker as we drank coffee and waited for a fish to swim underneath the shack.

"What do you mean, Freddie?" Jason asked.

"Well, take all those public buildings that burn power 24 hours a day - whether anyone is in them or not."

"Well, if you're talking about leaving the lights on, we don't," Big Al replied. "All the lights go off as soon as the cleaners finish working." Alex is a lawyer for the Provincial Government, however, because of his well-known handy-man skills, he is in charge of the Maintenance department in the office building where he works on University Avenue.

"Sure, the lights go off, but the air conditioning runs, the heat isn't turned down . . ."

"Wait a minute," John interrupted, "You know darn well that it would cost more to stop and start those air conditioners and heaters than it does to leave them on."

"Well, that's what the Electric Power people tell you. They are the same ones that say it would cost more to install automatic sensor switches on the street lights than you would save by turning the lights off. Personally, I don't believe that."

"I agree with you, Freddie," Pierre said as he signalled Nick the bartender for another jug of Upper Canada Rebellion. "There is absolutely no reason to have street lights burning all night."

"I thought they left them on to stop crime," Jason said.

"No, that's not so," Pierre replied. "Remember how all the schools used to leave the classroom lights on at Halloween? Ever see that now? No, somebody finally figured it out that if vandals wanted to be out and about at night, they would have to see where they were walking, what they were doing. If they carried a flashlight, the police could see them as easy as could be!"

"Gee, I never thought of that," John said. "So how come we haven't figured that out for street lights?"

"Well, that's a little different," I said. "You have people out walking on the streets who aren't criminals."

"At three o'clock in the morning?" Freddie asked with a grin.

"Well," I said.

"Look, Bill, how many times did you ever need the street lights after one in the morning?" Freddie asked.

"Other than the one time . . . not very often," I admitted.

"And you could have used a flashlight then, too, I'll bet."

"Except he was in no condition to be stopped by the police, if I remember the occasion," my friend Alexander said, referring to the night we held a stag party for one of our friends and we all walked home. I thought he had forgotten that by now. WUI is a seldom used part of the criminal code.

"But how much difference would turning off the street lights really make?" Jason asked Freddie.

Freddie paused while he refilled our glasses with the cool amber liquid. "It might make a big difference. I'm not talking just about our town, but all across the country. The power generators could cut back on their costs because of reduced demand, and in the case of the fossil-fuel fired operations, that could mean huge savings."

"As well as reducing air pollution," Pierre added.

"Right. The wear and tear on equipment would be another saving. Perhaps with some conservation like this, Ontario Power Generation could cut back on all their expansion plans - reduce some of that big debt load they are carrying."

"Most of that comes from those damn nuclear plants," John muttered.

"Well, I agree that if there was a better way to produce power, I would be against them too. But there just is no way we can meet the demand for electric power any other way," Pierre said.

"How about solar power? How about wind turbines?" Jason asked.

"Have you not noticed how little sun we've had this last spring?" Big Al asked. "All we've had is rain, rain, rain. No, we aren't in an area of the country where we could take advantage of sun, wind or the tides."

"So the answer has to be - cut back on consumption," I said. "I suppose every little bit helps. Like those new lights bulbs they are promoting . . ."

"Sure, but did you check out the price?" Jason asked. "The very people who need to save a few bucks on their hydro costs can't afford to buy the darn things!"

"I agree," Pierre said. "But there are lots of ways of saving - better insulation, keeping doors closed, turning down the heat a few degrees, as well as turning off lights."

Just then Nick arrived with a fresh jug of draft ale. I don't know how he does it, but Nick can pick up the thread of a conversation anywhere in the room and then add something to the chat as he delivers his brew. "You know I heard a fellow talking about his hydro bill the other day. He was saying how he had done all those insulation things that hydro recommends, but his bill didn't go down much. He lives in the country and the hydro people told him that it would not likely save him much money because he was in a 'billing block'.

"What's that?" Freddie, who lives in the country, asked.

"Well, apparently Hydro averages the usage costs over a service area and everyone pays for their hydro based on the rate for that area, not on what they use individually. So it didn't help much by insulating his house. In fact, the guy will probably never get his money back!" As usual, Nick then left us with another piece to the puzzle that might extend our visit to the Disraeli by a few more thirsty minutes.

"You know, I had heard something like that before, but I never believed it," Pierre said. "I'm going to check that out with Hydro. A person could pay more for his electricity just by having neighbours who are heavy users. There's got to be some way we can cut down on the amount of electric power we use!"

"Right. Turn off those street lights at one a.m. or sooner if it's a really cold night," Freddie said.

"What's the temperature got do with it?" John asked.

After we all explained, in exaggerated detail, how the current flowing through the metal lines meets resistance and gives off heat, loses its efficiency and generally is very wasteful, John suggested that the city should hire an Energy Auditor. This was met with an equal barrage of comments about increasing the costs to save money - a typical response of our government. Just then there was a building-shaking crack of thunder from the storm outside and the power failed.

In the total darkness of the Disraeli pub only one voice was heard: Freddie said, "Did somebody up there hear me and turn off the lights?"

Bambi

(2002)

By pure coincidence, Thelma, Freddie's wife, brought home a movie video that has had some far-reaching effects on our fall hunting expedition. Thelma claimed that it was their seven-year-old granddaughter, Melissa, who picked out the old Disney movie, but the rest of us in the Club knew Thelma too well. The granddaughters come to Thelma's home after school because both the parents work. Thelma has been after Freddie for a couple of years now to give up hunting or follow my example and hunt only with a camera.

The discussion at the Disraeli on the Tuesday evening before the hunt ended with some strict instructions to Freddie. "Freddie, you make sure you don't shoot at anything with spots on it," John warned.

"And no shooting at mommy deers, either," Jason said.

"Watch out for Thumper and Flower - they're Bambi's friends and they will spread the word if they see you pointing that big ol' gun at poor little Bambi!" said Big Al and then demonstrated how Thumper would hop around waving his finger ears, telling everyone to watch out for Big Bad Fred.

Every member of the Club was going hunting that fall at our new Hunt Camp we have up near Little Loon Lake. Actually, we have a very poor chance of getting a deer since Pierre comes along to do the camp cooking and play cards and I only hunt with my Nikon camera, although I do a fair imitation of a Basset hound for the fellows if I do happen to see a deer. Big Al, Freddie, Jason, and John are the hunters in the group. Jason is such a poor shot that his chances of hitting anything are rather slim. John gets his annual attack of 'Buck Fever' at least a week before the hunt and only recovers after he misses at least one deer. Pierre takes along my old .303 Enfield for a camp gun in case he has to scare a black bear away from the old log cabin.

Last year, he was the only one even to see a deer and it woke him up from a snooze he was having in the warm afternoon sun at the back of the cabin. The deer was eating the potato peelings out behind the cabin and Pete's first impulse was to shoo it away because the camp scraps belonged to the Jays and chick-a-dees. The .303 was still inside the cabin in its carrying case and I suspect that Pierre was just as happy that he did not have it with him.

Early Saturday morning we headed out for our posts. The hunters dropped me off first, with instructions to start the hunt in thirty minutes, when Alex would start dogging from the opposite side of the swamp. We would make a sweep supposedly to drive the deer towards Freddie, Jason, and John who were spread out along the Red trail.

I sat down and checked over my camera, making sure that the cable attached to the trigger was properly releasing the shutter. Alex had made up this camera mount for me when I gave up hunting with a gun a couple of years ago. He took an old stock off an old Mossberg .410 shotgun and mounted the top of a camera tripod holder into the wooden stock. I use a telephoto lens and Alex placed a rubber wheel for focussing on the fore stock so I could aim the camera, focus, and pull the trigger, just like a real gun.

At precisely seven-thirty I took a light reading, reset the "f" stop, and started into the woods. I had hardly taken twenty steps when I heard a snort - a big buck jumped up about thirty feet from me. I flipped up the Nikon and had time to set the focus and pull the trigger. The sound of the automatic film advance spooked the buck; however, out of the corner of my eye I saw another small deer. I aimed and tried three quick pictures but the little deer flagged his tail and was gone. When my heartbeat got back to near normal, I let out my Basset hound howl and started following the deer. From across the swamp I could hear Alex's tenor voice yipping like a terrier. I was going to have to invest in one of the new digital cameras that took video and audio as well as still shots.

After I had followed the big buck's tracks for about two hundred yards, he took a sharp turn to the left and doubled back towards the 'terrier' who was making all the noise but apparently not sounding like much of a threat. In a few minutes I heard the boom of a high-powered rifle - John's .306 Remington, if I wasn't mistaken. He let out a yell and began to bark, a sign that the deer had turned and was heading towards another hunter.

In a couple of minutes Freddie's gun boomed twice and he began howling. Either we had stirred up a whole herd of deer or else one deer was making the rounds of our watch positions. I found a rocky area with a good view and sat down to watch for the deer in case it came back my way. The woods were quiet for a couple of minutes until Jason fired three shots and began barking. Alex, the terrier, started yipping again to turn the deer back towards the men waiting on the watches. I figured the only quiet spot in the bush was where I was sitting. I checked the light meter and closed the "f" stop a notch.

A branch snapped. There were a few quick, light steps on the wet leaves that carpeted the ground just below me. A small deer, it sides heaving from panting, was picking its way through the under-brush. The deer sniffed and froze. Evidently it could smell me but as long as I did not move it was unable to find me. The black-edged ears moved around, searching for the smallest sound that could reveal my location to their owner.

As the animal slowly turned its head in the direction of Alex's persistent yipping, I raised the camera and focussed in on a young deer that still had traces of its fawn spots showing through the fur. Bambi! I clicked the auto-wind off, took one picture, and sat still as the little deer walked past me towards safety.

Back at the camp the three hunters who had shot at and missed a 'really big' deer all told and retold their stories. When they had all committed themselves to their over-sized exaggerations, I said, "Well, you fellows will be happy to hear that I got an excellent picture of that deer."

There was a moment's silence, then John said, "Are you sure it's the same one?"

"Yes, I startled it and a big buck up. The bigger one turned back towards Alex, while the smaller deer headed right for you, John."

"Oh," he said. "Well, I don't know how big that other one was, but this one was trophy size! I fired one shot and it turned and ran towards Freddie . . ."

"And it just kept on going when I missed it. My shot hit a tree."

"As I said," Jason continued the saga, "I didn't have a very clear shot, and it was somewhat far away from me. Looked like a good deer though."

"Yes," I said, "A good deer - a real Bambi! That little deer still had its fawn spots!"

"You're kidding!" Freddie said.

"No, that deer was winded from all the running and dodging. It stopped right in front of me. I'm sure that I have a perfect photo to prove it."

"Oh my gosh! Am I glad I didn't hit it," Freddie breathed a sigh of relief. "Thelma would have had my head if I had shot a Bambi!"

"Mais oui," Pierre said from the kitchen where he was just taking a fresh apple pie from the oven, "And that head of yours is surely no trophy!"

"Is anyone interested in a game of Liar's Dice?" I asked.

No Frogs

(2003)

"Well, I don't care what they say," Big Al continued, "frogs must have feeling. Putting that hook into them has to hurt!"

"Not according to the professor up at the University," John replied. "I was talking to him last week and he says there is an initial shock but the creature's natural pain defences block out continuing pain almost immediately." (This was the same professor who would take us on a Crow Hunt a few years later.)

"I agree with Alex," Pierre put in. "I think we should ban the use of frogs for fishing. Top up my glass, will you, Bill?"

Pierre, the gourmet cook, may have had other feelings about frogs, but I did not mention anything about his gourmand frogs' legs and garlic butter. Martha and I had dined with Pierre and Irene when he cooked up his cuisses de grenouille. From the size, I would guess we ate delicious bullfrog legs.

I poured the cool, golden, Rebellion Ale from the proper height to create just the right amount of head on the glass of draft beer. It was early spring and we had gathered at a special meeting of the BSBSC to plan a field trip into a new lake that we might fish later in the year. Access was by air only, so we wanted to be certain that the lake had some fish before the whole gang paid airfare to this wilderness lake. A fellow we know who flies for a local charter company had told us about the lake that no one seemed to fish, even though it drains into a well-known waterway system that has produced some trophy size fish. We thought it was worth investigating. John and I were going next Friday afternoon and being picked up the following Sunday.

"You know," I said, "I have to admit that I don't like using frogs anymore, either. It is not that I worry about the pain, because if we are going to start considering that, we are going have to include worms, crayfish, minnows, even leeches. The fish itself, come to that, and I am not about to stop fishing. No, it's just that frogs seem to know . . ."

"Yes," agreed Alex. "The way they won't swim after you cast them out – I don't think it is the cast and following belly-flop from fifteen feet that stuns them, I think they know that if they swim, some big bass or a hungry pike is going to get them."

The debate degenerated from saving the frogs to which kind of frog made the best bait. The final consensus was that bull frogs were the best for pike while the smaller spotted leopard frogs were ideal for bass. Freddie, Alex, Pierre, and I vowed not to use live frogs while John and Jason said they would let us know after the fishing season. After they had caught the most fish.

The flight in the small Cessna floatplane took just under an hour on Friday. It was a perfect spring day, the northern bush starting to show its sheen of pale green. The pilot circled the lake a couple of times as we all looked for any hidden reefs or floating logs that might obstruct our landing. The lake was crystal-clear and quite deep down the centre. We had no problem landing and then taxiing over to a small beach where we could pitch our tent. The lake was up on a plateau with rocky outcrops running along the north side. The opposite ends of the lake, where the inlet and outlet flowed, were low and swampy. The southern shore, where we were, was high and dry with a gently sloping shore. There was no sign of life anywhere along the lake; no access roads could be seen from the air; no used campsites. Our sandy beach did have the remains of an old fire pit, a sign we took as promising.

We unloaded our tent, camp and fishing gear, and the inflatable dingy, bid the pilot good-bye and began to set up camp in the remaining hour of daylight. We had a good fire glowing by dark when we cooked our steaks and warmed the baked beans and tea biscuits my wife had sent along for our dinner. The peaceful quiet of the wilderness was a pleasant change from the noise and clatter of the city, with only the crackling of the fire and gentle slop, slop of the waves on the shore to break the silence. John, to his feigned surprise, found a mickey of French brandy in his duffle bag so we laced our camp tea, sipped, and talked until the fire was low.

"The lake sure looked good from the air," John said as we were crawling into our sleeping bags.

"Yes, it certainly is peaceful and quiet. We'll get an early start in the morning so we can explore the whole lake tomorrow. Say good-night, John Boy," I said. The quietness was bothering me, yet somehow I fell asleep as I listened to a barred owl and its mate calling to each other in the night woods.

After a very cold and very quick dip in the lake next morning, we ate a leisurely breakfast of crisp bacon, deep-fried eggs, and properly charred camp toast. The camp sounds had attracted a pair of Canada Jays who finished off the bread crusts. They shared one piece of bacon between them.

"I didn't hear any loons last night," I said. "You would think a lake this size would have at least a couple of families, wouldn't you?"

By way of answer, John gave his loon call. He does respectable loon and duck calls. The eerie noise echoed off the far rocky shore, but there was no reply. We pumped the rubber boat full of air and set out to explore the lake, dragging a Mepps along behind us just in case there was a hungry fish looking for trouble.

The lake was deep but very clear. Along the shore, we could see bottom quite easily, twelve to fifteen feet below the boat. We pointed out a number of excellent places for bass to spawn; thought that the lake might even have trout, but saw no fish. After lunch, we paddled up the inlet. The creek flowing in had volume to supply the lake with plenty of fresh water, even a place for pickerel to spawn. John thought he saw a fish or two, but we never had a single bite.

Why it did not register sooner, I cannot say, but the answer came as we ate our dinner that evening. I had seen clear lakes before. Dead lakes. Lakes killed by acid rain. "John," I said, "that explains why there are no loons! Or ducks! There are no fish in the lake. It's dead!"

We finished John's brandy and then my emergency mickey of Glenfiddich scotch as we mourned the loss of another of our lakes. It was with sad hearts that we left the lake next day, never to return to such a postcard perfect place.

The BSBSC had reconvened at the Disraeli on Monday evening for a special meeting called to receive our report.

"Damn!" Alex muttered, "That sounded like such a promising place."

"Well," John advised them, "It would be a nice place to go to camp with your kids – if all you wanted to do was swim and hike. We never even saw leeches at the beach."

"Are you certain the lake is dead?" Jason asked.

"Yes," I replied. "In fact, I guess I knew the first night we were there, even before we paddled around."

"How?"

"No frogs! We never heard a single peep all night. Frogs are some of the first critters to die from acid rain shock. When the snow melts, the acidity is highest, killing the frogs in the egg stage. No frogs, no lake. It is dead."

We drank a silent toast to the lost lake.

"Well, guys," Alex announced, "I've got something to show you." He pulled a contraption out of the cardboard box he had with him. Alex is always making unusual things. He placed it on the table, saying that it was a fishing lure. It was indeed shaped like a frog, but it had a little toggle switch on the top. Alex flipped the switch and the lure began to 'swim' across the tabletop, trailing a treble hook behind it. That thing had about as much chance of fooling a fish as . . .

"What do you call it, Alex?" Jason asked.

"I made it from my nephew's 'go-bot' – I call it my 'frog-bot!"

"That settles it!" I said. "No more live frogs for me! Alex, I'll take two of those – one bullfrog model for pike and one leopard model for bass!"

Carpenters
(2003)

I'm not sure if it was their persuasive feminine powers or just simple blackmail that the women used to get us to agree to their trip to Las Vegas. I know my wife made some pretty strong points about the cost of my fishing gear, the trips we made to those ideal remote spots that took us away from home for whole weekends and finally, the amount we spend on our annual trip into northern Ontario or Quebec. The other male members of the Club reported similar approaches by their spouses so I can only assume that it was a well-coordinated effort that broke down our defences. Not that any of the BSBSC thought the women did not deserve a trip - it was just that we wanted to go too. Martha asked if we would want the women to join us on our annual week-long fishing trip. That settled that.

The ladies had looked after all the flight arrangements, the hotel reservations, traveller's cheques and all the other details for a successful trip to Vegas. Today they were having their final meeting at Irene and Pierre's home. Pierre was at a church board meeting, something to do about a complaint about the quality of the Communion wine, so I had wandered over to Alex's and watched him working on his latest project, making a fibreglass fishing rod.

We got into a discussion about the high cost of buying fishing tackle in Canada. After a careful analysis of the question, by tracking the product from design to manufacture, from American wholesaler to Canadian wholesaler or jobber and finally to a retailer, we believed there were just too many hands out there grabbing a piece of the action. Big Al's answer to the over-marketing was to make as much of his gear as possible, using the parts and pieces he could purchase in bulk, but few in the Club had Alex's skill or even a workshop that could compare with the one I was now in. I suggested to Alex that he could make me a rod or two but when he confided that the cost would be darn near as much as the store price, I said I would stick with my old rods a little longer. He made no comment about a workman only being as good as his tools but I think he was talking about someone else.

My wife had asked me to pick her up at eight-thirty so I left Alex's in time to arrive right exactly on time. They were not quite finished with their meeting when I rang the doorbell.

Irene greeted me at the door and invited me in. I could join them in the den and watch the rest of the video or make myself at home in the kitchen and talk to their cat, Thomas. Thomas is not much of a conversationalist so I said I'd watch the rest of their video. The ladies were studying a tape on 'How to Win at Blackjack'. I wisely kept my mouth shut and tried to pick up a few pointers for the next camp game of friendly poker that we occasionally play after a hard day of fishing or hunting.

When the tape ended the ladies compared notes and asked me for my opinion on doubling. "Well, when we play, we don't have to follow the table rules that they use in Vegas," I said. "Because the dealer has to draw if he or she has 16, it depends on what cards you hold. I'd say an 8 or more is a good choice, unless your luck has been running good - then try anything."

"Are you saying that luck is the deciding factor?" Thelma, Freddie's wife, asked.

"Well, unless you can remember all the cards that have been played in four decks of cards, yes."

"What about letting your winnings ride?" Cindy asked.

"The way I would do it is to pocket the amount you started out with and then shoot the winnings!" My wife gave me a look that summed up my card-playing philosophy. Irene came into the room with the coffee and home-made desserts that Pierre had made up for the meeting and all the ladies complimented his cooking ability. The conversation then somehow turned to how well the other husbands cooked.

I never knew that John was a complete disaster in the kitchen however Cindy said he could only cook when he was camping. Somehow, I thought that John had managed to fool Cindy because I know he can cook pancakes. Although, come to think of it, last spring he almost set the camp afire by putting the bacon on some paper towelling in the oven, forgetting that the ignition point of greasy paper is somewhat lower than the 400 degrees he had selected. Fortunately, we have an office safety officer, Jason, and his quick response with the fire extinguisher saved the day. The only damage was to the pound of bacon and John's reputation.

Thelma said that the only thing Freddie could cook was cold cereal and even then their two girls insist on getting their own breakfast. Claire said Big Al preferred not to cook and she was happy with that arrangement since Alexander was very helpful around the house with any repairs or renovations.

"Repairs!" Thelma exclaimed. "That Fred is the worst person I know to ask to fix something!" Somehow I had thought that Freddie was a pretty good handyman, living out there on his farm in the country. "I asked Fred to fix the door on the bathroom last week. It was sticking and squeaking. I thought it only needed some oil on the hinges, but no, Fred said the wood had swelled from the moisture in the bathroom and he would have to plane it. He spent the whole weekend trying to fix that door!"

"Gee, Thelma," I said, "Doors are hard to hang . . ." A look from my wife reminded me that I was to be seen and not heard.

"First he removed the door and then scratched the paint on the hallway trying to get the door down to his workshop. Somehow he bent one of the hinges and had to go into to town to get another one. It wasn't the same size so he had to drill new holes for the screw nails. The holes were too big and now the door won't close at all because the top hinge is really loose. Now he's going to have to move the hinge down, fill the old screw holes with plastic wood and of course that means we'll have to paint the door. I'm sure all it needed was a little oil."

"That sounds just like John," Cindy said. This was very embarrassing, hearing about my friend's little failures. "We did our rec room last fall and so help me, I could have done it better and faster without John! He said it would be easy to put wood panelling halfway up the wall, using half a sheet of panel for each section. Didn't he cut them wrong! He tried saying that the floor wasn't level, that the pieces of wallboard weren't square - really!"

"Uh," I said, "I've found that rec rooms are the hardest to work on because the floors are hardly ever level . . ."

Martha and the others ignored my comment. "We ended up having to buy extra wide trim to make the whole thing presentable. And I put the trim on after he went and cut all the angles the same instead of making them complementary. It'll be a long time before we tackle anything like that again." I felt some sympathy for John since I had that same problem once, trying to get two 45 degree pieces to make a square corner. It's not as easy as these women were making it out to be.

"Well Pierre admits that he's not much of a carpenter so we usually hire someone to do that kind of work. But Pierre likes to paint," Irene said. She went on to tell how Pierre had run out of paint and had to pick up another quart to finish painting one of their bedrooms. Apparently the lad in the paint store gave him the wrong paint and Pierre didn't notice the subtle shade difference until the whole room was dry. On the second try he had upset his step ladder and it cost them sixty dollars to get the rug cleaned. Those things happen, I said to myself.

Cindy then started a story about how John had tried to fix the plumbing and had somehow installed a sink that wasn't level. It cost them a new vanity top by the time he was finished and I guess it still drips a little. I could see that the story telling was working its way around the room and it would be my wife's turn next. There was no way I was going to sit through her telling about the time I tried to level the legs of a wooden antique table. I excused myself saying that I would go and talk to Thomas.

That damn table still wobbles. I even tried gluing those felt pads on the left side, but no . . .

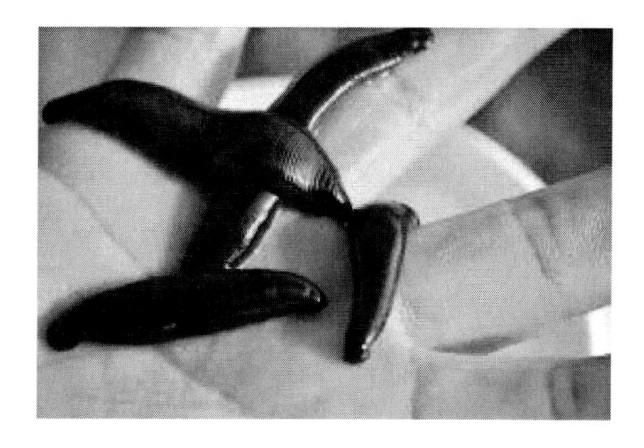

Leech Lake
(2003)

Alexander had heard about this secret fishing spot some two hundred and thirty kilometres to the east of the city from a friend of a friend who knew a farmer who claimed there were largemouth bass in his small, seldom-fished lake. It has been our experience that farmers are an excellent resource of bass fishing knowledge. Farmers are too busy in the spring with ploughing and seeding to fish for walleye (or pickerel as Alex prefers to call them), much too occupied with haying and harvesting to go after late summer pike, but quite at leisure around the opening of bass season. When it comes to bass fishing, most farmers are purists, preferring to use a simple worm for bait, thus ensuring a tasty catch every time they head out in search of bass. Alex and I are inclined to use artificial baits, not only to give the fish a challenge, but to get past the farmer's natural reticence about telling us where the best bass fishing spots are in his particular area. Any farmer who sees two city dudes with our tackle boxes, extra rods, fish-finder and comfortable Tracker fishing boat, knows it is safe to tell all.

Alex telephoned the farmer to ask permission to use the road into the lake and he assured us that it was all right as long as we stopped at his house to get the key to the gate. He asked Alex to be sure to close the gate afterwards so the cows would not escape to greener pastures, although when I saw the adjoining field I thought the cows would stay where they were even if the gate was ajar. Alex said we would stop at the house in any case, as we thought it best to talk to the fisherman and try to get some specific information about the lake. Very early on an August Saturday morning we arrived, just in time to meet the farmer, a man in his late sixties or early seventies, coming in from his morning chores.

"Hi," Big Al introduced himself, "I called last night about going into your private lake to do a little bass fishing."

"Oh, yes. You said you had heard about the lake from old Sammy Armstrong, didn't you?"

"Yes, I think it was his nephew, actually."

"That would be young Richard. Hope you didn't take their word for gospel. Those Armstrong boys all tend to exaggerate just a mite."

"There are some largemouth bass in the lake, though?" I asked.

"Oh, sure, sure. I usually catch a few every year. Not too many left in the lake, though." The old gentleman scratched his head, something that my brother does when he is stretching the truth a little, then replaced his Toronto Blue Jays ball cap. "There`s been quite a few fellows into the lake, earlier this year."

I thought that this might be a hint that the farmer was not too keen on sharing his fish with us.

"Well, we only do catch and release . . . all we're looking for is a little action. It's hard to find a good largemouth lake in our area . . ." I said. I explained that we were from the Toronto area and we usually fished north of the City and he said he was sorry to hear that.

"That's true," he said. "The largemouth prefers water that is a little warmer than what you get up north." He seemed to relax a little and went over to examine our boat.

"You fellows got a nice rig, here." Alex gave him a five minute tour of his boat, explained all the gadgets, and finally got the information from the old farmer that the north end of the lake was the best place to look for a really big bass.

"By the way," I asked as we were about to leave, "Does your lake have a name?"

"Leech. Leech Lake, same as that one they were always talking about down in Ottawa."

I thought that the reference to the failed Meech Lake Accord of 1990 had finally faded from the memory of Canadians, but I guess I was wrong.

"I think that one's actually called 'Meech'," Alex corrected him.

"Nope, Leech . . . named after all them blood-suckers that hang out around the Parliament Hill." The old guy had a glint in his eye and before I could signal Alex to let well enough alone, Alex had to try one more time.

"No, it's Meech. The Meech Lake Accord was named after the conference held at Meech Lake. It's a little lake just up in the Laurentians."

"Afraid you're wrong on that," the farmer said. "There never was any Accord. Those fellows never could agree on anything, let alone a formula for a Constitution that some of them never wanted in the first place. Nope, it was some reporter who dreamed up that name. His brother owns the Honda dealership in Ottawa, so I heard."

"Oh," Alex said.

"Besides, that lake where they went - used to be called Leech Lake but some Englishman built a resort on it, years ago. He couldn't invite his high-flautin' friends to a place called 'Leech', so he renamed it."

"How could he do that?" Alex asked, forgetting that we should have been out on the water by now, trying for some of those big bucket-mouths that were in the north end of Leech Lake. However I could see that the farmer had set the hook.

"Story goes that he ran the Post Office - just changed the 'L' to an 'M' and pretty soon, that was it. The local folk who were mostly French-speaking continued to call the lake Lac de Sangsue but as more people from Ottawa came to the lake, the English name stuck."

"Gee, that's really interesting," I said and then to Alex, "I guess we'd better get going."

"Yep, you fellows are going to miss the best fishing if you don't get out there. Come on up to the house and I'll give you the gate key." Big Al left with the farmer, still discussing something about Meech Lake.

Twenty minutes later we launched the boat on the pretty little lake that did indeed appear to be the ideal habitat for largemouth bass. There was plenty of weed growth, the water was clear enough that we could see logs and rocks down about eight feet, and there were leeches swimming along the shore. I had selected my 'Hot Craw' Bass Magnet lure and was about to make my first cast when Alex said, "By the way, you owe me five dollars."

"Oh?" I said. "You haven't even cast yet, and already you're claiming biggest fish?"

"No, not that. It cost us ten bucks to use the road."

"You mean he charged us?" I asked, just a little surprised at this piece of news.

"Yeah. Says he puts the fee towards the cost of maintaining the road."

"Well, the road was in good condition," I acknowledged. "But still, ten bucks . . ."

"Yeah. And another ten for a deposit on the key."

"This guy is a real businessman."

"I also had to sign a waiver."

"You're kidding!"

"No. He claims his insurance company makes him do it; otherwise they won't give him Liability Insurance coverage. I think there was something on the bottom of his form saying that he didn't guarantee we'd catch any fish," Alexander said.

"I don't suppose there is anything else on that form that you haven't mentioned," I asked.

"Well, the farmer said that he usually charges two dollars a fish, but since we are releasing all our fish, he said there wouldn't be any charge."

"Let me see that paper," I said. "I want to know exactly what you got us into!" Even though he is a lawyer, Alex had taken a night school course on Business Law a few years ago and since then we cannot trust his interpretation of anything that vaguely resembles a business document. Alex reached into his pocket for the paper.

"He stroked out the part about the $20 penalty for keeping under-sized fish, too," Alex said as he handed me the paper.

I could not believe all this, just to go bass fishing! I unfolded the paper. All it had on it was a hand-written title, 'The Leech Lake Accord': no printing, nothing.

"What the . . ." I said.

"Ha! Got you, too! It was just a joke - the old farmer's idea of a joke! He was laughing at the way you were believing all that crap about Meech Lake!"

I flipped the Hot Craw at a patch of weeds. "I didn't believe that for a moment," I lied. "I mean, who could ever believe anything about a place called Meech Lake?" I saw the flash of a big bass. "Five bucks for the first fish," I said, then set the hook.

Ducks and Deuces
(2004)

We were sitting at our table at the Disraeli Club, our favourite bar, having an after-work beer. Jason, John, Alex and Pierre were discussing the upcoming weekend when they planned to trek to an old remote cabin that Pierre owned on Pine Lake for their annual duck hunt. Each year they head out, armed to the teeth, over-supplied with food and full of optimism. Each year they bring back fewer and fewer ducks. They always expend all their ammunition but as Pierre confided to me, most of the shells were fired at sticks or empty cans that they threw into the air, not at ducks. He also said that the poker games were the highlight of the weekend. I was quietly practicing with Jason's new 'Mallard Deceiver' duck call while they talked.

"Bill, will you lay-off with the quacking?" Alex asked.

I quacked an 'okay' in mallardise. He turned to the others and said, "We should get some more decoys. Some of the Mallards are badly shot-up."

"Yes," Jason agreed. "And I can clearly recall who shot a couple of them."

"You guys still don't believe me, do you?" John said. "I swear those decoys were moving. There had to be a current, or something . . . they looked like they were swimming to me!"

"I hate to admit it," Pierre put in, "but they did sort of fool me, too. It was very foggy that morning and we did hear some ducks come in. I was giving the feeding call and they were answering. You really can't blame John for blasting away. If they had been ducks, he would have doubled our count right then and there!" (Pierre goes 'hunting' to use the duck call and cook the meals – he gave up shooting birds although he will shoot at an empty beer can.)

"I guess you're right, Pierre," Alex admitted. "The loss of four decoys to John's shooting would not have mattered so much except for the disaster at Freddie's place."

"What has Freddie got to do with your decoys?" I asked. Our friend Freddie does not duck hunt either.

"Oh, he said we could store them in his workshop. We needed some place to work on them – Jason and I repainted them this spring – and Freddie's big workshop seemed like an ideal place to work." Freddie has a farm north of the City where he has converted an old barn into a workshop and storage shed.

"Sure," Jason said, "until that damn dog of his chewed the heads off half the ducks."

"You must have done a good job painting those decoys," I said, "It takes a lot to fool that old half-blind Basset hound."

"Yeah, well anyway," Alex continued, ignoring my last remark. "We should get another six or seven decoys."

"Canadian Tire has some on sale," I offered trying to get back into their good graces.

"Those darn phony things!" Jerry muttered. "Styrofoam decoys are no good."

"Why?" I asked.

"Float too high in the water," Pierre said.

"Bounce around too much in a wind," John added.

"Wrong colouring for northern ducks," Jason said.

"Besides, they're sold out," Alex concluded. "I checked last night."

Nick, the bartender, brought us another jug of Upper Canada lager. Sleeman, the new owners of Upper Canada Brewing dropped the Rebellion line, our favourite ale, so we switched to the lager. Like all good bartenders, Nick is a great source of information. He eavesdrops on his customers quite often.

"Do you know anybody that has wooden duck decoys for sale, Nick?" Alex asked.

"Decoys, eh? Let me see . . ." Nick scratched the back of his head, a trait that I have noticed often leads to a joke. "Yes, as a matter of fact, there's a fellow out on the 12th line in Vaughan Township who makes decoys. Darn good ones, too. The last time I drove by his place he had a dozen or so Golden Eyes and Buffleheads in his front yard, but that was a month ago."

"Hey that's great! Just what we need," Pierre said. "That would give us a nice variety." The others all agreed.

"Well, I don't know as he has any left now. Old Jim South – you know the guy with the full beard, smokes a big hooked pipe, always orders Guinness – he was telling me about his brother-in-law's decoys. Some hunters from the City drove by one morning while it was still foggy and saw those Golden Eyes sitting on the grass – I guess they never even saw the house right nearby – they jumped out of their car and shot four of the decoys!"

"You're pulling our leg, Nick!" I said. "Decoys couldn't fool even city slickers that much!" Everyone looked at John.

"But the guy must have had more than four decoys," John said.

"Sure, he had about 20. But when those guys started shooting, they all flew off!"

I laughed. Nick went back to the bar. Jason pulled out his new duck call and gave Nick a well-deserved raspberry in the words of a Hooded Merganser. The four duck hunters were still going over their list of supplies when I left a few minutes later.

Early the next week I called Alex to see how well the weekend hunt had turned out.

"I lost 56 bucks!" he said. "John had the cards working for him. I think he came out of the camp with close to a hundred dollars of our money. Every time he got the deal, he'd play 'Deuces are Wild' and win. That used to be my favourite game, but not after this weekend."

"Did you get any ducks?" I asked.

"Not a single duck! I don't know if it was the weather or if the northern ducks aren't down yet, but all we saw was a pair of mergansers that live on the lake. Even Pierre, with all his culinary expertise, wouldn't offer to cook them."

Pierre had told me about his experience cooking a merganser: His French recipe for Canard de Poisson instructed the hunter to clean and prepare the duck with home-grown herbs, adding salt and pepper to taste. Place the dressed duck on a cedar cooking plank and slow-bake at 250 for three hours. Remove from oven, cool, throw the duck away and eat the cedar plank.

"That's too bad," I said, even though I no longer approved of duck hunting.

"But you won't believe this," Alex said.

"Let me guess – John shot some more decoys?"

"No, no. Sunday afternoon, when we were cleaning up, Pierre went down to the lake to throw some leftover bread out to a seagull that had been hanging around, begging, all weekend. We had packed the guns in the truck and so what do you think we see – right in the middle of the afternoon?"

"A flock of ducks?" I guessed.

"A flock of geese! About 20 Canada geese came flying by, low, right over the camp. Pierre is down there at the dock, doling out bread to his seagull, so he starts 'honking' at the geese, throwing slices of bread out into the lake. The geese circled around and headed right back towards the camp. I ran to the truck to get the Browning and all the while Pierre is still 'honking' and throwing bread. By the time I got the 12 gauge out and loaded, the geese had landed! The damn things were tame! They came right up to Pierre and were eating the bread as fast as he could deal it out to them."

"Imagine that!" I said.

"Yeah. I wanted to shoot a couple but the guys talked me out of it. They said they were probably somebody's pets."

"Could be," I said, "or they might just be wild geese that have come to trust people. In this case, I guess it was okay."

"Yeah, I suppose . . ."

"That's what Pierre said. In fact, when we got talking about it later on the way home, we agreed that maybe all the ducks that we were after could be considered 'tame'. Pierre pointed out that all summer long we are friendly towards the ducks, talking to the ducklings while we paddle around their lakes looking for fish, or out on a golf course when the little puff balls walk across a green. It hardly seems fair to suddenly decide in the middle of September to start shooting at them."

"That's true," I said. It was one of the reasons why I had given up duck hunting, but Alex already knew that.

"I think next year we're going away for a weekend of poker. We won't tell our wives, but that's the plan. You could come too, Bill," Alex offered.

I thought about it. "Yes, sounds great. I may just take up 'Duck Hunting' next year," I laughed.

Besides, I do fancy the occasional hand of 'Deuces are Wild'.

Crows
(2004)

The BSBSC were sitting around a table at our favourite tavern, the Disraeli, washing the taste of the day's work from our mouths when someone mentioned the subject of fall hunting. We each (there were six of us at that time) have our own favourite game species. It ranges in size from moose to rabbits and in speed from the wily woodcock to smart crows. It was the mention of the latter that brought the fellow sitting at the next table into our conversation. He was John's professor friend who told John about frogs. I ought to have known better, but I topped up his glass of draft beer.

"Crows," he said, "are the most intelligent birds native to this area. And I'll bet that you fellows hardly ever shoot one."

Well, I told him, quite politely, that we indeed got two last year. We (John) shot up our only stuffed owl in the process, but we did bag two. We were, however, stymied this year since we did not have a replacement owl decoy. Besides, we don't really enjoy shooting crows - it's just an old thing we do each fall - go hunting. The rationale was that crows eat the farmer's crops and we were trying to keep the number of crows down to guarantee our food supply. If we didn't kill any crows we certainly put the fear of the sound of a 12 gauge in them.

The Professor pulled his chair over to our table (he was sitting alone) and offered to set up a crow hunt with guaranteed results. We poured him another glass of Sleeman's Silver ale on speculation that maybe he knew whereof he spoke. It turned out that this fellow worked at the University of Toronto up on University Avenue and he knew all about the behaviour of crows having extensively studied lab rats and he knew about some dogs that belonged to a fellow named Pavlov. He introduced himself as Jim Lawlor and he knew my wife who works in one of those ivy-covered building on the campus. He said his field of study was psychology and Freddie said he was sorry for him, but it was better than being a lawyer. Freddie had a run-in with the law profession lately.

"The thing with crows," Professor Jim claimed, ignoring the jibe, "is that they can count. Well, actually they can recognize the number of things without counting." He paused for effect and a sip of our beer. "People," he continued, "can recognize four things without counting. Crows can do three, maybe even four." All you had to do was confuse the crows and they could be shot from a hide.

I tried the counting thing with my wife when I got home that evening but the best I could do was 3 sometimes and 5 once, although the beer may have confused my counter. Martha said there are only 3 kinds of people: those who can count and those who cannot. But I digress.

The hunt was set up for the next Saturday. Professor Jim sent us, via email, specific written instructions on how to dress. We were to all wear ball caps and be at a farmer's corn field in Maple at 10 a.m., (n.b. map attached) shotguns at the ready. The 'Professor', as we now called him, was there when we arrived. He was dressed in army fatigues and carrying a clipboard with a few sheets of computer printouts attached. There were about twenty crows feeding in the field near a hide constructed from cornstalks by the Professor and the farmer. The farmer was there in his red plaid jacket and ball cap, the same as Pierre, John, and Jason. The rest of us wore blue jean jackets.

The Professor explained his plan right after he let out a holler that treed all the crows. For a rather small fellow he had a very large voice. I wondered if he had ever 'dogged' in deer season and made a mental note to ask him later. We would, in selected groups, walk out to the hide. Go inside, wait three minutes (the attention span of the average crow as printed on an Excel spreadsheet), then return as instructed. Since the crows could recognize three, the Professor planned on shuffling us around until the crows were confused into thinking the hide was empty. They would then fly down and the men in the hide could shoot at them.

"Why the hats and the coloured jackets?" I asked.

"Well, my theory is that crows can recognize colour and form as well, so I'm testing this hypothesis at the same time." It turns out that this scholar was writing a paper and we were a control study group. John and Jason were muttering rebellious words at this disclosure but I said, let's give it a try.

The great crow hunt began. 4 guys, 2 with caps, went out to the hide. 2 with caps returned. 3 red checks went to the hide. 4 returned. 3 red checks were next, followed by 2 jeans, 3 jeans returning. Counting heads I realized that we now had three hunters in the hide. No crows flew down but one was calling "caw, caw, caw!" I mentioned this to the Professor but he muttered something about superfluous data and sent out 3 with hats and checks. 4 returned - 2 checks and 2 hats. Halfway back they were met by the farmer and a hunter, who in plain view of the crows, changed jackets, added 2 hats, split into two groups, 3 returning to the hide, 3 returning to the jumping-off point. One crow was now calling "caw, caw!" either meaning he had lost count or he was counting the number of men in the hide. I mentioned this to the Professor but he just said to come with him. The 2 of us went to the hide, changed jackets and 6 men returned: 3 with checks, 3 with caps. I waited in the hide. The crows had stopped cawing. I put a round of #5 into the chamber of the Remington, thinking that this was it.

Suddenly there was a great uproar of caws. All 20 or so of those crows (I never did get an accurate count of them) were cawing. As a flock, they flew off to the other end of the field. The farmer said he had seen an owl fly into a tree a moment ago.

The Professor said something about trying again next weekend with 3 more hunters and green checkered jackets. Some unkind words were said by Big Al, normally a mild-mannered fellow, advising the Professor what he could do with his crows.

Next weekend I'm going grouse hunting. Have you ever tried the 'noise' method of grouse hunting? I met this guy at the Disraeli who assured me that if you make lots of noise when walking in the bush, the grouse will sit still or even walk right out into the open to see what is happening and you are sure to get your limit every time. He said wearing a red checkered jacket helps too.

Tina's Cold Feet

(2004)

Canoeing in the hinterland is one of the most restful, relaxing and satisfying ways to get away from it all. A few hours paddling on a quiet lake or river, watching for wildlife or speculating on the possibility of where a big fish might be lurking usually recharges my batteries for at least a week. Camping out overnight is an added bonus. Never mind the work of packing a canoe and your supplies over a hilly portage or the occasional black fly or mosquito; the enjoyment of the peace and quiet is worth it.

No doubt these were the determining factors in my mind when Jason called to ask if we, my wife and I, were interested in a canoe trip over the long August 1st weekend. Jason's new lady friend, Tina, was really keen on the outdoors. She was learning how to paddle a canoe and felt that she was ready for a canoe trip. Jason had already called John and Cindy and had enlisted them. He needed another couple for the three day trip through the chain of small lakes not far from Halliburton. My wife had been making noises about a shopping trip to Buffalo and I thought this might stall her. Temporarily.

Camping with the ladies always means more baggage. Not that we leave the coolers behind, but we men do not take the Coleman stove, the propane light or the collapsible port-a-potty. Or more than one change of clothes. Or any cosmetics. I am certain none of the BSBSC use cosmetics although there has been a rumour that Thelma has been trying to camouflage Freddie's greying hair. Apparently her hairdresser had told her that the easiest way to keep her young looks was to dye Freddie's hair so they looked like a happy young couple . . .

I felt sorry for Jason before we even put a paddle in the water. "Jason," I asked, "You didn't forget anything, did you?"

"No, I don't think so." He rolled his eyes helplessly to the heavens.

"If you want to wait a few minutes," John offered, "I can go home and get the one-man raft - you could load some of your supplies in it and tow it behind your canoe."

"Sure, sure. Never mind, we'll manage. Let's get started."

Cindy and John are veterans and soon had their yellow Scott canoe securely packed and were ready to go. My wife, Martha, tends to like her comfort more than Cindy so we had a little more to stow. Tina came well prepared and a couple of sacrifices had to be made but she took it in good spirits. It was, after all, her first trip. She hardly flinched when we had to leave her folding chairs behind - along with the Hibachi and briquettes. And the extension for the tent that made a netted dining area, although I think that was Jason's idea for keeping the deer flies off his friend.

We paddled for an hour and a half, reaching the first portage about six. Tina had found her canoe balance and was paddling very well. We sang some voyageur songs for her, adding in a few of the rowdy verses that we usually kept for ourselves. My wife splashed a little cold water on me as a signal to 'cool it' but I knew she did not really mean it.

We camped that night under the pines and Tina was as excited as a youngster. The hooting of a pair of barred owls off in the distance was the last thing I heard until dawn. It was cool that night and by morning I was thinking that I should have brought my heavier sleeping bag. Tina said her feet almost froze.

"Jason," my wife scolded, "didn't you show Tina how to use a rock to keep her feet warm?"

"I never thought of it," Jason admitted.

"A rock?" Tina asked.

"Yes. What you do is find a nice rock, about the size of a water bottle, put it near the campfire in the evening so it absorbs the heat. Then, when you're ready for bed, you wrap it in a towel and put it in the bottom of your sleeping bag. It will keep your feet warm all night," my wife explained.

We had been pulling Tina's leg a few times so she was a little dubious about this latest piece of woods lore. "We'll show you tonight," Martha assured her.

We spent a pleasant day, not paddling too hard and managed to reach our second night's campsite late in the afternoon. While we set up the tents and gathered wood for the fire, the women had a swim and picked blueberries. They also found a rock for Tina's cold feet. It was somewhat larger than a water bottle but a very nice piece of granite with quartz and feldspar tracings through it.

We could see a weather front approaching so just before dark we secured everything in the camp, double-checked all the tent fastenings, and securely tied down the canoes. There is nothing worse than waking up in the middle of a storm with your tent collapsed over you. By ten p.m. we could hear the distant rumble of thunder. The loons on the lake took up their cry, warning each other of the impending storm. Cindy and my wife helped Tina get her rock wrapped and we all retired to our tents.

Watching and enjoying a thunderstorm from the comfort and safety of one's home is one thing, but when you are in a nylon tent with the rain beating down inches from your head, the wind tugging your tent pegs accompanied by the flashes of lightning and crashes of thunder, it can be a little frightening. My wife and I always count the seconds between the flash of light and the thunder clap to determine the distance of the lightning strike. 'A thousand and three, a thousand and four' is a good four fifths of a mile away. That night we were counting 'a thou . . .' and then jumping in our sleeping bags as the ground shook with the nearness of the lightning. We were well away from the trees but I hoped none of the branches would hit our canoes if a tree was struck. In a few minutes the storm passed, the rain slowed to a drizzle and we dropped off to sleep.

The next morning we examined the remains of a large white pine about a hundred yards away from the camp. The power of the lightning bolt that had virtually exploded the tree was awesome. We were gathering up some splinters as souvenirs when John smelled the smoke. Down in the roots of the tree, a fire was smoldering. We assigned the women to pack up the camp while we carried pail after pail of water to douse the area around the tree.

There were three short portages that day and by evening we were all tired. I was feeling a little sorry for Jason because he was carrying more gear than the rest of us. Tina had her cosmetic case to look after as well as the sleeping bags but it still left Jason with quite a load. The bottle of brandy that we had saved for the last night was all we needed to relax our tired muscles. The women wrapped their feet warmers and we all retired for a good night's sleep. Tina was becoming a real camper. She had even found another rock that looked strangely like the twin of the one they had found yesterday.

The last leg of the trip had the longest, hilliest portage but since most of the food and all the beer had been consumed, the packs were much lighter. The women were to carry the sleeping bags and a small back pack while we carried the canoes on the first trip. The men would then go back for the empty coolers and remaining packs.

John and I had less to carry so we offered to share Jason's load so he would not have to make three trips. We stopped at the crest of the trail for a breather. "Jason, I don't know what you've got in this pack, but it sure is heavy!" John said, easing his load to the ground.

"What do you mean?" Jason asked.

"Well, you lift this one. If there's a heavier pack here, I'll trade anyone!"

Jason hefted the pack, doing a double-take at the weight.

"What can it be?" He said, unfastening the straps. He dumped the contents onto the trail.

I was still puffing from the climb, but I had to join John in laughter that had us both lying on the ground. Jason's face turned red in embarrassment and he muttered a few choice oaths. There, wrapped in its towel, was Tina's foot-warmer. The granite one with the quartz and feldspar tracings!

"I thought that stone looked familiar last night," I said.

"You mean I carried that damn thing yesterday and today!" Jason asked. "Of all the dumb . . . !" Jason was about to throw the pretty stone into the bush.

"Aw, come on, Jason," John said, "be a sport! You might as well take it all the way home."

"Yes," I said, "It will make a great doorstop – and a wonderful conversation piece."

New Wheels
(2004)

I was sitting at my desk, pondering the merits of writing a sub-routine to tie into another of the client databases on the computer. What if I tied a client's most recent purchases to the account balance and grouped the purchases by type? All the groceries together; all the automobile costs; all the hairdresser appointments, and all the sporting goods. I will bet the clients will love that. The telephone buzzed me back to reality. It was Freddie who works at York Fine Cars calling with another 'hot' lead on a new vehicle. Last week it was a Porsche Cayenne and a Land Rover, both well beyond the budget Martha had set for me.

"Bill, we just took in a last year's model Ford Explorer yesterday. It looks like it has everything you would want on it. You should check it out."

"It's not a demonstrator, is it," I asked, thinking that some salesman had been bouncing it around back roads for six months.

"No, almost brand new – it was on lease and the people had to turn it in," Freddie said. "The former owner failed his road test when he had his 80th birthday."

"Well, thanks a lot, Freddie. Maybe I will take a look at it."

Normally I do not get the urge to buy a new vehicle until I have the old one paid off and have a couple of dollars in my pocket for a reasonable down payment. The normal cycle takes me about four years and this was just a little early. But I was having a problem. My little mid-size Jetta just would not push my new boat up the driveway without a lot of protesting. Protesting and whining in the form of a slipping automatic transmission.

My friends at my workplace, who are into the outdoors thing, all recommended a four-wheel drive truck as the answer to my problem. Most of them drive Toyotas, that foreign model that makes people jump up in the air whenever they say the 'T' word, but there were a couple of die-hard Truck owners in the group who claimed the only way to go was big, North American style. Nor were the Club members of any help in my dilemma. Freddie drives an old beat-up Dodge half ton that he calls his 'farm truck' - for tax purposes, I think. He has a very nice Jaguar sedan for work. Jason has a new Toyota 4x4 that he really likes, Big Al has his Suburban and John has a Chevy Yukon. The consensus was that I needed a four wheel drive, but there was no clear cut winner as far as models went.

I started making the rounds of the car dealers, test driving, getting their ridiculous sticker prices, and keeping notes of the pros and cons of the various four-wheel drive vehicles. In a month I had an impressive list but really could not find the singular outstanding feature that would persuade me to buy a particular truck. They all had warranties, offered many options, and all claimed to be the best. The Volkswagen and the boat trailer almost got bogged down on a back road one Saturday late in May, so I spent the next week making my decision.

By Friday evening I was so desperate that I put the question to the Club members at the Disraeli. They all knew of my problem and had been good enough to research the truck market for me. Big Al was the first to offer his opinion. "Well, Bill, I think you should get a full-sized truck. You never know when you might have to haul something really big around, and those little trucks just wouldn't be up to it."

"No," Jason said. "A medium-sized truck is much more practical. You're not hauling all that weight around, every day, day in, day out. You have to consider the gas consumption, you know."

"Jason's right," John said. "You can always make two trips if the load is too big. A mid-size truck is all you need to haul your boat."

Freddie picked up the pitcher of Sleeman's Silver and topped up our glasses, giving himself the last few drops then signalling to Nick to get us another jug. "Well, the box size is important, Bill, but the engine power is something you'll have to consider as well. If you are going to pull that boat around, you'll want enough power to cruise along the highway without holding up the traffic." We do some extensive highway driving to reach our fishing spots, I thought.

"That's right," Pierre, who only owns an old Buick Park Avenue, put in. "There's nothing worse than getting stuck behind some guy hauling a boat or trailer who can't keep up to the speed of the traffic." He took a sip of his beer and added, "And for crying out loud, buy a truck with signal lights that work on a trailer!"

"It's not the vehicle that causes those flickering signal lights," Alex said. He went to explain how it was simply a matter of installing a heavy duty flasher in the signal lights circuit to push the power the added distance to the trailer. He was wandering into something about ohms and resistance but we soon got him back onto topic. Alex reads Popular Mechanix Illustrated.

"Well, guys," I said, "I have compared costs, warranty, mileage, engine power, options - everything - and I really don't see much difference in these vehicles. The Consumers Reports are ambiguous because they tend to put too much emphasis on low cost - not on performance and the pleasure of driving and owing a vehicle. I think it's a matter of deciding to buy foreign or domestic, and I may have to toss a coin to make that decision!"

I could see that Pierre was uncomfortable with this totally unscientific, arbitrary method. He is a strong nationalist and the thought of me accidentally buying an import, based on the flip of a coin, was bothering him. He cleared his throat. "Bill, I have just a couple of questions, and then you can make up your mind. One: what's the most famous four wheel-drive vehicle?"

We were quiet until Nick the bartender who was bringing us our second jug of ale said, "The Jeep: Famous because of the war."

"Right," Pierre said and continued, "What tough vehicle did the Desert Rats drive?" I think we all watched that TV show.

"Jeeps," Jason said.

"Right. What vehicle did Eisenhower ride on when he entered Paris?"

"A jeep," Jason said. "But that was more than fifty years ago!"

"Right again," Pierre said. "And they are still making them. That goes to show how successful the vehicle has been. And," he continued before anyone could interrupt, "The Jeep Company has recently been bought out by a rather famous name."

"Chrysler," I said. I recalled Lee Iacocca taking over, but he was gone now.

"There you are. Name another automobile company's President other than Edsel Ford! You can't. There you have it. The best known name in four wheel drive vehicles and the best company name in the business. I rest my case."

Monday morning I found myself at the Jeep dealership and two weeks later I had them backed into a corner, begging me to buy a Jeep. After I straightened them out on the real meaning of 2X4 and 4X4 (I was raised in a lumbering family and 2 by 4s and 4 by 4s were pieces of wood that you used to build houses), I bought a four-wheel drive Jeep Cherokee.

I soon found out why my friends raved about four-wheel drive. It became a challenge to find a mud hole, a rocky hill, or a stream to ford. Right after the fish stories, our usual Monday morning greetings at work are the stories of getting 'stuck' or finding a new bush trail to explore.

I called Jason one morning to tell him about a new road I had found and how there just happened to be a little lake at the end of it.

"Oh, that one," he said. "John and I were in there two weeks ago. Just a few small bass, nothing of any size in that lake."

I made a note of that, thinking that where those two could catch small bass, Alex and I could get some decent fish. "You didn't get stuck on that creek bed?" he asked.

"No, I went right through. Of course, I didn't have the boat on behind. Shouldn't be any problem, though," I said.

"No, with that big motor, you should walk right through it," Jason replied. He is a little awed by my 4 litre engine that is just about twice as big as the one in his Toyota. "But, do you know the worse place to be stuck on a day like this?" he asked.

"No," I said.

"In this bloody office!" he replied.

I had to agree.

Mad Fish Disease

(2004)

Hard on the heels of the news of a Mad Cow discovered in the United States was my experience last week. Imagine my dismay when I saw the sign at the Joey's Sea Food restaurant saying that their product was guaranteed not to have Mad Fish Disease. "Mad Fish?" I asked my wife.

"I think there was something on the late news," Martha said.

I have seen a few really angry fish in my days of casting a line. Nothing disturbs a large northern pike like a red and white Daredevle spoon splashed right in front of him during his afternoon siesta. Or dragging a large jointed-pikie past him when he is out for a little morning exercise. A gold #2 Mepps spinner does the same. I have even met a few smallmouth bass that get mightily miffed when you tease them with a hula popper. On some days they will attack just about anything you throw their way. But Mad Fish? Not really.

My goldfish will give me a glassy stare when I arrive late with their food, but I cannot say that they look mad – more like ‘dismayed’. I am supposed to feed them no later than 6:00 p.m. every day. So I was somewhat surprised to learn that some little-known scientist had announced that the cod living just off the Grand Banks in the Atlantic were mad. They had Mad Fish Disease.

We were taught as children that eating fish was good for you. It was called ‘brain’ food; fish supposedly helped the neurons or synapses or gray matter develop. I guess I didn’t eat enough fish when I was young. I ate a lot of carrots too, and still I ended up wearing eye glasses.

Hard on the heels of the Mad Cod announcement was a news release that Mad Fish Disease (MFD) had been found in swordfish and marlin. Within days the same scientist claimed that early studies indicated that MFD was suspected in red roughy and Chilean sea bass. Using the same clinical methodology, a scientist in Japan supposedly found traces of MFD in Mahi Mahi and bottlenose dolphins. In Norway, a group is looking at whales, even though they are not fish, just in case MFD is carried in those leviathans of the deep that are only caught ‘for scientific purposes’.

I immediately began to worry about MFD disease in sardines. You see, I like nothing better than a sardine sandwich – sunflower seed bread, real butter, garnished with a little Dijon mustard, topped with some fresh radish sprouts and then washed down with a nice light lager – ah! Martha says sardines are not fish. They may smell like fish, look like fish, but they are not, in her book, a fish that is suitable to eat. Besides, the empty tin smells to high heaven in the garbage bin.

MFD is a very serious matter. Consumption of infected fish points to deterioration of the brain. Not a deadly disease of the bovine nature, Creutzfeldt-Jakob Disease, but a lessening of the ability to reason in adults over a certain age. It apparently affects that part of the brain that causes women to buy things on sale while men refuse to buy an item until the sale is over and the price is back to a normal markup. I could see where this might be true in our household.

However, the theory of MFD was quickly debunked when reporters discovered that the whole thing was a ploy by environmentalists to save the world's rapidly declining fish stocks. The foreign seiners and factory boats too near our East Coast likely brought this on. The fish huggers saw what Mad Cow Disease did to the Canadian beef industry and thought to apply the same strategy to the fish industry.

We should have sympathy for any effort to save the natural fish stocks. The rapidly growing world population is devouring our resources faster than they are replenished by nature. Fish are one of the main resources of protein for poorer nations and as we plunder the seas, we will eventually starve millions of people.

The answer may lay in commercial fish farms or aquaculture. But one thing is bothering me. What are they feeding these farm fish that we will eat? Not, I hope the same things they fed those mad cows. BSE has been traced to the practice of feeding cattle ground protein – from slaughtered cattle – as a means of quickly adding weight to the cow.

My pond fish seem to be happy with their pellets of solient brown, but I don't plan on eating my goldfish. Whatever they feed farm fish, I hope it is something the fish eat naturally because I don't want any Mad Fish in my sardine sandwiches.

On the Rocks
(2005)

It would have been acceptable to tarry a few minutes longer than the others if Alex and I had been catching any fish, but to wait until the last moment before pulling up the anchor and heading back to the camp when you are not catching anything, was not a good plan. Freddie and John were the first to leave, saying they had to get back to clean all the fish they had caught and they thought it might take them quite a while. Pierre and Jason left soon after since it was Pierre's responsibility to cook the pickerel that night. Actually, we all prefer to have Pierre do as much cooking as he wants since he is by far the best cook in our Club.

Alex made a couple more half-hearted casts and then said, "Okay, Bill, let's go back and play some cards. The fish just aren't biting this evening." We had two small walleyes in the live well but neither belonged to Alex.

"Shall we let these two small ones go?" I asked.

"Yeah, Freddie had enough for a feed," Alex replied as he carefully lifted the two pickerel from the live well and placed them back into the lake. "I don't know how some guy can sit fifteen feet away, use the same bait as everyone else, pay as little attention to his fishing as Freddie does, yet catch all the fish!" Alex does not usually complain, but he was having poor luck on this trip.

"He keeps saying it's all in the wrist action, but I think he was just sitting over the right place tonight. This river system is so broken, you never know just how much water you're in."

"The old river bed wanders all under this flooded area. There is a control dam down at the end of the lake." I said. A statement that would come back to haunt me in about five minutes.

We plugged in the running lights since it would be getting near dark by the time we docked, some eight or nine miles up the river. Life jackets on, we headed back to the warm camp, the Ol' Walt Kelly cruising along at her usual 25 knots. Although this was new water to us, we thought we had all the hazards marked, referring to the map the camp owner gave us and to advice from some local fisherman who suggested areas to avoid. With a sudden boat-shaking crash, we found another rock.

The engine flew up, revving madly; the control levers yanked from my hand by the force of the impact of the engine on the hidden rock, fell to the deck. The crash threw Alex forward but he managed to grab onto his seat for support. The motor was still running at top speed as I scrambled to the back of the boat and pulled the fuelling connector from the engine to stop it. By then Big Al had righted himself and I found the switch to turn off the ignition.

"Holy cats! What the hell did we hit?"

"Had to be a rock, just under the surface. I never saw a thing." The fish finder was still on, showing a slightly cluttered screen but eight feet of water and no fish. Alex and I both looked into the dark water but could see nothing of the rock we had hit.

"How much damage to the motor?" Alex asked. The motor had settled back down to its running position, but I knew we had sustained a lot of damage. I pulled up the engine. The complete bottom end was missing. No housing, no propeller – just a few rods hanging down.

"Damn," I said, and added a couple of expletives. After checking to see that neither of us had taken anything more than a couple of bumps from the sudden stop, we assessed our condition.

"The guys will come back for us," Alex said, "As soon as they realize we're overdue."

"Sure," I said, thinking that it would be pitch black by then and there was no way any of our group could find their way safely down that river system with only flashlights. "As soon as the hockey game is over."

"Oh, yeah. It's the final game tonight, isn't it?" The Stanley Cup semi-finals were on the camp TV. "They might not even notice we're missing until after the game."

"Well, let's get as far up the river as we can with the two horsepower," I suggested, getting the little trolling engine ready. The small engine would push the Ol' Walt Kelly along at about three miles per hour, full open. After a couple of false starts, the little outboard ran smoothly, and we began the long slow trip up the river. The problem was a stretch of fast water that the little engine had no hope of pushing the big boat through. If we even made it that far in the dark. It was getting darker by the minute, the overcast sky in the west dampening the twilight to a faint glow.

"You do have insurance, don't you? " Alex asked as we putted along.

"Yes, but you know how it is with insurance - you always end up paying something. Either now or by increased premiums later," I said.

"I guess we're lucky that the hull didn't hit the rock. We could be taking on water or be in the water right now. And that water is still very cold." The thought of spending a few hours soaking wet while we waited for a rescue did not appeal to me. Alex was right, it could have been worse.

"Yes, we could be on shore with the mosquitos, the bears, the wolves . . ." A loon called nearby, its eerie mating call echoed from the shore until it was answered by another loon farther down the lake.

"Alex, have you got your lantern? It's getting hard to see the shore line," I said.

"No, I must have left it in the camp," Alex replied after digging through his pack. "Don't you have one?"

"Yeah, it's in the storage area, up front. Get it out will you?" The little engine, mounted off to one side of the now defunct 30 horsepower, wanted to push the boat in circles and I was not making an exactly straight line down the lake.

Alex found the light but somehow I must have stowed something on the switch, because the bulb only made a pink glow when switched on. We were not going much farther without a light. The running lights on the boat only ruined our night vision by illuminating the area around the boat. It looked as if we might have to go ashore or spend the night in the Ol' Walt Kelly.

"You got any matches, Alex?" Neither of us smokes so we didn't carry lighters. Or matches it turned out. I used to carry a package in my tackle box but last fall when I accidently dumped it into the lake, everything got waterlogged. I had not replaced the matches that might be very useful if the guys did not come for us. Or could not find us.

"It's too dark, Alex. I can't see where we're headed. We could end up in a bay - the guys might not find us it we get off the main system."

"Let's anchor right here. We might as well stay away from shore so the flies won't bother us." Flies don't bother Alex that much. Was he afraid of the bears or wolves?

"I guess we're okay for a while out here. But if it gets much colder, we might be better on shore, out of the aluminium boat. I don't think there are many bears around here," I said, wishing I could check the reaction to my words on his face. The area around Chapleau is full of black bears.

"I'm warm enough. Are you cold?"

"I'm okay."

"Did you hear an engine?"

There was nothing but the night sounds. "No."

Another half an hour passed. "Geez, where are those guys?" Alex asked. "They should have missed us by now."

"Hey, Alex, why don't we try a few casts? Any true fisherman would be using this time to practice his night fishing skills."

"Uh, sure, why not. Did you hear something, just in there by the shore?" There were some noises in the brush, probably some old bank beaver getting a late night snack.

"Sounds big, doesn't it? Maybe a moose or a bear." Big Al didn't take any chances. He let out a loud holler that almost scared me right out of my seat.

"Holy smokes, Alex what are you trying do?"

"Scare away that bear."

"All you'll do is attract them making noise like that!"

"Oh, I never thought of that," he whispered. I was right. Big tough Alex was more than a little nervous out here in the dark. "Listen, do you hear a motor?"

"No, Alex, I think that's a train engine. The tracks are only about ten miles to the south of us. I'm going to turn on the stern light and put on a surface lure. Are you going to try fishing, too?"

We both geared up and then turned off the light to conserve the battery. After about a dozen casts Alex said, "I think I'm hooked on something."

"Well, I hope you don't expect me to start up the little engine and putter around in the dark while you try to find that old jitterbug of yours! How the heck could you get a surface lure snagged in the middle of the lake, anyway?"

"I don't know. I never did like night fishing. I'll just give a quick yank and maybe the line will hold . . . Holy smokes, Bill, I've got a fish out there!"

The next ten minutes would have been exciting in daylight, but in the dark of night with just the stern light showing its globe of soft white light, things really got hectic. The landing net somehow got caught in Big Al's pack, so I had to net the packsack from the water before it sank. The big fish, a very large pickerel as it turned out, went around the boat twice, Alex stumbling about, following it, trying to keep it away from the anchor line that was somewhere off the bow. Of course, I could not see the fish in the black water and the shadow at the side of the boat. This fish was big enough to cause some severe criticism if the guy with the net fouled up.

"I think it's tired now, Bill. I'll try to get it to the surface. Slide the net into the water, right in front of me." I did as I was instructed. "Okay, I'll reel it in straight towards the boat. You pull up the net when you think the fish is over the net."

"That'll be a neat trick. I can't see anything down there. You say when, and I'll lift the net."

"Okay . . . now!"

I felt the net hit the fish and lifted. Alex's line 'pinged' as it snapped, but the fish was in the boat. There was much congratulations as we measured the walleye, (Alex called it a big pickerel), at 26 inches. We estimated it at eight or nine pounds, took a couple of pictures of the fish with the small Kodak flash camera, that while a little damp from the trip into the drink in Alex's pack, still worked. Alex held the fish in the water until it revived and then let it go. We were thinking of continuing the fishing when we saw a bright light, almost like a search light, reflecting off the clouds, up the river.

"Wow, somebody must have a big light. That's no flashlight," I said. "Maybe the guys got the camp owner to come and look for us."

"No, I know what that is. Jason bought this hand-held search light - another of his toys. He was telling me about it last week. 250,000 candle power, he said."

"How many batteries does that take?" I asked, impressed by the light that was flickering up the river.

"You have to hook it right to a 12 volt battery. I guess he has it wired to his boat battery."

The guys were searching the shoreline as they worked down the river towards us. All we could do was wait. When they finally came around the last corner, I flashed the navigation lights on and off until they spotted them and came running straight towards us. It was Jason and Pierre, a more welcome pair, I had never seen.

"You guys okay?" Pierre yelled to us.

"You should have seen the pickerel I just caught," Alex said.

"Yeah, we're okay. I hit a rock and smashed the motor," I said.

We towed the Ol' Walt Kelly to shore and made it fast to a tree with a rope that would hold until morning when we would return for the salvage trip. The big, bright lamp led us back to camp where we had to relate our story once more for Freddie and John. With each telling, we realized just how lucky we had been. And how fortunate it was that Jason had bought that big lantern. The guys also confided that we were lucky that the hockey game hadn't gone into overtime since it was a close game and everyone was hoping that Chicago would win at least one game.

"I don't suppose you two would like a drink?" Pierre asked, knowing very well that both Alex and I needed a stiff bracer after the evening we had had.

"Yeah, I'll have a double rum and coke," Alex said.

"Scotch," I replied.

"You want it straight up or on the rocks, as usual, Bill?" Pierre asked.

"I think straight up tonight. I've been on the rocks once too often tonight!"

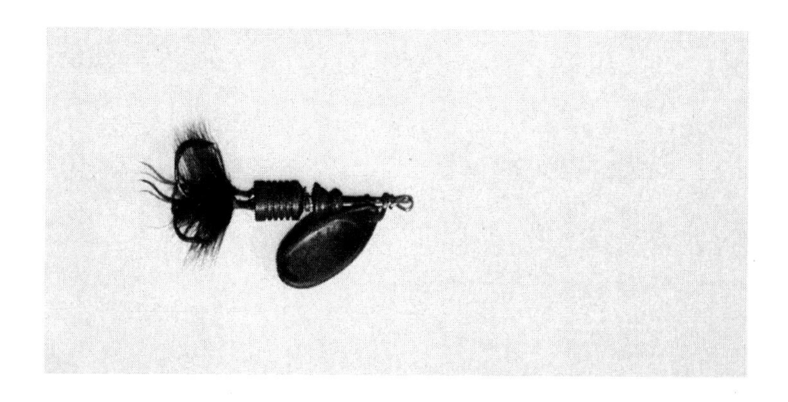

Plugged In
(2006)

We were sitting around a table at the Disraeli one Thursday evening near the end of June trying to figure out what had happened to us the past weekend. All six of us had been fishing on Little Pike Lake, a lake known for its walleye - pickerel, as Alex insists on calling them - and we had not caught a single fish.

"I just can't believe it!" Pierre said, nursing his glass of Sleeman's Silver. "I think that this is the first time we've been skunked."

"Hey, just a minute," Jason said, "I caught that little pike."

"Pierre's right," Freddie agreed. "We were skunked! What went wrong?"

"Uh, Jason's fish . . ." John, his fishing partner murmured.

"Will you be quiet about that 8 inch minnow that he hooked through the tail? You can't call that a FISH! Besides, he hooked it - it didn't even bite that weird-looking green and yellow contraption he had tied to his line," Big Al admonished John.

"Well," I said, "I washed everything in my tackle box and never got a bite. We could see them on the Garmin scope, too. Maybe live bait would have been the answer."

"Yeah, whose idea was it to try using only artificial baits?" Freddie grumbled, looking at me.

I raised a hand to catch Nick's eye and dug into my pocket to pay for the next jug of beer. I had thought it a good idea to try using only lures and jigs to practise for the upcoming fishing tournament but all we had netted from the experiment was a baby pike.

"You know," Jason said, "I wonder if we had used some good fish formula . . ."

"I tried Walleye flavour, Bass flavour and even some Crappie Come," Freddie said. "Nothing worked."

"Yes, I tried everything I had too," John admitted, "But Monday I went down to the *Bites and Bucks* and talked to Amelia. She had some new stuff that she and Geraldine had tried out last Sunday. They caught their limit just off Wilson's Point." Geraldine and Amelia usually can only go fishing on Sunday when their store is closed.

"Aw, come on," Alex grumbled, "You guys will believe anything those two women tell you. One of the junior lawyers at the office fished off Wilson's on Saturday and never got a thing." Lawyers, in my opinion, are not much of threat to the fish. They talk too much – Alex being the exception. Fish are not interested in the techniques used during summations, the many ways of wooing a jury, or what brand of scotch whisky Judge Martin likes.

"Hey, I'm only telling you what Amelia said. This new goop apparently sticks to the lure much better than anything else on the market. In fact, if you use those little sponges just in front of the lure, soak them over night in this stuff, the scent will last for up to half an hour, Amelia says." The idea is that the fish will 'smell' or taste this greasy trail in the water, follow it to your lure, and bite it. I had moderate success using sardine oil one week. I caught a bullhead or catfish, as Alex calls them.

"Well, if it lasts that long, it might help," I admitted. "The trouble with fish formula is that it washes off before the lure gets anywhere near the fish."

Nick arrived with the jug of ale and as we topped up our glasses we discussed the problems of using fish formula. Everything from its lack of adhesiveness to the lure, to how it smelled, was sticky when spilled in the boat or worse still, when the lid came off and the concoction ended up in your tackle box.

Alex was drawing designs on the table with his finger and the moisture from his glass.

"Hey, fellows, I think I've got it!" Big Al announced.

We all looked at his drawing. "What is that?" Pierre asked, "The fish of your dreams?"

"No, it's a lure. Jason was mentioning those little sponges . . . well, they may help hold the scent, but I don't like the way they interfere with the action of the bait when you slip them on your line ahead of a swivel snap. I wonder what would happen if we drilled a hole through the lure, put a plastic sleeve in the hole, then packed the hole with sponge soaked in the fish formula . . ."

"That might work," Pierre mused, "If the sponge were flush with the sides of the lure . . ."

"Yeah, and then scent would slowly dispense as the lure was retrieved . . ."

"You could use coloured sponges to match the colour of the lure . . ." I said.

"Maybe you could pack the sponges in a bottle of fish formula and reuse them as the formula rinsed out . . ."

We commissioned Alex to experiment on a couple of lures. Jason was going to see if Geraldine and Amelia would donate some of the new formula and perhaps a couple of lures. Pierre was to see if the idea could be patented and Freddie wrote something down on a scrap of paper about a 'Development Grant' but I could not make it out, having only recently taken up the art of reading upside down. We set a meeting date for next Tuesday at the Disraeli to assess Alex's idea on the sponge plug. We would wait until six p.m. so the women could join us.

Monday morning Freddie called me at work. He had contacted the manager at the local office of Northern Affairs and had ascertained that we might be eligible for a grant.

"We?" I asked.

"Well, I had to use a name for our company that will manufacture the scented lures. I thought if we could get the ground work done we could sell the idea to someone."

"Gee, Freddie," I said, "I don't know if the guys want to get that involved in this. Maybe you should wait until we have our meeting tomorrow night."

"I've already talked to everyone else! Alex has three models made from the lures that Geraldine and Amelia donated, Pierre's over at the library right now checking on what we have to do to apply for a patent. John and Jason are working with the girls to set up a couple of meetings with some tackle people."

"I get a feeling that we're rushing this, just a little," I said. It must be my conservative accounting background.

"If we get started right away, we can be manufacturing this fall and have our product ready for next spring." Before I could complain any further he continued, "What we need you to do is to check on all the tax implications, see about the incorporation and talk to your friend in Ottawa."

"My friend in Ottawa?"

"Yeah, you know, your Member of Parliament. He can pull some strings on the grant application."

"Hold it! I don't know him that well. Hell, I never even voted for him!"

"He doesn't know that. You went to school with him, that's all you need to mention. See you tomorrow night," he said and hung up before I could object further.

I was leaving the office Tuesday evening when my phone rang and I had to spend ten minutes helping one of the steno's who was working late with a formatting problem. I was late arriving at the Disraeli Club tavern. There were two guests at our table: Amanda who worked at the Hudson's Bay store and Catherine who was the head caterer for the Royal York Hotel. They had met the owners of *Bites and Bucks* who invited them to the meeting. John formally introduced me to all of the ladies as I had only been in their store once or twice and did not know them as well as some of the other members of the Club. Alex's modified lures were on the table and I examined them as Freddie brought me up to date on all the activity since our last meeting.

"What it amounts to is an opportunity to get into the tackle business with a very small investment. The Federal government will give us a non-repayable grant for creating jobs, a low-interest loan for capital manufacturing equipment and a tax holiday for the first two years. The Provincial government also will get us a grant for setting up in the northern part of the province and Amelia has a cousin in North Bay where there is a vacant building that we can get for a song!" Freddie explained.

"Whoa. Just what are 'we' going to manufacture? All we started out with was a couple of lures with holes in them."

"Geraldine has talked to the Rapala Company. They've been thinking of setting up a branch office here, under a separate name, and suggested we meet with them," John said.

"And I think we could talk one of the American companies into a partnership under the Free Trade deal if we want to pursue that route," Amelia said.

"I could check with my bosses at Hudson Bay – maybe they would be interested in this," our newest member Amanda said. "After all, the Company was founded on trapping, fishing and hunting." With that wild idea, I could see that she would fit right in with us.

"I think we should be independent of any other company. If the Rapala Company, or any other company, for that matter, wanted to have us manufacture for them under license, we could discuss it, but I think we should be our own bosses," Alex said.

"I wouldn't mind putting a few dollars into a business," Pierre said, "But I haven't the time to get fully involved in running another business."

"My feeling too," Alex said, "But I think maybe there is a good opportunity here for someone."

"Well, I don't really want to get tied up either," Freddie said, "but it just seemed that each of us had some connection that allowed us to plug into the system and make it work for us."

"That's true," Jason added, "Hell - we've covered almost everything in two days. It doesn't seem very hard to get a business going. Alex knows a lot about manufacturing, Freddie knows advertising, Pierre can keep the books, Bill can use his influence with the Federal Government to get the money, Geraldine and Amelia have a lot of connections in the tackle business, and John and I can test the product . . ."

That last statement caused a sudden dryness in my throat. I took a long draught of the Sleeman's Silver from my glass and reached for the jug for a refill. "Pierre," I asked, "How much do we need to get incorporated, for equipment, a plant, materials - all the basics? We will have to start looking for some funds."

"Well, I can do the incorporation papers myself but we'll likely need an independent lawyer for the grants and legal work that the government will foist on us. If the ten of us want to form a Limited Liability Company we'd have to have shares, the usual stuff, like a President and Secretary-Treasurer. That part is cheap enough: four or five thousand dollars. But we'd have to have some serious capital before we start looking at a building and manufacturing equipment such as extruders, presses, and a paint shop. The government won't give us quite everything!"

"We'd have to have some operating capital to keep us going until sales started coming in. We'd have to build up an inventory, pay wages, heating, overhead," Geraldine said.

"I'm just guessing at some figures," Amelia added, "but I think we'd need four or five employees just to start, and then hire part-time help to do finishing and packaging. I'd say we need about $250,000 to get seriously into the business."

We were all quiet as we each summed up our investments, and ready cash. Each of us realized that we were not ready for this kind of commitment.

"Whew," Freddie said. "I don't think I can get my hands on that kind of money." Every member of the BSBGSC Club echoed his comment.

"It's too bad," Alex said, fondling one of his renovated plugs. "I think we should have a tackle company here in the north. I even had a name - Northern Ontario Tackle and Supply."

"I like that!" Amanda said. "'NOTS', that's really catchy. What do you think, Geraldine?"

"Yes, that would work. We could specialize in fresh-water tackle – a speciality line, special colours, and our own brand of fish formula for the northern waters. There certainly are some possibilities here."

"Well ladies, I'm afraid we're long on ideas and short on cash - something that often plagues this Club!" I said.

The two women from *Bites and Bucks* exchanged glances and then Geraldine said, "I think we have a solution. You men are plugged into all the business circuits - you have all the contacts that we need to get a business started. All you lack is the time and the funds. Amelia and I have some experience in marketing and in running a successful business. Are you guys interested in being shareholders, albeit minor ones, in NOTS?"

"What do you have in mind?" Pierre asked.

Geraldine motioned to Nick for another round and then outlined their plan. "We know that this whole idea came from you fellows and it would be your ideas as much as ours that would be used in developing new lures. We need your help in getting the grants, because believe it or not, women still have a hard time getting grants from the government or loans from the bank. No pun intended, but we are not plugged into the business world and the back rooms of politics the way you men are. Amelia and I have some capital that we are willing to put into this company - about $200,000."

"Are you sure you want to risk that much money?" Pierre asked.

"I think so," Geraldine said. "We think it is worth the chance. If you will each put up a thousand dollars, we'll give you each two percent of the company. We can work out a deal where you can buy more shares later, up to twenty percent of the business, but we would remain the major shareholders and control the company, each holding forty percent of the stock."

I had always thought I would end up owning part of a tackle company, not by buying shares, but simply because of my annual purchasing of lures. "So we'll do the up-front work to help get the business started, and then you two will look after the operation once we start manufacturing?" I asked.

"Yes, but we would want to have your input on all the decisions about licensing or partnership manufacturing with other tackle companies. Any cost involved in meetings would have to be covered from the business funds. What do you think?" Amelia asked.

We agreed to talk it over with our spouses and each other but everyone seemed excited at the chance to start a business and get some of that 'free' government money. After all the years we had contributed our income tax dollars, it would be good to get some of the money back - especially if we could get some 'free' fishing tackle in the process. Catherine and Amanda were new to the Club and they thought they might defer for the time being.

My wife Martha thought I had lost it altogether. Apparently the other wives had similar opinions. NOTS would have been very successful, I am certain of that.

Death of a Pachyderm

(2007)

My wife had heard, via that grapevine that women use to keep informed of all things important, about a new restaurant just outside town that served absolutely the best food in our area. She was now talking on the telephone with Irene, Pierre's wife.

"Well, if the food is even half as good as Cindy said it was, it will be a real treat. It's just so hard to get a decent meal at a restaurant anymore."

"And Cindy said that it wasn't that expensive, either. John had the Seafood Supreme and Cindy had the Half Duck."

"And the pastry was just out of this world," she paused to see if I were listening or really paying attention to those two nitwits on Great Lakes Fishing who were raving about the fight put up by a five pound pike they had just landed. "No, Irene, Cindy said the bill only came to eighty dollars, and that included a bottle of good wine."

I could picture John's face as he forked over eighty bucks for a restaurant meal. John's idea of dining out is to go to the Golden Arches, order a Big Mac, extra fries, and a cup of cola. It must have been a special occasion. Or maybe Cindy had found out how much John had paid for his new Shimano reel. I knew from experience that one Shimano reel equals one dinner for two.

"Okay, Irene, we'll see you Friday night, about seven," my wife said and the replaced the receiver. "Bill, we're going out to that new restaurant on Friday with Pierre and Irene."

"Sure, okay," I answered just as one of those guys on the TV accidentally hooked a decent size fish. "I suppose this is a fancy dress affair?"

"No, but you could wear a sports jacket and tie. It's Pierre and Irene's wedding anniversary . . ."

"Oh," I said. It looked about twelve to fourteen pounds and the guy with the net was going to lose that fish if he . . . sure enough, he hit the line and the pike was gone. They cut away for a commercial. "Are we picking them up?"

"No, Pierre will drive. Our car is just too uncomfortable for Pierre." It was true that the little foreign job my wife drives was not designed for Pierre's generous size. We could have taken my Jeep but the women, who would no doubt be wearing dresses, did not like stepping up into the vehicle because of its high road clearance. Pierre drives an old Buick, one of those monsters that date back before the energy crisis, a '77 Park Avenue Buick. I continually tease him about applying for 'Antique' plates, but the darn old thing runs like a top. He had the car rust-proofed when he bought it and that undercoating treatment seemed to be working.

Friday evening I was dressed and relaxing once more in front of the TV, watching a documentary on the Ivory trade, when Pierre and Irene arrived. My wife was still putting on the finishing touches upstairs so I poured us each a liqueur glass of du Bonnet while we watched the plight of the elephants. Poachers were killing these magnificent beasts just for their tusks, leaving the carcass to rot in the hot African sun. The number of wild elephants left in the world was alarmingly small and there seemed little hope that they could survive the slaughter. I told Pierre and Irene about the show as we ate Martha's appetizers before we drove to the restaurant.

"Boy, we sure are something to be proud of, aren't we?" Pierre asked and then answered his own question, "Man just destroys one thing after another."

"It's hard to believe that we can be so ignorant. Don't those people know that they are wiping out a species?" Irene asked.

"Well," I said, "I suppose that they don't really understand. They can only see their immediate future, their immediate area. They don't have the over-all view that we can get, sitting here in front of a television. They have always had elephants. Their folk lore doesn't record a time when the elephant was not there . . . it's always been a part of their way of life. Now it's a way to earn some dollars."

"I guess we can't blame them if they don't know what they are doing," Pierre agreed. "But why don't they know? We go over there and find ways to 'civilize' those people, teaching them one of our religions, our style of politics . . . why haven't we stressed the importance of the ecology in their daily life?"

"I guess the animals just aren't that important to our mission people. Or they haven't been until now. Don't forget that we've made a pretty good mess of a lot of our own wildlife. We killed off most of the wild buffalo, whooping cranes, all of the passenger pigeons, damn near got rid of the peregrine falcon, the mountain lions, the burrowing owls . . . " I said. There was a pause in the conversation as the fellow doing the documentary showed footage of a small factory in Singapore where women were grinding small pieces of ivory into earrings and a man was selecting pieces for piano keys.

"I wonder if there is any hope for any of the big animals," Irene commented. "It seems we just won't give these creatures the space they need. I feel badly about the way the big cats are disappearing. I guess the elephants are next. The rhinos are virtually beyond saving!"

"Yes," my wife said as she made her grand entrance, all dolled up in her new dress, especially bought for the evening. 'On Sale', she had said. "They killed those poor rhinos just for their horns - because some ignorant man thought the powdered horn would improve his sex drive! Really, you men are so . . ."

"Let's get going," Pierre said. "I'm getting hungry."

Pierre had a little trouble starting the old car and only succeeded after soundly kicking the accelerator pedal and muttering his favourite string of French-Canadien oaths. Irene broke the silence by saying, "Pierre, I wish you would get rid of this old car!"

"There's nothing wrong with this car. It just needs a tune-up," Pierre said in defence of the old Buick. The car engine coughed and the ancient beast surged ahead, running smoothly. "Besides, they just don't make them like this anymore. The new cars are all compact and I'm not."

"The new ones are really very spacious, Pierre," I said. "The new Chevy Impala would be a good car for you. They get pretty good mileage, too," I added, knowing that this was a sore spot with Pierre. The old Buick sucks back about ten gallons (not litres) every hundred miles.

"Well, I like this car. It will last another five or six years. Besides, those Chevrolets look terrible! How anyone could design such an ugly car . . . ?"

"Do you have any problems getting parts?" my wife asked.

"No," Pierre replied, "There are a few of these old girls around yet. As they finally breakdown, the auto wreckers strip them of the good parts. As I said, she's good for another five or six years."

"I'll bet the wreckers are glad to see you coming. They can go out to their heap of parts and pieces and salvage another forty or fifty dollars from that car graveyard," I commented.

"That's almost like the elephants' graveyard," my wife mused. "A resting place for the old behemoths."

The old Park Avenue must have sensed something in that remark because the engine coughed, backfired and was silent. We coasted to a stop on the side of the road. Pierre tried the starter but the solenoid would not engage. Pierre and I got out and raised the hood, knowing full well that we couldn't do anything to revive the old car. I flagged down a passing taxi and we left the Buick at the side of the road, a problem to be faced in the light of the next day.

We had a very pleasant evening, enjoying the excellent food and ambience of the new restaurant. We celebrated Pierre and Irene's anniversary in style, even going so far as to toast the couple with champagne. We never once mentioned the old Buick although I thought my wife was pushing the metaphors a few times as we continued our discussion about the plight of the pachyderms.

Pierre called the next morning, about eleven. "Bill, they've stripped her!" he exclaimed.

"What are you talking about?" I asked.

"My car! Somebody jacked her up, stole all the wheels, took off the chrome grill, broke the window and ripped out the radio. The battery is gone, my air horns - everything!"

"My goodness, Pierre," I sympathized, "Did you call the police?"

"Yeah, but there wasn't much they could do. They said this often happens with these older cars. They promised they would keep an eye out for any of those chromed wheels on the few '77 Buicks around here, but they thought the parts would likely go to somebody who was restoring a car."

"That's too bad, Pierre. What are you going to do?"

"Well, she's sitting out there on the side of the road waiting for the wreckers to haul her away. Guess I'll have to start looking for a new car. Damn shame. That car was good for another four or five years – I'll never find another like that one!"

"Yes," I agreed. "She was the last of her kind. Too bad the poachers got her!"

Winter Bass

(2007)

An escape to Florida in mid-winter is something we in the BSBGSC had talked about for a couple of years, but saving up the required funds and getting our holidays coordinated had been a problem. It is more fun to travel with another couple, a couple whose interests are similar to your own. Alex and Claire were likely candidates - Alex and I fish together, do a little winter sports at the YMCA and even strike a few golf balls together if the fishing is slow in the dog days of August. Claire is an administrative assistant where my wife teaches at the Trinity College. They are both into Tai Chi so they had some things in common as well.

The plan was to fly to Orlando, find a motel with a large pool and absorb a few rays. Also to go the Epcot centre, do some shopping, slip over to the Kennedy Space Centre, do some shopping, visit Busch Gardens, and do some shopping.

A week before we were to leave on a well-deserved vacation, we met the rest of the Club members at the Disraeli.

"You two are sure lucky to get away from all this snow," Pierre said.

"Yeah, and I heard the long range forecast is for more snow and colder weather," Freddie added.

"Well, you fellows could have come along," Alex replied, "We certainly invited you all often enough."

"Yes," I said, "If you guys would just loosen up your purse strings a little . . . it doesn't cost that much to fly down there anymore."

"Mentioning purse strings - make sure you pay your annual dues before you go to Florida," Pierre said. "I don't want you complaining that you spent all your money in Florida." Our annual dues go 50% to the investment fund and 50% to covering incidental costs like buying the turkey for the Thanksgiving dinner at Freddie's place, prizes for the annual shooting contest and for camp maintenance at Little Loon Lake.

"Well, for my part," Jason said, "I don't think all that sun is good for you. It is not good especially for you, Alex – remember to wear your hat." Alex has a receding hairline that has receded all the way to the back of his head.

"I agree," John added. "You guys will look like a couple of rotisserie chickens when you get back. All that walking around in the sun and sleeping by the pool is not good for you."

"From what I heard about this trip," Pierre said, "Alex and Bill will have a better chance of getting a fluorescent light burn inside the malls than an outside sunburn."

"What do you mean," I asked.

"Irene says that your wife and Claire have some pretty heavy shopping excursions planned." Obviously my wife had been listening to all the stories her snow-bird friends told about bargains to be had in the clothing departments of American stores.

"That's right," John said. "I heard Cindy giving her dress size to Claire the other night. You guys are going to spend most of your holiday inside shopping malls!"

There were a few chuckles at Alex's and my expense, but as I signalled Nick to bring us another jug of ale, Alex reached into his jacket pocket and pulled out some brochures. "I hate to do this," he said, "but I thought you might be interested in looking at some of these fishing ads," he said to us.

He displayed a dozen or so flyers that he had written for as soon as he knew our trip was confirmed. It appeared as if there might just be a little bass fishing in Florida. In fact, it turned out that Alex had already booked a day of fishing for us. He had told our wives about it, he had just neglected to tell me the details.

"Holy smokes, Alex," I said, "I haven't made any arrangement to pack my rods, get my tackle sorted . . ."

"You don't have to do a thing," Alex replied. "We're going on this trip here," he said, indicating a brochure on the table.

Pierre picked it up and read, "Professional guide, all equipment supplied, lunch and cooler facilities on board. All boats are 17' Bass Boats with 150 horsepower motors, swivel seats, full tournament equipment. We will arrange for your Florida fishing license and take you to the home of the 10 pound bass!"

Now I knew I was really going to enjoy Florida. The rest of the Club members made some disparaging jokes about us having to hire guides and there were a couple of comments about alligators and swamp mosquitoes, but I knew they were all wishing that they too were headed for a week in Florida.

Geraldine said, "I think you will have a great time. Amelia and I went to a Fishing Tackle and Gun Show conference in Tampa last year in February. We took one of those bass fishing trips and had a ball."

"There is such a thing as a Tackle Conference?" Freddie asked.

"Absolutely. Next year it is in Las Vegas," Amelia said.

"Can anyone go?" Katherine asked. "Maybe Amanda and I could join you two ladies. I hear there is some decent fishing in Lake Meade."

Amanda had been quiet but I could see the idea of a trip to Vegas appealed to her. Maybe she could write off the expense as a fashion show trip for the Hudson Bay Company . . .

"Well," Pierre said, "you can tell us what it is like. Maybe we could all go south for a week next year. There must be some resort that can accommodate 12 fishers."

"Yes," Amelia said, "I am certain we can find something. There are plenty of places that offer deep-sea fishing, for instance."

"I'm not one for the ocean," Jason said. "I get seasick bobbing around in the big waves on Lake Simcoe."

We adjourned for the evening with promises to report to the Club about winter bass.

Lake Apopka is a small lake by northern Ontario standards. And it is much more polluted. The water was hardly the quality that you would even consider dipping a cup into to have a drink, but it did look like a great place for largemouth bass. There was plenty of heavy weed cover, extending well out into the lake, growing in seven or eight feet of water. The minnows were numerous, so many in fact that I thought we might have a hard time attracting a bass. Our guide, Orville, assured us that we would have no problem getting bass.

The boat was everything the advertisement promised. The guys in the Club had often made fun of these high-powered, squat boats, saying how they would not handle well in heavier waves, but for zipping around these Florida lakes, they were great. The equipment that Orville had for us was another story. I do not use my level wind equipment that much, preferring to use my spinning reels. Alex was more at home with the heavy bait caster than I, but as Orville pointed out, you needed heavy line to get your lure through all the weeds. He also hinted that eight pound test line just didn't hack it with the big bass we were after.

"Y'all throw thet bait ritt over thar," Orville said as we drifted to a stop near some weeds. He sat back and cut himself another chaw of tobaccy as Alex and I worked the weeds with buzz baits.

Alex got the first one. A large bass came up out of the water like a Cape Kennedy rocket. He also went back into the weeds before Big Al could follow Orville's advice and 'kip him on tuh top!' The trick was to keep the bass from getting down into the weeds where it would wrap the line around the greenery.

We had caught about half a dozen four to five pound bass, already a good day by our standards, when Orville decided that we needed to move. He headed for a small river that fed the lake and deftly ran the powerful bass boat through the channels into a small bayou off the main lake. "Don't usually take anybody in here, but seein' as you Kenadjuns come all the way out har, I figured y'all might like this har spot." It sounded like the same kind of guide story that you could get from any decent guide anywhere in Canada to me.

"You boys seen any gators yet?" he asked. When we shook our heads he turned the boat toward the shore. "One big old Daddy ritt thar," he said, pointing at what I had thought was a log. The alligator was about ten feet long. It sat there, ignoring us and then suddenly headed for the water. And us. Orville just laughed as he backed the boat away, saying that the gator was probably just looking for a hand-out as some of the fishermen often threw fish to the big reptiles. I edged more to the centre of the boat, thinking that anything that big with so many teeth was something to stay as far away from as possible.

We found some big bass, 'bucket-mouths', as Orville would say. In the two hours we spent in that little pond, Alex and I pulled in nine bass, all of them over five pounds and one that I caught, near the ten pound mark. Our time was almost over but Alex asked Orville if he could make one more cast. Big Al hooked into what Orville said was a 'gran- daddy'. It was definitely the largest bass of the day. It walked across the weeds three or four times, each time Alex managed to keep the line taut enough to prevent the big bass from throwing the lure. Then it decided to go down. The line flowed off the reel as the bass ran. Then it suddenly stopped. The brake on the reel did not stop fast enough and Alex had a back-lash. The fish was into the shallow water now and I was all for going in after it until Orville reminded me of the gators. It would have been good to have a picture of that bass to show the guys back home, but it was not to be.

Alex and I would have liked to have spent another day fishing but our full vacation agenda did not allow it. We promised ourselves that we would return some day for a real Florida fishing vacation. We arrived back in Toronto just after a ten-centimetre snow fall and I could feel my tan peeling away.

Back at the Disraeli we went through the fish story routine, telling the rest of the Club members about our bass fishing exploits. We had the photographs to prove most of our claims, but no picture of Big Al's big bass that got away.

"So why didn't you just pull the line in, hand over hand?" Freddie asked Alex. "At least you would have had a picture of it."

"Well, uh, by that time, the line was, uh, broken," Alex said.

"I thought you guys were using 20 pound test," Pierre said. "How could it break that?"

"Well, by the time Alex got the back-lash untangled, he had more like eight hundred pounds on his line," I said.

"Eight hundred?" Jason asked in disbelief.

"Yeah," Alex admitted, "That would be close. And it was about this long," he said, extending his arms to their over six foot spread.

There was a silence until Amanda said, "You don't mean to say you caught a fish that big! Come on, Alex!"

"No," I said, relishing Alex's discomfort, "But the alligator that ate his fish was just about that long!"

Getting the Lead Out

(2007)

It was Friday evening and we had gathered at the Disraeli Club to celebrate the end of another work week and arrange for the annual duck hunt. I gave up shooting the little quackers many years ago but I had not given up the gracious habit of sipping a little draft ale with the fellows as they made their plans for the annual foray into the cold, damp marshes late in September. John, who is a real estate salesman and often works Saturdays, and could not go on the hunt this year because of a good prospect, was telling me about last year's hunt when he had actually shot a decoy. I had heard other versions of the story from the rest of the members but it was interesting to hear John trying to justify that moment of poor judgement.

"I'm telling you, Bill, that decoy was moving - and the rest of them were as still as could be. There was no wind so I figured that it had to be swimming," he explained.

"Maybe there was a current?" I suggested.

"Not in a marsh on the lake. Man, it sure looked real to me."

"Pierre says you did make a good shot, though," I said.

"Yeah. Took the head right off it. Cost me twelve fifty for a new decoy," he complained.

"Plus the shotgun shell," I said. "They must be getting close to a buck apiece now."

"That's right," Big Al said from across the table. "And now that we have to use the steel shot instead of lead shot, we'll be paying even more."

"Well, you should all be using steel shot," I said, it being easy for me to criticize since I was not buying shotgun shells anymore. "I was watching Michigan Outdoors the other night and the Americans in Michigan must use steel shot."

"I presume this is an environmental safeguard?" Jerry asked.

"I guess so. All that lead lying around in the lakes is slowly going to poison us. And poison the rest of the creatures who eat fish." I was thinking about myself, of course.

"We've known for years that when waterfowl eat the lead shot, thinking it is a pebble as a digestive aid, they get lead poisoning and either die or produce defective offspring," Freddie said as he passed his empty glass to Jason for a refill from the draft jug. "I can't understand why it takes us so long to get the legislation in place to out-law lead shot. I, for one, am quite willing to pay a few cents more to protect the environment - and the ducks."

"Well, you don't need the legislation to stop using lead shot," Alex said.

"That's not quite true, Alex," Geraldine said. She is a partner in *Bites and Bucks*, the sporting goods store. "We have been trying to order steel shot for several months now and it is always back-ordered. They will send us lead shot, and we have to have something on the shelves or our customers will shop elsewhere."

"That's right." Jason added. "I went down to your store last week, looking for steel shot and Amelia said it wasn't available. It seems we need the legislation to force the manufacturers into giving us the right product!"

"True," Alex admitted, "But I bought my shells in Windsor when I was down there last summer. They sell it there because many Americans use steel shot. It is manufactured in Canada so it must be available to the local shops. It's likely that they just don't get enough demand for steel shot to bother carrying it."

"Typical attitude of some of our manufacturers," grumbled Pierre. "They can't see past the end of their noses."

"Only as far as the cash register," Freddie agreed with him.

"Believe it not," I said, "There are some people who are opposing the use of steel shot."

"Sure, the people who mine and smelt the lead . . ."

"No. An animal rights group in the States."

"You've got to be kidding!" John said. "Everybody knows that lead is poisonous . . . hell, it virtually wiped out the Roman aristocracy." That caused me to wonder about the wisdom of using that pewter beer mug I won at Darts last year – wasn't that tin and lead?

"Oh, they're not arguing that point - they claim that the steel shot will wound too many ducks."

There was a murmur of disbelief around the table that quietened down only after Nick the bartender brought us another jug of draft.

"That's the truth," I said. "The steel shot makes a tighter pattern and the animal rights people claim that because of this, more ducks and geese will be hit by single pellets and not be killed outright."

"What a bunch of crap!" Big Al said and slapped his big hairy hand down on the table for emphasis. Everybody cautiously lifted their glasses from the table, knowing that when Alex gets excited he often thumps his fist on the table. "I checked out the pattern of the shot and it is tighter - but all you have to do is adjust the choke on the gun. By using full choke instead of the half choke that I used to use, I have exactly the same pattern of shot!"

"What makes the pattern different anyway?" Pierre asked. "Is it the weight of the pellets?"

Geraldine replied and we all paid attention. The owner of *Bites and Bucks* was a championship skeet shooter. "No, that's not it. When you fire lead shot, it bounces off the sides of the barrel and off other the other pellets. The soft lead is deformed by the contact. Because it is no longer perfectly round, the aerodynamics are poor and the shot flies through the air in an irregular pattern. Steel shot, because it is hard, does not deform when it is in the barrel and it keeps its close pattern longer."

"And those dummies think that more ducks are going to be wounded with steel? I'd think it was better for the ducks - less area of shot, fewer random pieces of shot flying through the air!" Jason exclaimed.

I mumbled something about it being a whole lot better for the ducks if there weren't pellets of any type flying through the air, but the guys pretended not to hear me.

"That's right, Jason," Alex continued. "The steel shot also keeps its velocity better so if we continue to shoot at ducks within the same ranges as we do now, we should knock down more ducks and in fact have fewer wounded ones."

Pierre, who was obviously impressed by the technical explanations, looked at little thoughtful. "What's on your mind, Pierre?" I asked.

"I was thinking about those little steel pellets and what Gedraldine said about aerodynamics. Maybe they should put dimples on them - make them fly further and straighter still."

"You're joking," Freddie said.

"No. They do it with golf balls - why not with steel shot? They could hire some cheap labour; give them a small steel punch and a tack hammer. They could sit there tapping . . ."

Alexander, Geraldine, Jason, John and Freddie said in unison, "Pass the beer, Bill."

Wading for Trout

(2008)

It was the last Friday of the month, the day Pierre gave the BSBGSC the financial report. Six years ago we each had thrown in $150 and became Stock Market Investors. We invest one half of our annual dues into the Fund as well. Pierre, who looks after our finances whenever we trek off into the wilderness in search of better fishing, also manages The Fund. Using various 'hot tips' and avoiding brokerage fees, Pierre records our progress in a spreadsheet. The first year had shown that our original $900 had turned itself into $868.75. In 2003, we showed a gain of $335.00; 2004 the Fund was up to $1823.21; in 2005 we gained another $700.00; 2006 was a poor year and we dropped $326.75; 2007 showed the Fund sitting at $2,477.10. As soon as everyone had a glass of Sleeman ale at hand, Pierre began.

"As of this morning, we held 2500 shares of Golden Knight Resources, which I bought at 8 cents; 3000 shares of Precambrian Explorations at 15 cents; and 1200 shares of Echo Bay Development at 9 cents. I received a tip from an anonymous source this morning who said that there would be a run on Golden Knight, so I have sold Precambrian at $8^{1/4}$ and converted that to Golden at $11^{3/4}$. At closing today, Golden Knight was at $15^{1/2}$!"

"Hear, hear!" Alex said. The approval was echoed by the others at the table. Since it was my cousin who had given me the tip on Golden Knight, I too, applauded Pierre's strategy. Alvin works as a diamond driller and he had seen the core samples at a Golden Knight drilling site. Alvin cannot use any information about what they find as that would be insider trading information. I am an outsider who will make certain that Alvin gets a nice Christmas present again this year.

"I expect the stock to continue to climb into next week so we should be in a profit-taking position by closing Tuesday," Pierre stated.

"Let's drink to that!" Freddie exclaimed. Raising his glass of amber ale, Freddie toasted, "To Golden Knight."

Our financial plan is really quite simple. Pierre took a listing of penny stocks, compiled the data for a period of a month on his computer, and came up with the following method of becoming wealthy. Sell and cut losses if the stock drops 25% below purchase price; sell for gain if the stock doubles. If the stock does not move in three weeks, sell and try something else.

"How are the other two stocks doing, Pierre?" I asked.

"Precambrian looks like it is starting to move and Echo Bay dropped back to $1^{1/4}$ from $1^{1/2}$. I think we have some winners this time. However," Pierre said and the side conversations stopped. Whenever Pierre says 'however' in the Fund report, we shudder. "There are signs that the Sub-Prime Mortgages in the US are in trouble. This will likely have far-reaching effects on the stock market. I am therefore going into a 'Bear' position and holding all investments until I see where this is going."

"Hear, hear," someone said. I think it was Geraldine.

Freddie, Alex and Pierre then began to discuss their pickerel fishing plans for the weekend so I asked Kate if she was still on for our trout excursion, planned for the next morning.

"Yes, I'm all set. I even bought a new set of waders."

"It's about time," I said. "That old set had more patches than Joseph's coat."

"I don't see what you fellows get out of trout fishing," John put in.

"Just the best tasting fish you can find," I replied. I could picture a half dozen eight or nine inch Brook trout sizzling in a pan. "Brook trout, fried in butter, are just . . ."

"Scrumptious," Kate said.

"Delicious," Alex suggested.

"Delightful," Pierre added. "With a few capers, of course."

"Okay, okay," John said. "But what do you need waders for? I thought you just walked along the creek bank . . ."

"I guess you have never caught trout in a beaver pond." Kate said.

"I thought speckled trout liked fast-moving water."

"Mostly they do, but if there's feed in a pond, the trout will stay there. If the pond isn't too old, the trout will stay in the creek bed, feeding in the shallows. Once a pond dies, they move out. Most ponds are good for about three years - the time a beaver family will stay, too."

"The beaver will only travel so far from the safety of the pond for its food. In three years they usually reach the safe boundary from wolves," I explained to my city-slicker friend John.

"So you wade out into the pond?" John asked.

"Yes. You try to get close to the old creek bed, where the water is deeper. Kate caught two 14 inchers last week."

"Yes," Kate laughed, "I had quite a time landing them, too. It's not easy when you're up to your waist in cold water. I darn near fell in a couple of times."

"Yes, you should have seen her stumbling around!" I said.

"It sounds as if you had a good time. Do you think you could take me along tomorrow?" John asked. Kate and I told John what to bring for tackle, insisting that he use 4 pound test on a light rod. Kate said she would loan John her old waders. Kate and John are about the same size, a comment we never make to either one of them.

The next morning we were out wading in our favourite pond, instructing John in the art of trout fishing. With typical beginner's luck, he caught a 10 inch speckled trout and then a fat colourful beauty that was the match of the ones Kate had caught last week. But his beginner's luck also entitled him to step into what we call a 'beaver hole'. That's a channel cut into the bank by the beaver when the pond is new - a place where the beaver drags all his sticks into the water. The water in beaver ponds is not clear and you have to 'feel' your footing when in water up to your waist. Of course there are logs, slippery rocks and other underwater hazards, but beaver holes are the worst for dumping fishermen. John was still excited about his big catch when he stepped into a hole. He floundered a bit, got the waders full of water and had to go ashore to dry out. It was a warm evening, so he was soon back fishing.

But beaver holes are underwater. There are problems above the water, too. Because you are standing in water up to your waist, you have to use an over-hand casting motion. The presence of dead trees in the pond makes it even more difficult to get a line out to the trout. Sooner or later you end up hooking something - a tree, a limb or the backside of your own waders. Just try to free yourself from a hook in the sdeat of your waders while holding onto your rod, not losing your creel, keeping the worms reasonably dry, swatting a thousand flies and all the while keeping your balance on a slippery bottom. John managed to catch his waders and the hole he put in the waders let in a trickle of cold water, but it did not dampen his enthusiasm. He was becoming a trout fisherman. He wanted to come out again and I said I would give him a call some evening next week, if he was not working. Realtors work when their clients are available and we can never tell when John is going to have a day off.

The next Thursday morning I was talking to Pierre on the telephone about our stock market success with Golden Knight when the other line rang. I put Pierre on hold in case it was something important, like a Royal Bank customer.

"Bill, can you go trout fishing tonight?" John asked.

"Well, yes, sure. What do you have in mind?"

"I found out about a new pond from some of the guys at work. We can drive to within a hundred yards of it."

"Sounds good," I said. "Just the two of us?"

"Yeah, unless you want to call Kate."

"I was thinking of Pierre. If we don't have to walk too far, he might be interested. I've got him on the other line – something about those American sub-prime mortgages."

"Sure. It would be a great spot for him. Wait until you see my new outfit! I'll pick you up at six." John said.

"Okay," I said and then switched back to Pierre. "Pierre that was John on the other line. Are you interested in going trout fishing tonight?"

"Well, I guess . . . where are you going?"

Pierre is a little overweight and tramping through the woods has a limited appeal for him. "John found a spot that we can drive to. His source says it's full of trout."

"Okay. I'll check with Irene, but I think I'm clear tonight."

On the way into the creek we found a stake, driven into the ground and supported by a pile of stones. The squared piece of wood had some writing on it that was barely legible from months of weathering. We decided that it was a mining claim stake and Pierre tried to copy what information he could from the stake. He figured we might have some inside information in a mining stock. Or, as John suggested, a chance to invest in shares in the best trout farm in the area. Pierre always has an eye open for a good investment. There was no trout farm in our portfolio yet.

The pond did look good. It was quite large, probably over a hectare in area. I guessed the pond to be about two years old from the poplar tree line. The evening was calm and every now and then a ripple would appear on the mirror surface where a fish broke the surface. We all agreed that this pond was the reason for the claim stake. I offered to buy the first hundred shares on it. Pierre and John seconded the purchase.

John's new outfit was different. To the top of a pair of waders, that were about the same colour as those rubber suits worn by the firemen, was attached an inner tube. John got into the waders and then pumped up the tube with a small hand-held bicycle pump. I was concerned that he might overturn in that contraption and not be able to right himself or free himself from the waders. The floating waders had a safety plug that would deflate the inner tube in an emergency. He said not to worry because he had tested the outfit in his swimming pool. It was quite safe. It looked awkward, but in this pond he would be able to get out to the middle. Pierre jokingly asked if he had forgotten his flippers but I could see that John took the suggestion seriously.

Pierre did not have waders so he was going to fish off the beaver dam. I went upstream to where I could wade out and fish the creek bed. John floated out to the middle of the pond to try his luck there. The pond seemed full of chub, not a particularly good sign for trout, although they do live together. I was about ready to quit feeding the little fish when I got a real strike. It took me a couple of minutes to land it, but when I finally got my fish to shore, it was a hammer-handle pike! This creek must drain a lake with pike in it. I threw the pike back, advising him to eat lots of chub, and headed back to get Pierre and John. John was still out in the middle, casting out his bait.

"Any luck?" I called.

"Naw, just a couple of chub," he said.

I waved to Pierre to see if he had caught anything. We could not hear him for the water going over the dam but he held up three fingers.

"You'll never guess what I caught," I said to John.

But before he could answer, his pole bent and the line sang off the reel. Fifty feet away a fish broke water.

"Holy Moses!" He yelled.

I did not want to spoil the fun by telling him he had a pike on the line. A four pound test line takes some care when you are floating around in an inner tube, even for a small pike. John finally reeled it up to his floating platform. He did not have a net, so he was trying to get it near the creel. Somehow the fish got behind him and then through his legs. He dropped his rod once but grabbed it before it sank. He began thrashing his way to shore, all the way whooping and hollering about the big fish he had on the line.

I was laughing and Pierre could see the commotion, so he came up the shore to where I was standing. Soon we were both laughing.

"What's so funny?" John yelled. "I'm all tangled up and the fish is still swimming around my legs. I don't want to lose it! It's a real dandy!"

"Yeah, some dandy!" I called out. "This pond has pike in it! You just caught yourself a hammer-handle pike!"

"What? You mean . . ."

"Watch out for that tree, John," Pierre warned. But he was too late. John had backed himself into a dead balsam. There was a 'pop' and John suddenly began thrashing his arms to get to shore. The inner tube soon lost its air but John had made it safely to a solid footing. Our laughter continued while John tried to get himself untangled from his line and the fish.

"Just a minute, John," I said, "I'll come out and help you."

I was picking my way out to him, carefully feeling my footing through the murky water, when John said, "Wait!"

"Bill, I can see that fish. It's not a pike. It is the wrong shape."

"How big is it?" I asked.

"About 22 inches and pretty wide. Definitely not a pike."

"Maybe it's one of these," Pierre yelled from the shore. He held up a forked stick with three big black suckers on it. "You can keep your shares on this pond. It's strictly for suckers!" Pierre laughed.

Darning

(2008)

It was a hot, dog-day afternoon in late August and Pierre and I were enjoying a little relaxed fishing at his cottage. Pierre owns an old log cabin on Spruce Lake, generally referred to as "The Camp" because of its lack of amenities. Furnished only with rustic chairs and a table, and two bunks, the cabin is 60 kilometres northeast of the city on a small lake. Actually, the lake is more a widening of the Snake River but the small bay in front of the Camp does attract some fish that seem to move up and down the river, depending on the weather, the season, or availability of their favourite food. Pierre uses a small car-top aluminium boat, powered by misfit oars (one is two inches longer than the other) at the Camp, a craft that adequately supports Pierre's somewhat overweight body and one other adult. And a cooler of wobbly pop.

As so often seems to be the case with big, heavy men, Pierre has a delicate touch. He was exhibiting the fine art of fly-casting this afternoon. He would work out the line, flipping the long rod easily back and forth, spooling off line with his other hand, until he had the fly exactly where he wanted it beside a lily pad or deadhead snag. The little Royal Coachman Bucktail was catching one perch after another, and Pierre was having a pleasant time bringing in the little scrappers on the light tackle. He would bring them up to the boat and then release the colourful fish after telling them not to bother him again. Other than catching the odd horsefly that landed on my arm, nothing spoiled our idyllic afternoon as I fed the wounded flies to the minnows at the side of the boat. I was content to let my bobber and worm harness do my fishing. It was an afternoon for relaxing.

"How many times have you caught that one?" I asked as Pierre released a 10-inch perch.

"Four times, I think. If he comes in once more, I'll tag him!"

"There are so many perch in this bay a bass would have to be mighty quick to get your fly – they're probably eating the perch," I commented.

"Naw, this time of year they are more interested in crayfish or frogs – something small, easy to eat. I think they are like Muskies – getting their new teeth at the end of summer," Pierre said.

"That's an old fisherman story," I said. "Muskies don't lose their teeth."

"Then how come they don't bite this time of year?"

"Probably like your bass - having a change of diet. All you have to do is find the right bait and you'll catch them. You have to think like a bass," I said.

"Speaking of bass, your bobber just went under for the third time."

"Damn perch," I said and started to reel in. No sooner had I applied pressure to the line than I knew I did not have a perch on the hook. The brake on the reel gave its "wheeee" scream; was quiet; and then gave another whine as my line peeled off the reel. "Get the net, get the net!" I yelled, the afternoon's lethargy dispelled instantly by this sudden action.

"What is it?" Pierre asked, retrieving his line as quickly as he could.

"Must be a pike …" The line went slack as I frantically reeled in, trying to keep tension on the line. Fifty yards away the water erupted and a large black bass thrashed across the surface, dancing on its tail, shaking its head to throw the hook. The line went slack.

"Holy mackerel!" Pierre exclaimed. "Was that a bass, or was that a BASS!"

"Damned bobbers!" I said. "I keep saying I'm going to stop using them." It is my theory that bobbers do two things: they allow you to neglect your fishing and have a cool drink; they lose big fish because the slack in the line prevents a proper set of the hook.

The perch had all fled the scene so we decided that I should row over to another bay. This mode of transport reminded me of the 'olden days' and I suggested to Pierre that he could buy an electric motor if he was concerned about pollution from a gas motor.

"No, it's not the pollution – it's the noise we don't like. An outboard motor destroys the peace and quiet for everyone around." I had to agree that it was very quiet here at the Camp with only the sounds of birds accompanied by the soughing of the wind in the big pines along the shore. I could understand why all four cottagers around the little lake had agreed not to use gas motors.

"Besides, I think the noise of even an electric motor scares the fish," Pierre continued. I wondered about the squeaking of the left oarlock, but said nothing.

"Well, I don't know about that. I think they get used to the sound of motors after a while. You know, that reminds me of a story my Dad used to tell."

I went on to relate how they reportedly cut a long birch branch (why it was always a birch in the stories, I never did ask my father) and then they would thrash the water near a lily pad bed. The noise and commotion was supposed to attract the big fish. Small fish would be intimidated by the thrashing and flee the area, but who wanted small fish, anyway? My father thought perhaps the sound idea was to imitate a moose feeding on the lily pads: the fish would come to eat any creatures stirred up when the moose pulled up a plant.

"I wonder what they used for bait back then," Pierre mused. "Something that looked like it did the thrashing and splashing?" Pierre had that faraway look in his eye as he was searching the shoreline for a birch tree. I should have kept my big mouth shut.

"Oh, they used whatever they had," I said. "Dad said that he remembers his father catching bass with a piece of red yarn wrapped around a small treble hook."

"Really?" Pierre said another glint in his eye.

"There, Bill – there's a good birch – let's try it!"

When we went ashore we thought the birch was too big for our fish knives so I hacked down a nearby alder, all the while assuming that it would work as well as a birch. I rowed us back out to the edge of a weed bed. Pierre was rummaging in his tackle box.

"Look," he said, "I always wondered what this was for! My cousin, a fellow fly-fisherman from the United States, gave it to me a few years ago. I thought it was a joke." He held up a small card of yellow, orange, and red yarn. The kind of thing you might find at a Knit and Sew Shoppe if you were thinking of darning your wool work socks.

"Pierre, you're not going to . . ."

"Why not?"

I opened a couple of cans of Bud Lite by way of answer. Pierre wrapped the red yarn around what he said was a Black Nosed Dace, leaving a trailing strand of yarn about three inches long. He pulled it back and forth in the water beside the boat to persuade both of us that it was suitable bait. It did look rather interesting to me, thinking anthropomorphically like a bass.

"Okay, Bill, you thrash the water. When you get the branch out of the way, I'll cast out and draw the lure through the place where the big fish should be."

Thrashing the water with a ten-foot tag alder is no easy chore, but I did manage to make a commotion and raise some froth. Pierre cast the newly adorned Dace.

On the first pass, he only caught a weed but on the second try, all hell broke loose in the form of a largemouth bass on a light tackle.

In the ten minutes that it took to get the bass to the boat, it broke water four times, running across the surface, trying to shake the lure. Pierre kept the tension on, using the long thin rod expertly, coiling line by hand between his feet. Three times, he had to let out more line but the bass never got to the end of the spool.

I netted the large bass and we both agreed on seven pounds before releasing it back into the lake. "Bill, let's go home! Anything else today is going to be a real letdown. Man that was great! I'm going to make up some more of those red yarn lures tonight!"

"Yes, Pierre," I said as I applied the oars, "and just think what might have happened if we had used a real birch branch instead of that alder!"

Dowsing

(2009)

Pierre and I were fishing in what is humorously named 'Fish Bay', looking for largemouth bass and catching only a few small perch. We fish this nearby lake quite often, mostly because it is within an hour's drive, not because of its reputation as a great fishing lake. Our peaceful afternoon was disrupted by some young fellows playing with their boat. It seemed a great sport to make waves by circling the boat, then turning the boat into the waves, to make splashes of spray. They were far enough away so as not to disturb the perch but Pierre was beginning to make noises that the kids might be the reason why the bass were not biting.

"I wish those kids would go and play somewhere else," Pierre said. "They shouldn't be doing that anyway - they aren't even wearing life jackets."

"Yes, they should at least have jackets on. But I remember when I was that age, doing the same thing as they are doing. Mind you, all we had was a large cedar strip boat and a five horsepower motor. Not much chance of upsetting that old tub."

"No, I suppose not," Pierre said as he pulled up his line with yet another six inch perch hanging onto the end of his worm. If that worm had had some sharp teeth it would have given that perch a good tussle. "But those kids have a much smaller boat - and a bigger motor."

"Do you think we should go over and tell them to at least put on their life jackets?" I asked.

"There is not much chance of them listening to us, but I suppose we should warn them. I'll get the anchor," Pierre said. Before Pierre could haul in the mud-coated anchor there was a high-pitched roar from the little 9.9 engine on the kid's boat. We both looked up in time to see the motor come flying off the boat, bounce on the water a couple of times and sink out of sight. The boat rocked almost to the gunwales but righted itself, the two kids hanging on to the sides. It was very quiet.

"Well I'll be darned!" Pierre exclaimed. "Did you see that? The motor just came right off!"

"Yeah, it must have vibrated loose, then it cavitated. It pulled itself right into the air. Those kids were damn lucky it didn't land inside the boat!"

"I guess we'd better go over see if they're all right," I said. By this time the boys were waving and shouting at us to come to their rescue. "I'll bet they don't even have a set of oars in their boat," I added.

"Before we move let me get a line of site on where that motor went into the water," Pierre advised. He looked for a couple of landmarks, took some pictures on his cell phone, made a note in the little electronic notebook that he carries, and then motioned for me to start the motor.

The two young boys were about twelve or thirteen and indeed, had no oars on their boat. They looked like brothers, both with freckles and red hair, the one who had been driving being the older. The motor had fallen into about eight feet of water, but the murky nature of Fish Bay made it impossible to see anything on the bottom. The thick weed growth would make the job of locating the engine even more difficult. We moved upwind a little and Pierre dropped in one of my fish markers as a reference point in case the parents wanted to try to find the outboard motor. We then asked the boys if they wanted a tow back home.

"Actually," the one with most freckles said, "we just rented the boat at the Marina. Could you take us back there?" I knew the Marina owner as being a man who was a little excitable. I remembered him getting quite upset one day when Jason backed his boat trailer into a garbage can that was nearby, well, it was within twenty feet of the launch ramp. I thought maybe the lads were in for a bit of nasty reception when the lessor found out that the lessee, who was under legal contract age, had lost a thousand-dollar motor. While the boys were putting on their life jackets and being helped aboard our boat under Pierre's instruction, I looked at the transom of the rental boat. It was built up with two pieces of wood bolted through the aluminium, and well-worn from many years of rough usage.

"Damn," the Marina man said after the two boys had left on their bicycles, "that's the second motor I've lost this year! I guess I forgot to hook up the safety chain. My insurance agent is not going to be too happy when he hears this."

"We tried to mark where the motor went down, but with all the weeds . . ." Pierre said.

"Yeah, there's no sense in even looking for it. Chances are the engine sucked in water and the cylinder head would be cracked anyway. No, the insurance company just pays up on these losses."

"Gee, I'd be inclined to at least try to find it, if I were them," said Pierre, the Investment accountant, no doubt thinking of the hassles of writing off the accumulated depreciation and applying it against the loss recovery column in his books.

"Hey, go ahead. Finders keepers," the marina man said as he went back inside to sell some dew worms to a couple of fellows who said they were going out to try for bass.

Early the next morning, about eleven o'clock, the phone rang. It was Pierre. "Bill, I was talking to a guy at Church this morning and he told me how to find that motor. He said we could dowse for it."

Not being particularly religious, I made some comment about witchcraft being condoned by the Holy Roman Catholic Church but Pierre let it slide. "No, he showed me how you can find metal objects using two pieces of coat hangers."

"Pierre, you did say you were at church this morning, didn't you?"

"Yeah. Listen, this really works. It's just like dowsing for water, only you use coat hangers instead of an alder branch."

"Willow," I corrected him.

"Whatever. Do you want to try it?"

"Only if we take along our fishing rods," I said.

"Well, of course. See you in half an hour? I've already packed us a light lunch." Pierre's idea of a light lunch is a couple of sandwiches with at least three items for fillings, some crisp dill pickles, a few of his own homemade cookies, a fruit and a thermos of tea. Lunch and chance to catch a fish - what more could a fellow ask for? Besides, who would not want to investigate the weird world of dowsing?

I had been party to dowsing for water a couple of times and although I could never get the same response as the Dowser, I was sure that I could feel the forked willow wand move as I walked over the spot indicated by the Dowser. It seems that every rural community has a Dowser. Where I grew up, it was a Mr. Manson Kidd, a seemingly normal farmer, who had the 'gift'. It was amazing how often he could find water. In fact, he also carried a piece of binder twine with a couple of old rusty 2-inch hex nuts tied to one end that he would get out to gauge the depth at which water would be found. He would hold the string over the exact spot he had selected as most promising for water, swing the nuts and count the number of pendulum swings, convert this to feet and make his pronouncement. Old Mr. Kidd would never take any wagers on his ability, but his nephew who drove him to his dowsing appointments was known to have made a few dollars from doubters.

We found the fish marker and moved around the area trying to spot the motor but the water was just too murky. The motor was a Mercury - all black except for the name. A bright blue Yamaha or red Mariner might have been easier to see down in the weeds. I thought I saw a bass once and suggested to Pierre that maybe we should fish first but he wanted to try his coat hangers. Pierre bent the two pieces of metal into an 'L' shape, the method being to hold the shorter end loosely in your hands about six to eight inches apart. When the rods passed over metal, the wires would cross, indicating that the motor was just below.

Pierre stretched out over the bow of the boat, reaching as far from the aluminium boat as possible while I tried to make slow passes in a search pattern around the marker. I had just started to make snide remarks about the whole concept of finding metal with coat hangers when Pierre yelled, "Whoa!" The pieces of metal had crossed, no doubt. "Back up a little, Bill . . . there . . . shut it down. I'll drop the anchor."

Now that we had found the motor, we had to bring it to the surface. Since neither of us had the foresight to bring a set of swim trunks, I volunteered to make the dive in my underwear. I stripped down and asked for the exact location. Pierre moved his wires around and pointed just off the port bow. It was too murky to see much but the water was only about eight feet deep. After getting a firm commitment from Pierre that he would pull any leeches off me, I took a deep breath and jumped in. The water was warm and not uncomfortable. I dove to the bottom, parting weeds and looking around. Nothing.

Coming up for air, I asked Pierre, "Are you sure this is the right spot?"

"Yeah, look - the wires cross right here," he said, again demonstrating the action of the wires over the place where I was treading water.

"Okay, but I sure didn't see anything." I took a deep breath and duck dove again. I was parting the weeds, carefully so as not to stir up any sediment when I came face to face with a huge largemouth bass. I know water distorts size, but this was at least a five pound fish. I reached out towards it but it gave a flick of its tail and was gone. Just as I was about to return to the surface, my foot touched something hard. I turned around and felt about. Sure enough, something that might have been the bottom end of a motor. I had to get some more air so I went straight up, yelled to Pierre that I had found it, grabbed the rope we had for hauling the salvage to the surface, and dove again.

I found the metal object again but soon realized that what I had thought was the missing motor was a large anchor that someone had lost. I fastened the rope around one fluke and returned to the surface. "Haul away, Pierre," I said as I scrambled over the end of the boat.

"Well I'll be darned! It's an anchor!" he exclaimed.

"Yeah. No sign of that motor."

"At least it proves that the wires work. Say," he continued, "this isn't a bad anchor. It has to be worth at least thirty or forty dollars."

"It's yours," I said. "Just swish the mud off it before you bring it into the boat."

We tried to locate the motor again but the wires never moved in Pierre's hand. I told Pierre about the big bass I had seen down in the weeds so he immediately put down his dowsing rods and picked up his casting rod. We fished for half an hour without a nibble and I suggested that we move to a favourite spot just east of Little Pine Island, try there for half an hour and then call it a day.

"I just put on a Mepps with an orange and brown rubber worm trailer. Let me try one more cast over there to the right. I'm sure there's a big hungry bass just lurking in those weeds," Pierre said as he gave an extra hard flip to his rod, trying to send the bait out a little further.

It was that extra effort that caused the back-lash and it took Pierre a couple of minutes to free the reel of the snarled line. He started to wind in but was snagged. I got out my lure retriever, a gadget that slides down your line. It attaches its grapples to the underwater obstacle and by pulling on the heavy nylon line, dislodges either an old limb or whatever you have snagged. I pulled and whatever was down there, started to move. Pierre was looking down into the deep with his polarized glasses, trying to see his Mepps lure. He saw the motor before I did.

"It's the motor! Hold it steady while I throw in the anchor." In his excitement he grabbed the anchor we had found and threw it overboard. "Whoops. I'll just put this other one in too, in case we start to drift," he said, looking very sheepish.

I once more stripped off my clothes and slipped buck-naked into the water. I had discarded my wet underwear and was now swimming about in the weeds, totally exposed. We hauled in the engine and then the anchor. I didn't tell Pierre about the big bass that was watching me. I was not certain if that fish was just curious or if it was looking at one of my appendages, thinking it was a dew worm . . .

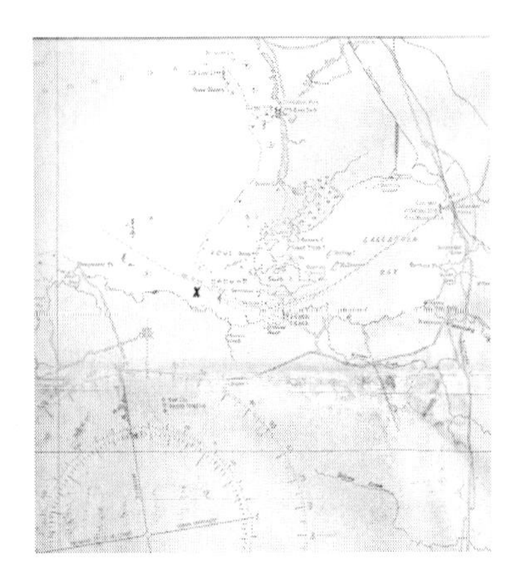

The Remote Lake

(2009)

"Did you see that fishing show on Channel 2 last week?" Big Alex asked as we sat down for a cool draft on a Friday night late last spring.

"Yes, I did," I answered, sipping on the glass of Sleeman Silver Ale that appeared as if by magic but it was only Nick's anticipation of our needs. "Could you believe the way they were hauling in those walleyes?"

"Pickerel." Alex insists on calling them pickerel.

"Well, I guess there are still some great fishing places left - all you have to do is find them," Pierre said.

"Sure," I said just a little sceptically, "those guys have all kinds of money at their disposal so it's no problem for them to fly into some remote place and make a video of fish jumping into their boat."

"Yes, you're right, Bill," Jason commented. "They edit their videos and make it look like a normal day's fishing - not three or four days condensed down to a half hour show." Jason works in the television field and knew whereof he spoke.

We all agreed that this had to be the case.

"Well, that may be true, but I looked up Horwood Lake on my maps, and it does seem accessible," Alex said.

As with most things on television, you need a large salt shaker close at hand when watching those professional fishermen catch their limit at some remote, exotic camp that can be reached only after bouncing over miles of backwoods roads. Or by taking the easy way and flying in to the 'Outpost'. The TV show that presented Horwood Lake last week was good. It depicted this remote lake in Northern Ontario that was just full of walleyes, walleyes so hungry for Rapalas and Bagley Big O's that they almost had to be restrained by the use of a landing net from jumping into the boat.

What really sold me on Horwood was the story in a fishing magazine that I read about two weeks after seeing the television show. The article told of the road that was only passable with a four-wheel drive vehicle, the remoteness of the camp, the perfect isolation . . . and lots of fish. Really big pike and pickerel. The story also provided a map - alongside the photo of a stringer of fish that would match anything our local lakes could produce. We had to give it try. Alex and I began planning a trip for the long weekend in August. After all, it was different when you read about a fishing place in Field & Stream than seeing something on TV.

We booked a Motel room in Timmins, needing a good night of sleep after the six hour drive before heading out at dawn to Horwood Lake. Alexander said I snored a little but also kept muttering something about a large pike I had lost two weeks ago. Martha says we are not having any stuffed fish on our walls but that would have been a nice mount by a taxidermist who some of the members use for a special fish.

Horwood Lake is southwest of Timmins on the road to Chapleau. It had been a long, long drive, but the promise of excellent fishing at this remote camp in the middle of the boreal forest was conversation fuel for the whole trip. We found the sign for the 'Outpost' right where the magazine article promised it would be. We also found the road to be every bit as challenging as the author had reported.

"Watch out for that rock!" Alex warned as we topped another little hill. We had been creeping along about as fast as a person could walk for the best part of an hour, dodging rocks, squishing through mud holes and clawing our way through old creek beds.

"Man, this is some road. I'd hate to have to come out of here in a hurry." I said.

"Yeah. We could make a little better time without the boat, but not much. You want me to see how deep that next pool is?" he asked.

"No, I think we're okay. Other vehicles have been through here recently - I'm sure the owner of the camp would have marked any really bad spots."

"Look, there," Alex said, pointing to the left. "Isn't that the lake?" A patch of rippling blue glimmered through the trees on our left.

"I guess we've made it! Look out fish, here we come!"

The camp was everything the article said - neat, clean, well-appointed cottages, Delco power, a beautiful main lodge, all looking out over a quiet lake. The camp operator was glad to see us and helped us launch the boat, recommended some lures that were working well only yesterday and supplied us with a map of the lake. He pointed us to a log boom about a quarter of a mile away. He had a cabin we could rent for the night if we wanted to stay over and fish again tomorrow.

"Bill, this looks great. Look at those hills! Did you notice how quiet it is? I've only heard one boat since we got here!"

"Alex, it sure looks good, but are there any fish? I'm going to try the silver Canadian Wiggler, like the camp owner suggested. What are you going to use?"

"Looks like a black jointed Rapala day to me," he said.

Three casts later we had a four pound pickerel in the live well. On my fourth cast I caught a three pound beauty. Considering it was 2 p.m., we thought we had found our dream lake. We decided to scout the lake, particularly looking for the falls that the television fishermen had shown us in the cold days of last winter. Five miles down the lake our dream was shattered. We met a 16-foot boat towing a small barge with a house trailer on it! We stopped at another fishing lodge on the pretext of looking for place to stay.

Alex called out to the young lad who was mixing gas and oil, a few feet away from the dock, "Hi there. We're checking out the lake. Any vacancy here?"

"Sorry, we're all booked. You might try down at the west arm. There are a couple of lodges, a trailer park and a motel down near the dam." Motels?

"How's the fishing been?" I asked.

"Pretty good. The pike are hitting and you can still get pickerel in the evening. Fellow here caught an eight-pounder last night, right off that island," he said, pointing at a small rocky island about a quarter of a mile away.

"I hear it's really good here in the spring," Alex offered.

"Sure is. There was a television crew up here last year, down at the Falls. They caught over a hundred pickerel in two days!"

"Must be a great spot - at the Falls" I said.

"Yeah, everybody goes there. The first weekend in June, I counted seventy-two boats there at one time!" So much for our remote resort.

We fished, half-heartedly, for another three hours and caught the whole sum of two hammer-handle pike. We cancelled our reservation, gave the lodge owner $20 for using the launch, released the two walleye, and opted to drive back out over that five miles of 'road' that led to the remote end of Horwood Lake late that evening. The fellow who wrote the article should have tried driving that trail at night if he wanted a real impression of the northern woods!

The next day we drove to the other entrance to this 'wilderness' lake. This place was busier than Algonquin Park in July! We talked to a couple of men from Rochester, New York who thought this was great - miles from the city, no cell phone service, no boss, no wife, no kids . . . no fish, but who cares? A bad day of fishing is better than a good day at work, one of them said. They motored off in their 22' pontoon boat heading to the 'Falls' that was marked on the same map I had thrown away, happy as could be.

We met the Club members at the Disraeli the Friday following our trip to report on Horwood.

"Sorry, guys, it wasn't that great," Alex explained. "The one end of the lake was quiet and peaceful, but twelve miles down the lake, it was like Coney Island."

"The camp owner did say he had private access to a couple of small lakes just off Horwood, but I got the feeling that it just wouldn't be worth the trip up there to try them."

"Well, we should save up and take one of those fly-in trips into northern Saskatchewan or Manitoba," Jason said. "That's where you have to go now to get really good fishing!"

John agreed. "Jason's right. Just last night there was a show on television where these guys were catching and releasing twenty pound pike . . ."

"You did say 'television', didn't you?" Alex asked.

"Uh, yes," Jason replied.

"And you did say, 'show'?" I asked.

"Uh, yes, but . . ."

"We rest our case," Alex and I said in unison.

Fenimore Cooper Gets Lost
(2011)

I grew up in Northern Ontario before moving to Toronto after University, and I always fancied myself a woodsman. In Boy Scouts, I earned badge after badge - as long as the requirements were based on woodcraft or camping. As a young man, I had read everything from Fenimore Cooper to Jack London to Farley Mowat. I faithfully stored every titbit of outdoors lore that these authors penned, not pausing to question or to sift out some of their more dubious suggestions on survival in the great white north. I thought I knew an ample amount about the woods, how to survive in the wilds, and generally look after myself in the northern woods better than most of my peers. I made no bones about my prowess around our office on Bay Street, and consequently talked myself into becoming the President of the Little Loon Lake Hunting and Fishing Club, a subsidiary of the Bay Street Boys and Girls Sporting Club.

Of course, my organizational skills helped in the management of this elite group of executives from Toronto. Beginning in early May and up to August, we spent our free weekends in the summer fishing on the lakes in central and northern Ontario. The first two weeks of the migratory bird season in September saw some of us at the camp hunting ducks. Then to round out the year, we reserved the most important first week of November for hunting whitetail deer. When I say that we spent those times fishing and hunting, I must confess that although we were keen at the start of any season, we soon found that playing low-stakes poker or Liar's Dice and drinking a few beers was just as enjoyable and a lot less tiring than playing at being sportsmen. I should note that I gave up hunting deer and moose several years ago, and after the following episode, gave up hunting birds as well. The Club members are getting on towards retirement age and are not as rambunctious as we were ten years ago when we formed our Sporting Club.

Little Loon Lake is not really remote in the sense of the northern lakes of Ontario, but for the investment boys from the big city, it was an absolute change from the noise, crush, and rush of downtown Toronto. The small quiet lake, with its clear emerald green water, is just south of the Algonquin Park border, accessible by a rough and bumpy gravel road that meanders off highway #7 until it peters out as a two-wheel trail about a quarter of a mile from the camp. There, a small stream has washed out the old log culvert, and the only way into the camp is by foot. We have not repaired the culvert in an effort to keep curious weekend drivers off our property. We do not have a 'No Trespassing' sign but one that reads "Caution: City Hunters!" seems to work for us. If there are heavy supplies to carry, we go to the aluminum storage shed behind the cabin, start the old grey Ferguson tractor with the 6-volt battery we bring in and using its wobbly-wheeled trailer, haul the goods up the trail to the camp. There are no other camps in the immediate area, the nearest camp being about six miles to the east of us on Big Loon Lake.

Each fall, the weekend before the deer season opens, we drive to the camp to remove windfalls and brush out the trails that we use when hunting. The trails were marked with those little plastic ribbons that surveyors use and we have developed a rather neat system of coloured trails, similar to the cross-country ski club method: RED trail is the longest and most difficult; GREEN is the most scenic; YELLOW trail is a modest walk for an afternoon hunt, and the PURPLE trail wanders in a lazy circle around the camp, laid out more for an exercise track for Pierre than for hunting. Each year I insisted that we check out the trails and refresh any ribbons that curious crows have removed. Using a spray paint can of the appropriate colour, we paint the trees. As the most experienced woodsman, I felt responsible for the rest of the men in the club and I did not want them getting themselves lost in the woods. Everyone carries a map of the area, with our trails neatly marked in the appropriate colours, and, of course, matches, and a compass.

There is no cell phone service at the camp. This is a relief for all of us except John who is in real estate and has left his phone number and business card with far too many strangers.

Freddie Smith and I were in charge of the trail marking this year and we had arranged to go to the camp the last weekend in October to prepare for the deer hunt in two weeks. We brought enough food and snacks for the two days we planned to be at the camp, telling our wives that we would be home on Sunday in time for dinner. I drove my fancy new Jeep Grand Cherokee pulling a trailer loaded with gasoline for the tractor and generator and some lumber we needed to repair the dock for the next spring. Freddie parked the car company's BMW X5 at the creek and we carried the food and our duffle bags into the camp rather than starting the tractor on a late Friday afternoon. The days were getting shorter and it was almost dark at 5.00 p.m. when we opened a Sleeman beer to relax before dinner. The Honda generator was soon purring away quietly in its nearly soundproof shed next to the tractor's garage. We ate our dinner of fresh cabbage rolls that Freddie's wife Thelma had packed for us and then played a few hands of cribbage before turning in for a peaceful sleep in the refreshing country air that was such a pleasant change from the smoggy stuff we breathe in Toronto.

There was a light frost overnight, but by eight o'clock the temperature had risen enough that we took only light jackets, thinking that the walking and work would keep us warm. The sky was overcast, that flat grey colour that will eventually turn to light drizzle, but not into a really heavy rain. The wind was calm and I said we should have fair weather until late afternoon, long enough to do the RED trail and then come back and do the YELLOW. The GREEN and PURPLE trails we would do on Sunday since they were not only shorter, but covered an area that had a lot of rock and open spaces that required little brushing.

We had not walked fifty yards into the bush when Freddie slipped on some frost-covered leaves and fell.

"Damn, Bill, I think I twisted my ankle!"

"It's not broken, is it?" I asked.

"No, I don't think so. I can put weight on it, but I don't think I can walk very far." He took a few steps and I could see the discomfort on his face.

"Freddie, there's no point in you stressing that ankle. You'd better go back to the camp and rest. I can do the trails. I won't spend too much time brushing. I'll mark more trees with the coloured spray paint - that'll be good enough for this year."

"Yes, that should do. We brushed quite a lot last year. I can haul the gas up to the shed and then maybe I'll finish painting the tractor if it warms up this afternoon."

Freddie gave me his cans of paint and the old .410 gauge shotgun that we carried in case we saw a grouse. I cut a sturdy oak walking stick for him and sent him limping on his way back to the camp. I said I'd be back before 4.00 o'clock. I thought that I could finish the RED trail by about 1:00, and then cut across to the far end of the YELLOW and work my way back to the camp. I should have told Freddie my plan, but I really only worked it out after I left him as he hobbled slowly and painfully back to camp.

The RED trail goes to the furthest point from the camp and by eleven thirty I was starting to move back towards the camp, to where the GREEN trail meets the Red, just below the big granite rock. However, there were several trees across the trail here and I spent some time cutting through them with the little Swede saw. This was the area where we most often caught a deer, so I wanted a trail cleared in case we had to pull the carcass out. Detouring through the brush is no fun when you have a 180-pound buck on a rope. I was a little tired after all the sawing, so I decided to take my break and eat my lunch. I took off my pack and placed it beside the rock where I sat comfortably as I rested and ate. The woods were quiet at this time of year, with only a few chickadees hopping from limb to limb as they watched me eat. I heard a jay call a few times, a red squirrel chattered briefly, then the harsh crronk, crronk of a raven as he sailed overhead.

I was just finishing my cup of tea and putting the lid back on my thermos, when I heard a few quick, light steps on the leaves behind me. I slowly turned and saw a ruffed grouse poking among the leaves, looking to make a snack of a late season bug. I carefully reached for the shotgun and took one of the three shells from my pocket. The click of the breech opening was enough warning for the partridge and he quickly scurried away, running in a straight line away from me. Since it did not fly, I thought I might sneak up close enough for a shot. Leaving my pack on the trail, I started following the bird. Using all my Fenimore Cooper skills, I moved through the brush, remembering to put my feet down carefully, toe first, lightly, making hardly a sound.

The grouse flew up right in front of me but I could not get the gun to my shoulder quickly enough to get a shot. I was about to cuss my luck when the bird landed, only twenty metres away. Again I began creeping through the light brush, keeping my eyes on the spot where the grouse had landed. Just as I was getting close, I stepped on a dry stick and the sharp crack of the wood echoed in the quiet, still woods. I froze, not moving for two or three minutes and then moved cautiously forward. I saw the grouse but as I took aim, it seemed to sense my presence and began to walk quickly away, looking around for the danger that was near. I started after the bird, watching for an open place where I could fire a shot.

One of the rules you must always follow when in the woods, is to look around, see your surroundings. That way you keep a map in your mind as you walk. You remember seeing a tall pine tree with a bent top or a particular outcropping of rock that has a trace of Feldspar running through it. You do not have to look at your compass to know that you are walking north or east because your mind will update that information for you if you are a trained woodsman. The other members of the Club are amazed at my ability to find my way in the forest, but really, it is nothing but a little practical woodcraft. Freddie says I seem to have a built-in GPS.

I had not been watching where I was going the last few minutes, but watching a partridge. The bird finally paused in an open space and I took careful aim just above its head and fired. I did not want to hit the bird in the body since the lead pellets make a real mess of that fine white breast meat. Aiming for the head means that you have to rely on the pattern of the shot spread hitting the bird and this usually works for me. This time the grouse was lucky and received nothing more than a good scare from the sudden blast of the small shotgun. The bird didn't wait around for me to load another shell and this time it flew far enough that I would not be able to find it. I turned around and began making my way back to the trail.

I walked about ten steps and realized I was not certain which way I should be walking. I glanced at the gray sky, but by now the overcast had become heavier and I could not really find the sun, although it looked brighter to my left. However, I felt as though south should be to my right. I soon rationalized that the brightness was only because the cloud cover was not so heavy in that direction. There was no surface wind to guide me, and the cloud cover was more like a thick fog than individual clouds, so I could not tell if there was any wind at the cloud ceiling. The low pressure that was moving in would come from the southwest but if the centre of the low pressure were to the north or south of me, the wind could be from the east. I stood there for a moment and then went with my feeling that I had to move to the right. I kept looking for a familiar tree or rock but nothing was registering on my senses the way it normally does. It was only a few hundred yards to trail and once I crossed it, I would know where I had left my pack.

When I did not cross the trail after a few minutes, I knew I had turned the wrong way. I took some bearings on a hill in the direction I now realized was south and started back. I came to a small swale filled with thick tag-alders and went around it. Funny, I had not seen this swale on the way in. I stopped cold, a slight shiver tingling up my spine. I had just committed the most common mistake of people who get lost in the woods. I had moved to my right to bypass the swale and I knew that I had moved to the right around a couple of downed trees before that. I was starting to walk in a circle! Right-handed people will inherently move to the right. I stopped and caught my breath. I had been walking a little too fast. Second mistake. I stood still for a few minutes, thought about what I was doing and then moved off to my left, being very conscious about not walking in a circle. After all, I told myself, I could not be more than a few hundred yards from the trail.

I walked for five minutes. I know because I checked my watch. Still, I did not cross the Red trail. How, in heaven's name, had I missed it? I reached for my map and then realized I had left it in the packsack. I thought the best thing to do would to make myself a map from memory, just so I would have a reference point. Stripping off a piece of white birch bark and using a small stick, I made a copy of our trail map from memory. I soon realized that I had moved north when chasing the partridge, then had swung to the west when I first started walking. I had turned north again when I had made the mistake of moving to my right. I now was likely only several hundred yards from the trail that should lie to the south. Except that where I had eaten my lunch was just about where the Red trail turned to the south as it headed back to camp. Therefore, I would have to bear to the east, my left, a little more to make sure I intercepted the trail.

I started off again and had only gone a few steps when I realized that I was making another mistake. I should have been marking my trail. I began to bend the branch tips in the direction that I was travelling. This would help me if I accidentally turned around again and came across my own trail. Twenty minutes later and I still had not found the trail. I looked for some high ground and climbed up a rocky outcrop to look around. Nothing looked familiar. I felt a twinge of panic, then realized that there was no reason anything should look familiar. When we hunted in this area, we always stayed within our trail system. I was now outside it looking at the terrain from an entirely new perspective.

I checked my wristwatch. I was stunned to see that it was 3:45 - I had been lost for over three hours! Taking a bearing on a tall white pine about a quarter of a mile away, I struck off, walking quickly. I had to find that trail before the light failed. Even then, I would be in for a long walk to get back to the camp. My foot caught on a root and I fell, landing very hard on my right shoulder and banging my head on a tree trunk. The shotgun flew from my hands. I slowly got to my feet and looked around. The trees were swirling around me, as if I were riding a carrousel, looking out at the forest. I rubbed my head and knuckled my eye sockets to stop the whirling. The shotgun was lying at least five metres from where I stood massaging my head. I started to ask myself how the gun came to be so far away, when I realized I had just broken another rule of survival - I had been running! Running, and not even to any specific place - just a tall white pine tree that I had singled out as a reference point. I took several deep breaths to calm my nerves. My heart was pounding. The last thing I needed was to exhaust myself! I picked up the shotgun, thinking how heavy it was, and for one fleeting moment, I thought of leaving it - to save my energy for walking. Somehow I calmed my nerves enough to realize that I might need that old gun. I could be out here for some time and the two remaining shells could mean the difference between eating and not eating.

I sat down and took a more realistic stock of my situation. With darkness only an hour away I was not going to make it out of the bush. Therefore, I had better prepare myself for the night. I felt in my pockets for my lighter but remembered that it was in my packsack - wherever that was. I had my pocketknife and the shotgun. The cell phone was useless. No Signal. No food. I would need water. As I began to look for a sign of water - a depression that might have a little creek, it began to rain. The big white pine would keep me dry for a while but if the rain continued overnight, I would suffer from exposure. I calmly walked the rest of the way to the pine tree. Breaking off evergreen boughs, I quickly began to make myself a shelter against the pine tree. I glanced at the branches over my head. They were within reach in case I had to climb the tree for safety. The black bears were still out looking for a last meal before hibernation. Moreover, the Park was full of timber wolves. I gathered up a large pile of dried pine needles from the base of the tree and made myself comfortable by burrowing into the heap of rusty red needles. Despite not having my jacket, I was warm enough. If I had that chocolate bar that was in the pack, I was certain that I could survive the night without a problem.

The woods were very quiet now that even the chickadees had gone to roost. As darkness crept over my pine shelter and me, my imagination began to work. I stood up and watched as the leafless trees crept closer to me, their grey branches reaching towards me, grasping at me like Poe-like monsters. I shook my head to clear the visions, knowing this was going to be a long, lonely night. The sudden splash of a raindrop on my face made me jump. I backed in against the rough pine tree trunk and sat, shivering slightly. The rain was not heavy, just a drizzle, enough to drip slowly from the branches around me, but when I stood tight against the trunk of the tree, I was dry. I had the shotgun nearby, a shell in the breach. I realized that this could be a mistake if I accidentally discharged the gun so I put the shell back into my shirt pocket. The rain might keep the predators in their lairs, I thought, trying to comfort myself. Then I remembered reading how scent travels better with more moisture in the air. I listened for sounds that were not to be heard. Why hadn't Freddie sounded the car horns when I failed to show up? Was I so far away that I couldn't hear them? The Honda generator did not make much noise, so I knew that I would not hear it, but surely Freddie would realize by now that I was not coming in. Of course he would not worry too much about me spending a night in the bush. After all, Bill was the great white hunter, a veritable Fenimore Cooper!

First thing in the morning I would climb the tree and find the lake. If I made it to the lake, all I had to do was follow it until I found one of our trails that came down to the lake in any number of places. Or if I could not see Little Loon Lake, I could surely see Big Loon Lake and make my way to it. There were several cottages on Big Loon and I could easily get back to our camp by walking on the roads. I was physically tired and thought I had better rest, but my brain kept whirling around, tracing out all the things I done wrong in the past few hours. I finally drifted off, curled up in the foetal position to conserve my body heat.

When you are used to sleeping on a mattress, the ground is a rough substitute. No matter how hard you try to make it soft, there is always a lump here, a bump there and no place to rest your head. The pine needles helped, but my body kept moving, trying for that one soft place that had to be there somewhere under the big pine tree. The discomfort kept me from falling into a deep sleep and that is how I first heard the soft movements in the brush nearby. I told myself that the sound magnifies in the bush at night in the dark when you are alone but this sounded like a large animal to me. Of course, it was pitch black and I couldn't see my hand in front of my face, let alone a hungry black bear or a timber wolf. A loud shout was my best defence, but in case I only raised some hungry bear's curiosity, I felt around for the shotgun and loaded one of my two remaining shells. The click of the breech silenced whatever was out there for a moment then the soft steps began again, moving towards me.

"Hey!" I yelled. "Hey! Get out of here!"

There was a crashing of brush as the startled creature ran away. My adrenalin count must have been almost at overload. My heart was pounding so loud in my ears that I soon could not hear anything but my heart beating. Several hours passed before I drifted off to sleep again.

The sky was turning to a light grey when I slowly awoke. I was cold now, having shaken off most of my pine needle cover during the night. I got up and stretched, trying to work out some of the kinks and get my blood flowing again. My urine smelled strong since I had not drunk enough water yesterday. The smell would mark my presence and I thought then that I should have used my urine to mark off my territory last night. I would do that tonight if I were still out here, but now that I could see where east was, I knew I could find my way out in a few hours. Funny, but I thought east would be more to my left. Maybe there was a thinner cloud cover in that direction and east really was about 40 points to the left. I caught myself in time to put that thought from my mind. I had to trust my observations, not what my worried mind was feeding me.

I scrounged around for some wintergreen berries and found a few that were not too withered. There was not much sugar in those berries but at least they eased my growling stomach. I knocked the seeds from a few pine cones and nibbled on them but they were not very tasty. This was truly different from my usual breakfast of shredded wheat, toast, juice, and coffee. Freddie was probably just putting on the fire in the camp. I thought it too early to climb the tree to see if I could spot some familiar landmark or smoke, but I might better hear a car horn if Freddie tried to signal me.

Freddie should have sounded that horn last night. Maybe he did not even think of such a practical thing to do. Freddie was, after all, not the best woodsman in our group. In fact, as I thought about what he would do when I did not return to the camp last night, I realized that he would likely panic. He would try to either find me or go for help. He had hurt his foot so there was no way he would try to walk the trails looking for me. Fred must have gone for help. As soon as there was enough light, there would be someone out looking for me. Perhaps even the police search team if I were still here tomorrow. They had tracking dogs, helicopters equipped with infrared searching devices and trained woodsmen that could track me once they found my pack. It was a reassuring thought but I didn't want to have my reputation tarnished any more than necessary. I would get out on my own today.

A fall mist had settled over the woods after the drizzle of last night and it would be several hours before this lifted enough to see very far. The sun at this time of year just does not produce enough heat to burn off a morning fog. And I could have used a little solar heat myself. I was chilled but not in danger of hypothermia. I did a few 5BX exercises to get the circulation moving but because I had not eaten since yesterday, I had to conserve my energy. There was a small brook a hundred yards from my pine tree and I drank my fill of the cold, crystal-clear water. I thought of turning over a few stones to see if I could find a crayfish but I was not that hungry yet. I ate some more bitter wintergreen berries, pretending they were bright, sweet cherries.

I was tempted to start walking a couple of times but forced myself to wait until ten o'clock when I climbed up my tree. White pines are easy to climb and I was soon above the tops of the surrounding poplars and birches. I knew I had to move to the south and I had east clearly marked in my mind now. I could not see the lake, but then it would likely be covered in fog. I could not see any low-lying areas that even suggested the lake, but Little Loon Lake is in a flat area and might not be that noticeable from a distance. Unless the sun where shining, making bright sparkles on the blue water. I picked out another pine tree about half a mile away as my target and scurried down the tree.

For the next three hours I walked, climbed trees and walked. I carefully marked my trail with bent branches in case I turned myself around but as the mist dissipated, I had no trouble keeping my direction. By one o'clock the sun was out and I needed a rest. I found a comfortable rock and decided to stretch out for half an hour. Awaking with a start two hours later, I cursed myself for wasting the precious daylight. If I didn't find a trail in the next hour, I would be spending the night in the bush again.

Why didn't I hear any searchers? I listened for the thump, thump, thump of a helicopter. Nothing. No rifle shots. I thought I had better yell in case someone was nearby, so I began yelling, "Help!" The only answer was a scolding chatter from a red squirrel off to my left. Taking a line on yet another large tree, I began walking quickly towards it. When I fell over a root, I realized that I had been running again. I was panting and sweating. My throat was sore from yelling. I began talking to myself, telling myself to calm down. "Think, McGyver, think!" I kept saying, repeating the phrase of my hero of a TV show. I had my pocketknife and that was all McGyver ever needed, although his was a real Swiss Army knife, not an Eddie Bauer special. I also had two shotgun shells in my pocket. I could take one apart and use the powder to start a fire. Why didn't I think of that last night? All I had to do was make a spark. If I didn't find a trail soon, I would stop and make a camp. Build a signal fire for the next day. Stay put, as I should have done 24 hours ago. I gave myself 40 minutes more before I stopped for the night. I was beginning to think that Mark Twain had been right in his criticisms of Fenimore Cooper.

I had not taken ten steps when grouse flew up in front of me. It headed in a generally south direction so I thought I could try for it. Use one shot and have something to cook over my fire. I was very careful now. This bird meant a lot to me. I could see the bird on the ground now, watching for me but still interested in finding its own dinner. I raised the gun and took careful aim. By habit, I glanced behind the bird to make certain that I would not be hitting someone or something else. I slowly lowered the gun. Just behind the bird was a red paint mark on a tree. I let of a whoop of joy that sent the partridge flying in panic and then ran crashing through the underbrush to the trail. I hugged the tree. Twenty paces to the right was my packsack.

I gulped down what was left of my cold tea and ate the chocolate bar and the one-half of a sandwich I had saved for yesterday's afternoon snack. A mouse had chewed one corner of the bread but I guess the sardines were too strong for him so he had nibbled instead on my apple. I took a couple of bites of the apple and left the rest for the mouse. There was less than half an hour of daylight left, and over two miles of trails to get back to the camp before dark. For one crazy moment I thought of cutting across country to the Yellow trail but then picked up my pack and began trotting along the Red trail, back to the comfort and safety of the camp.

There was no light in the camp, no purring of the Honda generator. I went directly to the shed and started the little gasoline engine. Under the glow of the sixty-watt bulb was Fred's note. His foot had swollen so much that he thought he had better get back to town and have it examined. He hoped I wouldn't be too lonely in the camp that night and even suggested that I could listen to the Leaf's game on the radio for company!

I washed and shaved as my dinner was heating on the gas stove. I had to clean up the camp a little before leaving but I was feeling much better just being within the four walls of the Little Loon Lake Hunt Club's cabin. As I drove back to Toronto that evening I came up with my game plan. Wednesday I would tell Martha that I had an out-of-town meeting and she should not expect me home until late. I would book off work that day and return to the camp to finish brushing the trails. There was no way I was going to tell anyone that I had been lost in the bush. No way.

Uncle Timothy

(2011)

I was at *Bites and Bucks*, shopping for a new rod. Amelia was showing me an ultra-lite by Azilda, a new line the store was trying. The manufacturers were the same people that made some of the best golf club shafts on the PGA circuit and they supposedly used that same technology in their new fishing rods. If a pro could hit a golf ball over 300 yards with their shafts, maybe I could make a 50 yard cast with more accuracy. That was the sales pitch Amelia was giving me when the entrance door opened setting off the little bell that announces customers. The door opener also starts the CCTV security cameras the ladies had installed after they noticed a few fishing lures had developed legs and walked out of the store.

I glanced up to see if it was John who said he might drop by the store that afternoon after work. It was a police officer who was accompanying an older man who was using crutches. The crutches appeared to be new and the man was being careful with them. "I'm looking for Amelia Restoule," the officer said.

"That's her down there at the back of the store with the feller testing that fishing rod," the chap on crutches said.

"Uncle Tim?" Amelia said. "What happened to you?"

"I had a little accident. The officer here, Mike, was kind enough to bring me to the store after they let me out of the hospital. I'm okay – just sprained my ankle and bruised my knee."

We found a chair for Uncle Tim and offered the Sergeant a cup of coffee. I explained how I knew Amelia Restoule and her partner Geraldine. The Sergeant was a novice fisher and knew the store as the place where he had bought some gear for his two children. He owned a camp up in the Muskokas and the children wanted to try fishing for bass. I handed him the rod and he flipped it a few times, saying it had nice balance. Amelia was talking to her Uncle so I asked Sergeant Mike de la Chastain what had happened to Uncle Tim.

"I got the case when the patrol officer who was first on the scene of the traffic accident filed the victim as *John Doe*, possibly a homeless person. An ambulance had transported the accident victim to the hospital with possible broken bones (leg) where he entered the system as again, *John Doe*. He had no identification. As was most often the case in the Missing Persons Unit, we had to establish the victim's bona fides. I was the only officer in the office as my crew was doing another investigation, so I went to the hospital.

"'John Doe' was resting comfortably in his hospital bed, eating his mid-morning snack when I arrived. I had already checked with hospital administration for registration details but the man apparently had no health insurance card, no driver's license, no cell phone, (nor home landline phone number), no Social Insurance Number and no street address. He had a leather pouch with $78.25 in coin and 8 small rocks, which may or may not have been gold nuggets. That was in the hospital safe locker.

"I stopped at the Tim Hortons kiosk in the hospital lobby and bought two small black coffees, one of which I offered to 'John Doe' as he introduced himself. The victim ignored the sugar and milk packets saying he took his coffee straight – when he could get it.

"I showed the man my identification and explained why I was there.

"What is your given name, sir?" I asked.

"Tim. Mother named me Timothy but most just call me Tim."

"Your surname?" I continued writing this in my service book.

"I go by my mother's name as my father left when I was young. Robertts – with two t's."

"Tim, you had no ID on you when the car hit you so we need to get something for the records. Do you have a driver's license?"

"Nope. Can't even drive, I suppose – I never tried."

"No health card?"

"Never needed one until now."

"Social Insurance Number – from the Canadian government?"

"Never needed one of those either."

"You don't pay income taxes?"

"Not yet. I figure why bother the government with all that paperwork until I hit it rich."

"Okay, do you know your date of birth? Maybe I can find a birth certificate somewhere," I said.

"I reckon I was born in 1956 or 1957. Mom always talked about how cold it was on that Wednesday, but she never put a date to it."

"Were you baptized in a church?"

"Not as I can recall."

"Where did you go to school? In fact, where were you born?"

"Larder Lake. I went to grade 4 before we moved. Mom home-schooled me after that."

"Where was that?"

"I reckon now it was about 15 miles south of Matchewan – on the Montreal River – where she had her trap line."

"Your mother was a trapper?"

"Yes sir. One of the best. She taught me all I know about trapping."

"Is that what you are – a trapper?" I asked.

"That and a prospector."

"Are you married? Do you have any next of kin?"

"No, never married and Mom is gone. I came down here to see about finding a wife a couple of times but nobody found the idea of living in the bush very attractive. Nor, me either, I reckon.

I have a nice house – Beaver Lodge - the folk along the Montreal River call it," Tim said.

"He was not that bad looking, I thought: his full beard was trimmed, hair cut short, seemed to have all his teeth, and certainly in good physical condition even if he looked like he might have been out in the weather too much.

"Okay, Tim, so you live in bush, trap, and prospect – living off the grid and on the land. What to do you do about supplies, clothes, and such?"

"Oh, I go into town about three times a year. In the spring, right after the ice is off the River. I go to North Bay and sell my furs. They pay me in cash, as I don't bank. Then, mid-summer and again in the fall before freeze-up, I make a trip in and come down here to Toronto and sell my semi-precious stones and a little gold. I visit with my niece Amelia; I buy some new clothes, rifle shells, a few books, and anything I need for my solar panels and radio. I do it all in cash which seems to suit everybody because they avoid the bookwork. I just got my hair trimmed and was crossing the street when I stepped in front of that car. I forgot to look at the traffic lights and thought I had time to get over the street but I guess that young lady was going faster than I calculated. Is she okay?"

"Yes, she's all right. You just made a dent in her fender."

"You think I should pay her for that?" Tim asked.

"No, don't worry about it. A couple of witnesses said she was speeding and talking on her cell phone. We have video camera at the crosswalk and she should have stopped. Of course, you should have pressed the button to cross . . ."

"I reckon I never noticed it. Not that many crosswalks on the Montreal River," Tim smiled.

"I'm just wondering - how do you buy ammunition without a gun owner's permit?" I asked.

"Oh Arthur South – he's just five miles up the river from me – we share his card. There's no picture on those cards – and anyway, we do look a little alike," Tim said.

It was not my problem – it was the RCMP's problem if those two old trappers abused the computerized system that the Feds had set up.

"Okay. I think I can file a report now. Do you have the money to pay the hospital? If you had a free health card, the government plan would cover this, but without it you have to pay for the services."

"I have a little pocket cash but I was on my way to the jeweler I know to sell some gold. There should be enough to cover my bill," Tim said. And then he added, "You reckon they'll let me charge it for a day or two?"

"I'll talk to them, but I think so. Maybe you should think about getting a health card."

"I did try that once but I did not have any ID to show them and they wouldn't do it without some ID. I reckon I can pay my way for a time. If I ever move into town from Beaver Lodge, then I'll do something."

"Okay, Tim. It just makes our job easier in case of accidents or heaven forbid, a death," I said.

"Forfend," Tim said and when I looked puzzled, he said, "The phrase is 'Heaven forfend' – most people get that one wrong. But yes, I can see what you mean. Although, when I die it'll probably be back in the bush and the wolves will eat me, so it won't matter."

"Okay, Mr Restoule. Do you have a place to stay?"

"I was going down to my niece's place. I reckon she will be at her store now."

"Does she work downtown?" I asked.

"Yes. She owns '*Bites and Bucks*'. It's just off Yonge Street."

"Okay, I know where that is. My shift is almost over – I'll give you a lift if you like."

"Yes, that would be good. I don't have much cash on me until I get the money for my gold and I surely do not want to give some cabbie a gold nugget!" he laughed.

"So I brought him here. He seems like a resourceful old guy so I guess he'll be all right," Sergeant Mike said.

"Sure," I said. "I'll give them a hand if they need assistance getting into the car."

The Sergeant shook Tim's hand and said, "Well, Tim, I hope you are feeling well soon. Good luck to you."

Uncle Tim helped at the store for a week and then was on his way back north. He had supplies to pick up in North Bay and then would be on to Latchford and the Montreal River. Tim came to the Disraeli Friday evening with Amelia. He did not drink alcohol but enjoyed the tonic spritzer that Nick made for him. Uncle Tim had some good fish stories and did invite us to try the Montreal River if we ever came north. We could camp beside Beaver Lodge.

Buck Fever

(2011)

Katherine, Amanda, Pierre, Freddie, John, Jason and I were at the Disraeli soon after the October Thanksgiving weekend. Deer hunting season was only three weeks off when John asked Freddie if he and Cindy could use the old gravel pit on the farm on Sunday to do some target shooting.

"No problem, John, anytime. Just check at the house to make sure the girls aren't out on their four-wheeler," Freddie said.

"Don't tell me you are going to teach Cindy how to shoot?" I asked.

"Sure. She has already passed her gun-handling course and has her gun license," John replied.

"She's not going hunting, though," I said, assuming that our city girl would not become involved in the autumn deer-killing ritual.

"She certainly is. She has heard us talking about hunting so often that she wants to try it."

"Umm," I said. "I thought she was not the type. I know she likes the outdoors now, but she does not strike me as the kind of person who would go out in the wilds and kill animals."

"You're right, Bill," Pierre put in. "I thought she was more . . . more, well, feminine."

"You guys are being sexist," John said in Cindy's defense.

"You're right, John," Jason said while topping up our glasses with the dregs of a jug of Sleemans and signaling Nick the bartender to bring us another jug. "There is nothing that says women shouldn't hunt."

"Well," I said a little weakly, "somehow it just doesn't seem natural."

"Nothing is more natural," Katherine offered. "If you look at nature, you'll see that it's the females that do most of the hunting. Lions, bears, wolves – you name it. The females have to provide for their young."

"What kind of gun is Cindy using?" Alex asked, trying to change the subject to save Pierre and me from any more embarrassment.

"Amelia gave us a good deal on a .300 semi-automatic – a Czech rifle – it's light but has good hitting power," John replied.

"You think you should give a novice a semi-automatic?" Alex asked. Alex uses a bolt action, saying that they are the safest in the bush.

"Well I thought about that, Alex, but I figured that the easier a gun was to use, the less chance of doing something wrong in the heat of the hunt."

"Would you mind if I came out with you on Sunday?" Jason asked. "I should check out my 30-30 before hunting season," he explained. At least Jason uses a Marlin lever action which is safer than a semi-automatic according to Alex.

By the time we left the Disraeli everyone had agreed to meet at Freddie's place at 2 p.m. on Sunday. They even talked me into going out by challenging me to defend my target shooting title. I had not fired the Ross-modified Lee Enfield .303 since last year. When I thought about it, I had missed the boom and kick of the old rifle that was designated as 'Army Surplus' after WWII.

Sunday was a typical fall day, a high thin overcast with a warm southerly wind that was rattling the dry brown oak leaves that like to hang onto their tree until the first snowfall. It was the kind of day when you can take off your jacket, knowing that next week could be 10 degrees colder. Big Al had thoughtfully brought along noise protectors for each of us. Alex is the safety and maintenance manager at his law office. Go figure. He was also acting as range captain, making certain that only one gun was loaded at a time and that that gun was always pointed in the right direction.

I knew my marksmanship title was as good as gone as soon as I fired my first round. There had been a major change in the past year – I was now wearing bifocals. Without the glasses, the bull's-eye was just too fuzzy. With the glasses I could either see the sights clearly or the target. But not both. I tried looking through the top of the glasses, through the bottom of the lens, without the glasses and even putting that damn split-line on the lens right on the rear sight, but I was in trouble. I also knew I was in trouble when I saw the gun Alex had brought. He has his Mauser .270, the gun he calls his 'Varmint Special'. He claims he shoots groundhogs at over 300 yards with that gun and his 4x scope. He did not have the scope on that day, but then Alex does not wear bifocals either.

Our shooting contest allows five shots. The standard target scoring applies but we add bonus points for grouping. We found out that Cindy could group her shots. Unfortunately they were all about two inches to the left of center. Had John sighted her gun correctly, Cindy would have picked up an extra 18 points she needed to beat Alex. Cindy certainly had a steady hand and good eye. The little Czech rifle was as true as my old Enfield. When we left to catch the end of the Argo – Blue Bomber football game, John was setting up a row of potatoes for Cindy to practice on – the idea being to move quickly and smoothly from one target to another. The quick barks of the seven-shot clip indicated that she was not having any problems.

A week after hunting season I met Cindy and John in the grocery store.

"Hi, how did the hunt go?" I asked.

"Oh great," John said. "We got two bucks and a doe for ten hunters."

"Did you get one, Cindy?"

"Well, no . . ." she hesitated.

"Buck fever," John explained.

"Oh," I said, understanding. "Maybe next year, Cindy."

"No, I think this was enough for me. The more I think about it, the more I agree with what you've been saying Bill," she said.

"Well I'm glad to hear that," I replied, "but it is unusual to make a convert of someone who never fired a shot."

"Hell," John said, "she fired all right. She got off seven rounds at a trophy buck!"

"What happened, Cindy?"

"Well, this great big deer came running through the woods. I was sitting down and when I stood up to shoot, it stopped – right in front of me. It stood perfectly still, although I could see it puffing, from running, I guess. It looked right at me with its big glassy eyes. I remembered to count the points, because John told me to make sure it was a buck and not just a single point fawn. It had 10 points. I took off the safety, aimed at the deer and pulled the trigger."

"You missed?" I asked, recalling how John has said that Cindy had hit all seven of his potato targets at fifty yards.

"I guess so. It just ran away, flipping its big white tail. It was such a beautiful animal."

"I guess you would have like to have shot it, but I'm glad it got away," I said.

"Me too," she said. Cindy left to find some special cheese for a fondue that they were to have that evening.

"Is that what happened, John?" I asked.

"Buck Fever, like I said. I heard the seven shots so I went over to Cindy's watch right away. From the tracks, that buck had stopped about ten feet from her. She fired all seven shots into a tree, about twenty feet to the right of where the deer was standing. Probably never even raised the gun to her shoulder, but she swears that she did. Put all seven rounds in a grouping that I could cover with my hand!"

"Nice shooting," I said.

"Sure," he said as he went off to find some Ritz crackers.

Alexander's Trout Trap

(2012)

It seemed to come as a surprise to most of us when Alex announced that he was retiring at the end of April. None of us apparently realized how old we were getting even though we had all been middle-aged when we started the Club back in 2001. Alex, who works for the government and has a defined benefit pension, would reach the magic number of 35 years of service, and as far as improving his pension, he might as well retire. He would continue to work as a consultant, but work from his home. He would be certain to come to any meetings at the Disraeli and would have more time for fishing. Pierre said he would get a retirement gift to give Alexander at the end of the month.

Irene, Pierre's wife discovered through Claire, Freddie's wife, that Alexander was a fan of Salvador Dali and Irene bought a print that she (and we) thought appropriate for the retired lawyer. It did have a fish in the painting. The framed print only depleted our Investment fund by $524.75 – a price my wife Martha thought very reasonable for a framed Dali print.

There was a new waiter serving tables as the BSBGSC settled in for a few glasses of Sleeman's Silver to celebrate the end of a long workweek. He was a young fellow, of about 20 years, just up from Tarpon Springs, who said he wanted to spend the summer in the Great White North, doing a little camping and fishing while picking up a few dollars for his third year of university. He was a nephew of Nick, the owner, probably working without a Canadian work visa, but it was all part of being good neighbours. He said he was studying to be a lawyer and Freddie said he was sorry for him, but supposed it was better than being a dentist. Freddie had a root canal on Monday and was still a little grumpy.

I introduced the Club to him, saying, "We come in once or maybe twice a week after work; we always drink Sleeman's Silver; and we only have two glasses each unless one of us is wearing the 'D.D.' cap. The Designated Driver can have one beer but must then switch to soda pop. The pop is free, you can check with Uncle Nick at the bar." Eight of us were present that evening so I called for two jugs of the amber refreshment. The kid seemed like a nice enough fellow for someone from Tarpon Springs, Florida, the sponge capital of North America.

"Three weeks until trout season," Big Alex announced after taking a long draught of the cool ale. "I think I'll head up to Barnes Creek on opening day. Anybody want to come?" Pierre is too overweight to enjoy 'creek' fishing so he declined the offer. Kate and Amanda were going into Algonquin Park on opening weekend for a canoe trip and maybe a little Lake Trout fishing. Geraldine and Amanda would be busy at the store so that left Freddie and me. We said we would try to make it.

"I'm going to use those red angle worms that the bait shop in Orillia had last year. The owner said they withstood the cold water better than the regular worms he gets later in the year," Alex said.

"Yes," I added, "those earth worms just curl up when they hit that cold spring water – no action to them at all. No wonder it's hard to get trout in the early weeks."

"Naw," Freddie put in, "it's the muddy water. The trout cannot see very far in that murky water. I'm going to try using some of that glop that the salmon eggs are packed in – rub it on the worms and use a small silver spinner."

Kate said she would be using plastic grubs as the Ministry forbid live bait in the Park Lake where they were camping. Amelia said to be sure to get fresh plastic baits as the plastic degenerated over winter and sometimes gave off a strange chemical odour. *Bites and Bucks* had a new line that had salt on them and they might be worth a try.

The new waiter had been listening as he cleaned the table behind us.

Pierre offered, "Why don't you use some of that shad-fly oil? It sure worked on the smelts."

"Yeah, but I used it all and Amelia doesn't have any left."

"Are you ready for another jug?" the waiter asked.

"Yes, bring us one more - that should do us," I replied.

Business had slowed in the Disraeli so the waiter had a few moments to chat as he delivered the beer. "I heard you fellows mention trout fishing. Are you going after browns?"

"Browns?" John asked.

"Yeah – brown trout. Isn't that what you have up here?"

"No, no brown trout this far north," Jason replied. "We're after speckled trout, or brookies, as some call them."

"They're small aren't they?" the waiter asked.

"Well," I said, "they do run smaller than a brown trout or a rainbow, but they are better fighters and taste the best of all trout. We get them up to five pounds around here."

"I heard you say you used worms. Do they take lures as well? I've fished for sea trout at home and they take a small spinner."

"Naw, worms, or flies later in the summer," Freddie answered.

Big Al mumbled, "Or the Trout Trap."

"Beg your pardon," the polite young man from Tarpon Springs said, turning his attention to Alex.

"The middle of the summer is a good time for the Trout Trap."

All of us have seen one or another of Alex's inventions, especially the Trout Trap. It has caught all of us at one time or another.

"Yes," I said, "Alex invented it. He has a patent applied for, too! Don't you have one in your car, Alex?"

"Um, yeah, I think so."

"Gee, I'd really like to see it," the American university kid said.

"Yeah, okay." Alex pushed back his chair, "I'll get it."

Alex had the package open on the table when the new waiter got back to us. Nick, the bartender, said he would cover for the kid while he looked at the Trout Trap. Nick had already seen it. He bought the first one Alex made.

"Geez, that looks just like a big mouse trap," the nephew observed.

"Nope," said Alex. "She's a real Trout Trap. Look - here is where you fasten on the worm, sort of like the place where you would put a piece of cheese if it were a mousetrap. However, this here spring lets the worms hang free without pinching them too much. This here is a 6 pound test, clear line – about 50 feet is what I use around here."

"But where is the hook?"

"There is no hook."

"But . . ."

"Works like this." Alex took a sip of the suds to whet his whistle and get into story mode. "It's got to be a bright sunny day. You find a pool, sneak up on it real careful, so as not to scare the trout, and look real careful." Alexander lowered his voice as if he were talking to a jury. "Sure enough, you'll see a big, fat, lazy trout, sunning himself, sitting there on the bottom over a patch of gravel. Watching for anglers, too. Real careful, you go upstream, past the head of the pool and get the Trout Trap ready. You put on a fresh worm, right here, you see?" The waiter nodded.

"Then you put it into the water, real easy and then let it float down, playing out the line as it needs it. What does the trout do?" Alex stopped for a drink. The people at the next table were all ears. We were feigning attention. Alex lowered his voice even more. "Well, that big lazy trout sees this piece of wood – see the brown colouring I put on it? – this piece of wood drifting on the surface of his pool. With a nice juicy worm hanging on for all it is worth. So up he comes to get a nice afternoon snack – and WHACK!" Big Al slapped his huge hairy hand down on the table, making the glasses and the waiter jump. "He's hit on the head, stunned! All you have to do is pick him up before he comes to!"

"Gee whiz," the waiter said, recovering somewhat from the scare. "Does it really work?"

"Yes," I replied. "I've seen Alex use the trap quite a few times. I have one myself."

"Hey, could you sell me one?" the would-be lawyer asked.

"Well, I dunno – I've only got this one left. Well, I suppose so, if you really want it.

"How much?"

"I usually get $6.50 for them but I'll let you have this one for $5.00 – it's been used a few times."

"Hey, that's great!" The university kid dug into his education money and gave Alex a blue Kingfisher five-dollar bill.

"Well," I said, getting up, "I've got to be getting home." We all bottomed up, left the money for the beer on the table, and got outside where we could all laugh.

Except John.

"I don't know what's so funny," he said.

"The Trout Trap," I said. "That kid paid $5.00 and he really thinks . . ."

"I think it's a good price," John said. "I got six trout with mine last summer."

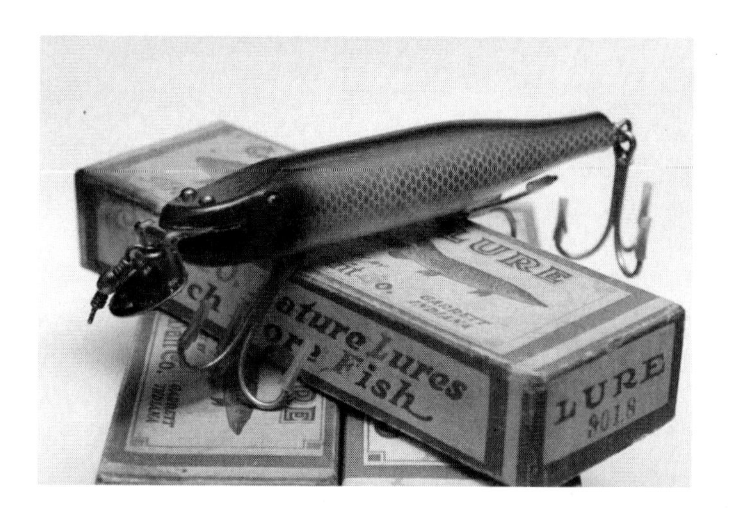

The Spook

(2012)

Katherine called Martha to ask permission for me to accompany her on a day of pike fishing. I did not have a fishing boat at the time and Katherine has a very nice Lund 18. Martha said I could go but would have to cut the lawn the next day.

I thought that I had a reasonably well-stocked tackle box until the day Katherine brought her new tackle box with her as we headed out for a day of pike fishing. My three decker has an extensive assortment of lures that, although perhaps a little conventional, afford me the chance of attracting a few fish. Perhaps the operative words here are afford and few. Fishing lures are not inexpensive, especially if you tend to lose them occasionally by casting too close to trees on the shore, rocks, boat houses, docks and various underwater snags where the fish are supposed to be hiding.

I have several of the common Rapalas, a couple of jitterbugs, two prettily painted Cordells, many daredevil spoons of various shapes and colours, a couple of big Williams, a selection of spinner baits and Beetle Spins that are always tangled up in each other, the traditional Canadian Wiggler and too many Mepps spinners. The box also contains sinkers, hooks, leaders, two bobbers, various swivels and snaps, a bottle opener, a spool of line, an old stringer that I should have thrown out years ago, a packet of water-proof matches and another bottle opener. Of course I have all my jigs and plastic worms and grubs in a separate single case.

Katherine had just purchased a new tackle box that could have passed for a small steamer trunk if it weren't for the Fenwick label on the outside. As we motored out to a weed bed that we thought should be sheltering a couple of big pike, she related how she had simply run out of room in her old tackle box and had been forced to get this new one just to be organized. She now found that she had some empty slots and obviously needed to round out her supply of lures by spending another sixty-five dollars on some special baits. Katherine was anxious to try out as many of the new lures as possible that day and was giving me the operating instructions for each lure as she held them up for me to see. These lures all had printed instructions enclosed in their little plastic boxes. I guess the days are gone when you would just ask your favourite tackle shop owner what was the hottest lure going and how you should fish it. Just throw it out and see what transpires is my method.

The weed bed looked good: a few weeds had grown right to the surface, but most were still underwater; the water was calm and flat as a plate. I selected a red and white weed-less daredevil as my first offering, while Kate attached a long, roundish lure that was supposed to represent a frog in colour, if not in shape.

"What's that one called?" I asked.

"This is your Zara Spook," she replied.

"Spook? What kind of a name is that! Was it made by the CIA? It'll probably scare the fish away!"

"No, I saw a guy using one on a fishing show. He was after bass but he was getting pike on it. So I thought I had better get one. Only $9.49 at *Bites and Bucks* – after our discount," she said.

"Won't it get caught in the weeds?"

"No, it's a surface lure. Watch, I'll show you how it's supposed to work." She flipped the Spook out about thirty feet and began retrieving it with a jerking motion. "That's not quite right," she explained, "It should be flopping around a little more." She cast again. This time she got the Spook to flop from side to side as she retrieved it. It definitely looked like a wounded minnow thrashing about. I flipped out the red and white, just behind the Spook, thinking that maybe the Spook would attract something.

My lure had no sooner hit the surface when out of the water surged a pike, grabbed the Spook and headed for the bottom. I guess the weeds helped the big pike to put the added pressure on the line, or maybe it was just too big for the tackle, but the line suddenly went slack. Kate cussed, something that she reserves for the fishing, not while she is catering unless someone drops a tray of flans. Blaming herself for not using heavier line, she reeled in.

"It feels like something is still there," she said, a puzzled look on her face. The Spook popped to the surface. She wound the lure in and then held it for my inspection. "Look at that! That must have been a monster!"

The trailing treble had been torn right out of the Spook.

"Wow," I said. "That's frightening! Just think of the size of that pike! He broke your Spook right in half."

Katherine was digging in her tackle box for something while I made one more cast out into the weeds. "What are you looking for?" I asked, not paying attention to my Red and White that had landed right on top of a lily pad.

"Ah, here it is," she said, holding up the little plastic box that once contained a lure. She took off her sunglasses and read aloud, "'Guaranteed to be free of defects'. . . I am going to send this thing back to them."

"Sure, Kate, I would too. Just make up a story about a huge pike breaking your Spook - they'll probably send you another one." I gave my rod a flip to dislodge the spoon from the lily pad. The water swirled and I set the hook. "But you know you just can't beat a Red and White for pike - get the net, Kate, this is a big one!"

Katherine looked at the bend in my rod, took a farewell glance at the Spook, and tossed it to the back of the boat. "Stupid name for a lure, anyway," she muttered.

GIGO

(2012)

I was sitting at my desk the other day trying to make some sense from a computer printout that was obviously garbage when my thoughts wandered to fishing. Actually, I was thinking about the garbage I saw on the side of the road on the way out from a small lake in the McConnell Lake area. Some thoughtless ninny had thrown a green garbage bag full of tins, plastic wrappers and bottles into the bush.

The scavengers had eaten all they could so I picked up the remains and stuffed them into one of the bags I always have in the SUV. Pop cans, beer cans, pork and beans, spaghetti, a plastic bag that once held Enriched White Bread, two plastic ketchup squeeze bottles and the blister packaging from three fish lures.

Why would anyone go to the trouble of packing their garbage out of their fishing campsite and then throw it into the bush on the side of the road? Were they afraid to take it home in case their spouse saw the empty beer cans? Or the empty boxes that once held a Canadian Wriggler at $12.49 each? Did they only care about their campsite and not the rest of the wilderness? People are funny.

Whenever we go into the remote areas, or even out on a local lake, we always bring back our garbage. Even though I lived 4 hours away, I always practice Garbage In, Garbage Out. It is probably a holdover from my computer programming, I thought, as I returned to the problem at hand.

What do you have to do to make people responsible for their 'garbage'? Obviously I had to add more controls to the input program to force the operator to make certain what he or she was entering was not garbage - only good data. The routine is to make the program 'user-unfriendly', have it force the person to do the correct thing by making 'beeps' and sending time-consuming messages that required answers before allowing access to the data update program.

Maybe that was the answer to the garbage problem too. Make leaving garbage in the wilds so onerous to fishermen and hunters that they will always clean up after themselves. Maybe have them keep an inventory of everything taken into the woods on their cell phones and balance it off when they come out. Make people file a list with the Ministry of Natural Resources that can be checked by a Conservation Officer at any time. Or reward them for being good citizens by increasing the deposit fee on returnable bottles and cans. Like, maybe three or four times what it is now? You would think just being proud of a clean environment would be enough, but . . .

Or put a surcharge on the retailers who insist on using plastic to enshroud everything they sell in blister packs. Surcharge everything from squeeze bottles to plastic bread bags. Definitely put a charge on those plastic grocery bags. Instead of offering five cents off each reusable bag you use at checkout, charge twenty-five cents for every new plastic bag used in packing up the groceries. If twenty-five cents isn't enough, try a dollar. Then send that Loonie to the municipality that has to try to dispose of all that plastic.

Maybe people would go back to carrying their own canvas shopping bags the way they used to before we found this wonderful way of turning our non-renewable fossil oil into non-decomposable plastic bags. Then there are those plastic rings that the handy six-pack cans are attached to, the ones that end up around the necks of our waterfowl.

The phone on my desk rang and brought me back to reality. I asked Alex to hold for a minute while I checked my program once more. I read the line of code I had just written.

Could I really get away with asking computer operators to send me a dollar before I would allow them to print the results of the mistake they had just made? Could I exact a charge for garbage they had just entered in my neat, pristine computer program?

Or just let them go merrily on their way oblivious to the mess they were going to have? Garbage In, Garbage Out. I erased the prompt that said 'Go to Jail, do not pass Go' and settled for one little 'beep' of protest and 'saved' the program.

"Sorry, Alex," I said, picking up the telephone. "I was right in the middle of a program. What's happening?"

"Are you busy this Saturday morning?" my fishing buddy asked.

"No, I think I'm free. What lake did you have in mind?"

"None. I am looking for volunteers to drive my Cubs around Saturday morning. I have the rest of the Club recruited and only need you and your SUV to complete my list."

"They're not selling apples, are they?" I asked.

"No, nothing like that - once a year we go along the creek bed and pick up garbage. The kids get their Citizenship badge and the city gets a good cleaning."

"Where and when?" I asked.

"Eight o'clock at the Uptown Mall. We'll be finished by noon. The lunch and beer is on me at the Disraeli. Then I thought we might just slip up to Bear Lake and try for some late afternoon bass."

That Alex sure drives a hard bargain.

THE BARITONE OF BASS LAKE

(2013)

My wife and I were camping on Bass Lake, a little lake just off Highway 35 that used to have some of the best bass fishing in the area. The lake gets overfished soon after the bass season opens in July, so by the end of August no one bothers to fish there - excepting a few loons and fish ducks that are interested in small fishes. It was the quietness of the lake that attracted us this time because we wanted to try out our new Nikon digital video camera on the birds. The young waterfowl were a little awkward and unsure of their flying and I thought we could record some of the splash-downs and take-off attempts.

We had had an early dinner at our campsite and had set out to paddle around the lake, following the shoreline. It was a very still evening, hardly a ripple on the water, a typical ending to an unseasonably warm August day. My wife was sitting in the bow, camera ready, while I paddled the canoe as quietly as I could. We managed to get very close to a family of Redheaded Mergansers before they all panicked and ran flapping across the water. I approached them again, very slowly, while my wife filmed the ducks. They dove, trying to hide from us, but I gave the canoe a couple of quick, hard strokes towards the place I thought they might surface. The young ducks began popping to the surface all around us. The mother surfaced, gave a couple of squawks, and led her family to flight and safety.

"Did you get some good shots?" I asked.

"Yes! Wasn't that great? Did you see that one surface right beside me?"

"You could almost read the surprised expression on its face, couldn't you?"

"It certainly didn't expect to see us right here!"

From the shore line, a hundred yards ahead, a bullfrog gave its late season 'garrumph, garrumph.'

"What's that?" my wife asked.

"Sounds like a really big bullfrog. Want to video it?" One has to be cautious identifying a bullfrog from a distance because the American Bittern makes a similar sound.

"Sure."

I eased the canoe near the shore and very carefully worked it through the weeds. 'Garrumph.' 'Garrumph.'

"I can't see it," my wife whispered.

It sounded so close, but I could not spot the big frog either. 'Garrumph.'

"There, just to the left of that piece of poplar," I said. The big black and green frog's throat swelled and he 'garrumphed' once more. "He's big enough to eat!" I whispered.

My wife glared at me. "Only kidding, honey," I said. I did not have the slightest idea of how to prepare frogs' legs anyway. Pierre knew how to cook them but there was no point in catching just one frog for the four of us.

We left the bullfrog and continued up the lake following the shoreline, watching for signs of wildlife. The piece of poplar that was near the frog had been cut and chewed by a beaver, so I was watching for an old bank beaver. Around the next point we could hear something splashing.

"What's that?" my wife asked.

"I don't know. Sounds like a large animal wading in the water," I whispered. "It could be a deer or a moose. Get your camera ready."

The splashing continued. Whatever it was, it was certainly sloshing around in the water a lot. Perhaps it was a moose pulling up water lily roots.

"Start the camera now," I whispered as we came up to the little rocky point.

Suddenly, just as we turned, a voice broke into song. "*Shall we gather at the River. . .*" boomed out across the lake. There, up to his knees in the water, was a portly gentleman clad only in soap suds. Oblivious to us, he scrubbed and sang. The camera was rolling and my wife was grinning.

The chorus ended and the man dove into the water to rinse off the soap. When he bobbed to the surface, I called out, "Halloo, the camp!"

The old fellow was startled but waved a hand and said hello.

"Beautiful evening," I commented.

"Ah yes, 'tis that. Would you be coming ashore for a visit?" He offered.

"Well . . ." Martha said.

"Oh my gracious goodness," he said, turning around. "Faith and I didn't know it was a lady in the boat!" He sloshed to shore and picked up a towel and a pair of glasses. "Come ashore, come ashore," he said. "I haven't seen a single soul all week!"

I landed the canoe on the little sandy beach. We got out and introduced ourselves.

"I'm Pat Murphy," he said.

"Ah ha. I thought you looked familiar. I mean after you put your glasses on," I said. "You're Father Murphy, from St. Rita's, aren't you?"

"Sure, and I'm he. You aren't my parishioners, are you?"

"No," my wife answered, "but Pierre and Irene go to your church, I think."

"Pierre . . . Oh, yes, Pierre and Irene, surely, surely."

"You have a good voice," I said, "We thought at first it was some animal splashing the water and were surprised to find you instead."

"I've been camping here all week. T'is a beautiful spot. Naught but God and the animals, and me. T'is like the Garden, I think."

"Yes," I said, "It certainly is a beautiful place."

"A man needs a place like this, a place to go and rest up, to be nearer his maker. T'is something to be here at the dawn, when the mists clear away and the sun breaks through! T'is like a revelation!''

It turned out that Father Murphy makes his own wine and we had a cup or two or three before leaving to get back to our camp before dark. Halfway across the lake, Father Murphy's baritone again broke into song. My wife, who sings a pretty respectable note, joined in. In a few minutes her high voice had a family of loons down the lake all excited, and they too joined in the vesper chorus. I reached forward and flipped the record switch on the Nikon and then added my bass voice to the chorus of *Onward Christian Soldiers*.

As we zipped up the sleeping bags that night I asked my wife if she had enjoyed her day.

"Yes, wasn't it just perfect? We got some good pictures and had such a nice visit with Father Murphy."

"Yeah," I said. "That was a pretty decent wine, too."

My wife laughed, "I can't wait to show Irene the video of her priest in the water!"

Women can be so . . .

On the other hand, I wondered if the Father would be interested in a copy of that video - say in exchange for a couple of bottles of his blueberry wine . . .

PIKE
(2014)

Depending on their size, and the credibility of the fisherman who catches them, pike are known as 'hammer handles' (anything under 3 pounds), 'pike' (that most sporting and quite delicious fish weighing between 5 and 15 pounds), and 'Great Northern Pike'. The latter title is reserved for those monsters whose spirit and fighting ability are challenged only by their brothers, the muskellunge. Pike season had been open for a couple of weeks when I found it at a garage sale.

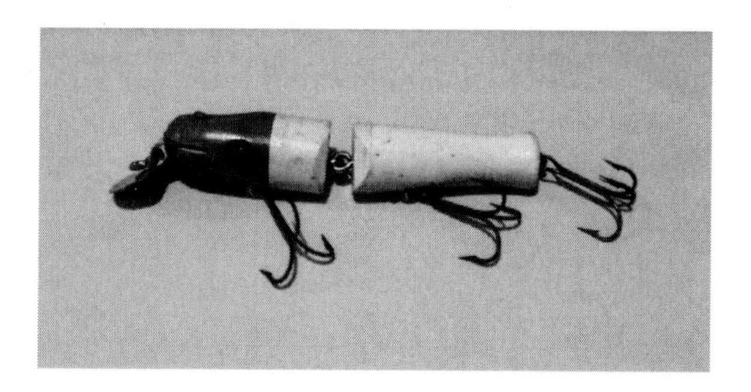

It was one of those treasures that occasionally surface at garage sales, where people preoccupied with cleaning out long-stored items, often have no idea as to the value of their so-called junk. I paid forty cents for it and after cleaning it and using the whetstone on the treble hooks, I now had it on the table for inspection by the rest of the Club.

"Holy smokes! Where did you get that?" exclaimed John, who knows fishing lures as well as anyone. He picked it up, examining it carefully from end to end. "This is a genuine A L & W Pikie!"

Geraldine, who certainly knows tackle, not only from *Bites and Bucks*, but from Tournament fishing, inspected it and agreed.

"A L & W?" asked Freddie who is more in tune with automobiles than fishing lures that are 30 years old.

"That's the name of one of the best tackle companies that ever existed. My Granddad knew Mr Alcock personally. This Pikie was one of their best . . . that trailing treble hook,'' John indicated, "was what caught the big pike. They would grab the lure and when they realized that it wasn't a fish, would try to throw it. They could toss out these trebles on the sides, but a good fisherman could always set that trailing treble." He fondled the 8" long red and white Pikie. "Bill, I'll give you $10.00 for it," he offered.

Now in anyone's books, that is a good return on investment.

Alex, who was now holding the lure, said, "$12.00."

John gave Alex a dirty look and replied, "$15.00. Tops"

Alex, now in the spirit of things and reacting from my kick in the shins, said, "$15.00 and a Trout Trap!"

John was about to explode so I interrupted the bidding, "Wait. I'll sell it to John on the understanding that I can keep it for a week. I want to make a copy for myself. $10.00, John."

The deal was sealed and I delivered the original pikie to John shortly after I had made my own copy. I did not think of the pikie until one Saturday near the end of August when I was out fishing with Alex, Freddie, and a friend of Freddie's from Toronto. The fellow was the Outdoors columnist with one of the big Toronto papers: *The Star*. He had all the trappings of a rich fisherman. Freddie is a bad one for gadgets but his friend had them all. He had things in his over-sized tackle box that I had never seen before and no idea what they were purported to do. He had brought only two of his three rods that were in the car with him. He brought three of what I think were seven different reels that were neatly secured in a travel rack in his car. We were out for an evening, hoping for bass or perhaps a pike or two. He had made a careful selection of lures, reading the weights off them and commenting on the lack of wind.

I drew the columnist, Jim, as my partner in my canoe, Alex and Freddie using Alex's larger canoe. Jim was a good canoer and he could certainly handle that extra-long light rod. He used small lures and a light line, flicking the bait out easily, right on target, near a lily pad or beside a dead-head log. He picked up a nice two-pound small mouth bass which we released, but that was all the action we could get. Alex and Freddie had released a 'hammer handle'. I suggested that we paddle down to the bay at the south end of the lake where I had had some luck pike fishing last year. The columnist was all for it, rigging his other rod and reel and selecting a large spinner.

As we paddled down the lake Jim talked about the time he had caught a 24-pound pike. It was a good story but somehow I thought that this fellow had never caught a really big northern pike. A pike maybe, but not a Great Northern. The lake was as calm as a mirror as we drifted to a stop in the area I had selected.

After a few casts without any action, I suggested that a surface lure might be the ticket on a calm night. It turned out that he had not brought any surface plugs so I looked in my old beat-up tackle box. I found a jitterbug that was likely to attract a bass, but not a big pike. Then I remembered my copy of the A L & W Pikie. On a slow rewind it would break the surface. I hauled it out of its box. His gear was too light, and I think he thought the big pikie too large of a bait, so I was going to try a cast or two with it while he paddled.

On the first cast, the big lure splashed into the still water and my bail stuck. The two seconds that it took to set the reel aright were too long. The water swirled and the pikie, with a large fish following, exploded from the water. The big pike shook, danced for a second on the surface, and was free.

"Damn!" I said. The columnist's jaw had dropped.

Acting like a true guide, I said, "There could be another one. They sometimes travel in pairs. I'll reel in slowly, then you try another cast." We were whispering.

"Did you see that!" Jim said, "That had to go thirty pounds!" I agreed. In fact, he could have been low in his estimate.

As I reeled in I glanced over to see that Alex and Freddie had witnessed the strike. They were sitting still, not wanting to disturb the calm water. The columnist had his paddle feathering the water, slowly turning the canoe around for me to cast in the direction of the last strike. The paddle was hardly moving, just making the smallest ripple on the calm water. I was going to suggest that he should stop - thinking that a large pike might like to investigate those ripples - when all hell broke loose.

The columnist yelled, grabbed the side of the canoe with one hand and tried to hang onto the paddle with the other, pulling on the paddle as hard as he could. The canoe tipped violently and we half-filled with water before we could steady it. He let go of the paddle.

Water exaggerates size. Freddie says it is refraction but I think it just magnifies things. However, when that pike arched out of the water right beside us, he was big! I let an excited 'whoop' out of me, but the columnist started swearing in awe. Jim had a vocabulary that he never uses in that newspaper. I started laughing so Freddie and Alex paddled over to see what had caused the big commotion.

"The biggest *@%¢&!! pike in the world just bit my paddle," Jim said, "I've never seen anything like it! It was huge! I'll bet it would go 50 pounds . . . it was five feet long . . . it had teeth . . ."

"It bit your paddle?" Alex asked, in disbelief.

"Yes! Pulled it right out of my hand!"

I fished the paddle out of the water then passed it to the columnist. He would have something to write about now. There were teeth marks right into the wood, right around the silver and red sticker that showed a maple leaf and said 'Made in Canada'.

We had to go ashore to dump the water out of the canoe.

When I suggested that we go back and try for that fish, Jim would have no part of it. There was no way he was going to share a canoe with a Great Northern Pike.

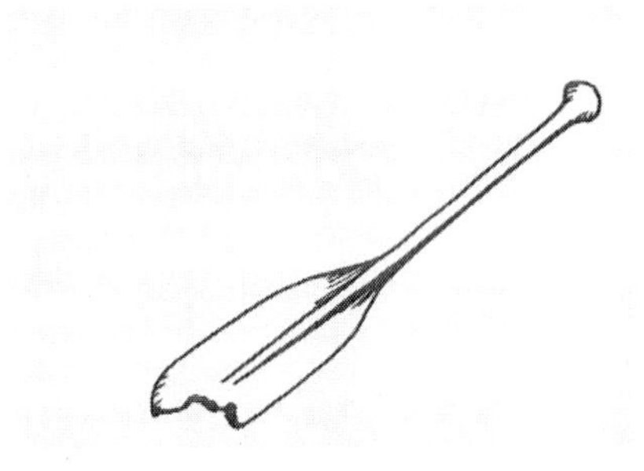

SMOKED FISH
(2014)

It was a hot, humid Tuesday afternoon, the kind of day you wished you were at the beach instead of sitting in an office half-heartedly working on a dull project. Even the rock dove that visits the ledge outside my window was looking bored and hot, his beak open, trying to cool himself. Why he did not go to the beach, I could not understand. When the phone rang and Jason asked if I was going for a beer after work, I felt better. The prospect of a nice cool draft or two was all I needed to make it through the rest of the afternoon. The BSBGSC was in summer recess as the vacation schedule took its toll. Jason was just back from a week's camping near Killarney but John and Pierre were away this week. Jason had something interesting to tell us.

Alex and Freddie had already sipped into a frosty glass of Sleeman's when Jason and I arrived at our favourite pub, the Disraeli Club. Nick, the owner-bartender, almost beat us to the table, him carrying a tray of draft to slake our thirst. Nick was retiring at the end of August. His partner would buy his share and continue operating the tavern. Nick was going back to Greece for three months, thinking about buying a house there.

After a pause that absolutely refreshed, Jason said, "We had a great week at Killarney. The hiking trails there are great. They have trails for all ages, marked on maps-how difficult, how long it takes, and what to look for. Lois really loved the place."

Lois is Jason's latest lady friend. We had all met her and she was certainly a nice person, well-educated, had a good job at a bank and could cook. Her only short-coming, in our eyes, was that she was a City girl who knew little of the outdoors. This week of camping was to be the litmus test.

"How did Lois like sleeping outdoors?" Alex asked.

"Great. She's a real sport. The bugs weren't bad and there's a good clean washroom and shower facility on the grounds. It was a bit like camping in your backyard for me, but she loved it. She wants to go again!"

"That's great," I said, "Perhaps you've found a mate at last."

"Could be. Anyway, at Killarney, you can buy fresh fish from Herbert's - the local commercial fishermen. We had fresh pickerel, white fish and pike - and smoked fish."

"I've never liked smoked fish," Freddie said.

"Well, me neither, until I tried this stuff. Lois said they used to buy smoked fish every week, down at the St. Lawrence market, so she had to try it." Jason said.

"Yeah, but that was probably salmon or some ocean fish," Alex commented.

"I dunno. Anyway, I brought some for you to try," Jason unwrapped a package from the folds of waxed brown butcher paper, exposing a large fillet of some sort for us to see.

Nick does not allow food brought into his bar so Jason called over to him, "Nick, could you bring us a knife? I've got something for you to try."

Nick was given the first slice after he had cut the fish into neat rows of dark meat. "Say, that's good! Where did you get it, Jason?"

Jason told the story and gave Nick a business card with the Herbert's address on it - in case Nick wanted to order some for the bar. We all tried a piece.

"Ummm," I said, "not bad, not bad at all. It tastes like trout to me."

Big Al chewed his piece carefully and said it was a great lakes salmon.

Freddie tried his second piece and said it was damned good and probably a cod or mackerel or maybe even whitefish.

"Nope, you're all wrong," said Jason, helping himself to another slice. "It's plain old pike."

We found this hard to believe and all ate another piece.

When Alex found a bone, the familiar 'Y' shaped bone of the pike family, we had to agree. It was pike; tasty, northern pike.

After discussing how fish was smoked and how the native people did their fish, we appointed Alex, who was now retired and had time on his hands, to study the problem and then design a fish smoker for the Club. Freddie was to assist Alex since he ate more of the smoked fish than the rest of us.

Two weeks later we got the official notice that the following Sunday we were to gather at Freddie's farm with samples of fish to be smoked. Please do not bring frozen fish.

The occasion was to be a family picnic as well as a test of the smoker that Alex and Freddie had built. Jason was to bring pickerel, Pierre a couple of bass fillets, John some pike and I was to bring some perch. Freddie said it was his job to find some cherry wood as this was to be the smoked flavour of our first effort. I thought I had the easiest job and waited until Friday night before I went perch fishing. Of course, just when you want them to bite, they won't, but I did manage to catch four nice catfish just as the sun was setting. I could see no reason why I could not substitute.

Big Al was explaining his fish smoker. "I had a devil of a time finding an old refrigerator with galvanized insides. All the new ones have plastic liners and they're no good."

"Why not?" asked Pierre, who was interested in all things culinary.

"Well you see that little hot plate? It smolders the wood to make the smoke that flavours the fish. But it also produces enough heat to melt the plastic while it slow-cooks the fish."

"You're not supposed to cook the fish first, are you?" asked Jason.

"No, no! What you do, is put the block of wood on the electric hot plate. The smoke and the heat combine to 'smoke, cook and season' the fish. The metals racks are where you arrange your fish. If you are doing different kinds of fish, you arrange it by density. I put a probe in here," Alex pointed to a gadget that looked like a meat thermometer with wires attached, "and connected it to a thermostat. If the heat exceeds

200°, the plate shuts off."

We all marveled at this piece of modern technology that was sitting out behind Freddie's tool shed. I was still pondering the density of fish when Freddie handed me a bottle of cool ale. The wood and fish were loaded and the hot plate plugged into an extension cord. We retired to the patio and pool to while away the next three hours while our fish smoked.

Alex had removed the latch from the door of the fridge so small kids could not get trapped inside and the door was temporarily secured by three bungee cords. There was a small vent drilled into the top of the smoker to allow just a little of the steam to escape, but not large enough to let air into the smoking area.

We all gathered around the smoker at six o'clock, three hours after we had placed our fish in the converted refrigerator. Big Al undid the cords and opened the door. A cloud of smoke and steam surrounded Alex. We could see him waving his arms to clear the air. There was a loud 'poof' and Alex jumped back, tripping over Freddie's dog that was sniffing the air. The fresh supply of oxygen had ignited the cherry wood. While Alex and the dog were getting untangled, John hooked the flaming wood from the smoker with a stick and kicked it aside. I unplugged the extension cord. Unfortunately, John had neatly booted the fiery block into some straw that Freddie had raked up and we all spent the next few minutes doing a foot-stomp on the grass fire.

When we finally got to test the fish, we determined that it needed an additional three hours in the smoker. Another piece of cherry was found and the process started again. The delay was not discouraging enough to spoil our appetites for barbequed steak. Nine o'clock would be a fine time to have a snack of smoked fish.

Freddie said later that he had not noticed any sign of a black bear (ursus americanus) on his property.

His farm was at the southern boundary of black bear habitat, but still . . . I suppose the smell of smoking fish must travel a long way on a hot summer's day. Just as we went to check on our fish at nine, we met the bruin. Black bears are notorious garbage eaters and can be dangerous if they become too accustomed to man. This fellow was a novice but he was in the process of carefully pulling the bungee cords off the smoker when we rounded the comer. We all stopped, watching in awe. The bear hooked the door open with his claws, only to be surrounded by smoke. The now familiar 'poof' and flame frightened the bear, forcing him to back away. The chorus of shouts and yells further upset the bear and he rambled off across the hay field. Freddie's dog, not knowing any better, took off after the bear, baying at the top of his lungs. The old dog came to his senses about the same time as he ran out of wind and left off the chase at the edge of the field.

We put the fire out again and collected all the fish. Once safely indoors, we tasted and commented on how good the pike was, how the pickerel and bass picked up the flavour of the cherry and how much my 'perch' tasted like barbequed chicken.

Alex said, "Freddie, we'll have to move that smoker - otherwise that bear will come back."

"Yeah," Freddie agreed, "But where can we put it?"

"I have some room in my backyard, but I'm not sure what Claire will say . . ." Alex mused.

"I'll take it," John said. "There's room right behind my storage shed. And it certainly won't attract any bears in the City. Cindy and I'll experiment with it and learn how to use the smoker for all kinds of fish!" Cindy nodded her agreement.

"Sure, I thought to myself, "No bears, but if the way my cat takes to smoked fish is any indication, you'll have a yard full of hungry, yowling, stray cats!"

Cold Weather Camping

(2014)

How do you keep a pound of bacon from freezing so hard that it becomes almost impossible to cook over a camp fire in the dead of winter?

Tom, a loans and financing officer at work, has a son who is into Scouting and winter camping and he asked me to give a short talk to the Scouts on how to prepare meals in the cold of winter. I mean, why bother with all the problems of feeding yourself in a winter camp when you could stay safely at home in the city, play a few video games, maybe take in a Netflix movie, play a little street shiny and then drop down to your favourite burger palace for a quick meal of fries and a mystery-meat burger?

Scouting is a great experience for young people so I said yes; I'd tell the young people a few of my Fenimore Cooper secrets. I guess there has to be something out there in the still, silent winter forest to attract people. Maybe it is just the challenge of surviving. After hearing of their last trip into the winter wilds, the Frozen Bacon Problem was the first topic I had to address.

Now unless you like sharing the bottom of your sleeping bag with a couple of pounds of premium bacon, you have to find a spot in the camp that stays just around the freezing point. My suggestion was to dig down in the snow, right to the ground, place your bacon on the ground, and then cover it with lots of snow. It will stay very cold but not so hard as to be impossible to handle. Of course, I never take bacon into the woods - it attracts too many unwanted guests in the summer time. I've seen campers come from campsites hundreds of yards away just at the smell of cooking bacon! I thought it best to check one of the BSBGSC members, Big Al, on winter camping about the bacon problem as well. Alex is the only one of the Club who goes camping during the cold winter months. In fact, the more adverse the conditions, the better he likes camping. He says it builds character. His answer was simply not to take anything into the bush that won't stand freezing.

Preparing for a winter weekend of camping requires a lot of fore-thought about food, clothing, gear and shelter, I told the boys and girls that evening. While food is usually our first thought, keeping warm is the priority for winter. Cold and exhaustion can kill you in the winter, so keep warm, carry as little as possible and be careful. A slight accident in a remote site during the winter can turn out to be much more serious than the same mishap in the summer. That's one reason Alex never carries a hatchet into a winter camp: A long-handle axe is safer because if it does bounce off a piece of frozen wood you are further away from the cutting edge. I pretended that this was one of my own maxims.

It sounds like heresy, but a small Swede saw will do everything you need as far as cutting wood and building a shelter. You are far less likely to cut yourself with a saw, whereas an axe or hatchet may bounce off frozen wood. If you insist on using an axe, always chop while on your knees, not standing upright – it's difficult to hit your feet if they are behind you! From my knees, I made a couple of swings with the old axe at the block of wood that I had brought along for the demonstration but the Scouter said one nick in the gym floor was enough to show the boys what I meant.

Packing a tent into a winter camp is another big drain on your energy. A brush lean-to will keep you just as warm, assuming you have a proper sleeping bag. Do not even think of going into the winter woods with a cheap, thin sleeping bag. I recommended the Hudson Bay store as a good place to by a bag from Amanda. Another key in reducing the weight of your kit is to take only the cooking utensils you really need. No cast iron fry pans, only a main-meal cooking pot and of course, a tea pot. I left out Big Al's recommendation of carrying a small portion of dark rum for the tea since these boys were either too young to know about such things or already had this piece of information handed down to them by the older boys.

The key to keeping warm is to keep dry. I highly recommended light clothing that 'breathes'. Dry footwear, I said, was essential. I could see that the boys knew all about clothing so I quickly switched back to food.

Alex says stew is the answer for a winter camp. A prepared stew can be heated in a single pot, will stay warm while you are eating your first helping and probably even improve with an over-night freezing. The same pot that cooked the stew can be used for heating soup for your lunch. There are any number of dehydrated soups on the market that are only improved with the smoke and balsam ashes from a camp fire. Follow up every meal with some hot camp tea or coffee, raisins or a chocolate bar for dessert and you can easily survive until Monday morning when you can cook your bacon and eggs in that big heavy cast iron pan at home.

Some little nipper in the back asked if I could come with them the next weekend but I quickly thought up a previous commitment I had to go shopping with my wife. Anything to get out of winter camping.

Mr. Grass
(2015)

It was just about five thirty on a Thursday afternoon one day last summer when Jason declined a second glass of Sleeman's Silver saying he had to get home to cut his grass. We had called the meeting to arrange a 'Micro' Bass Tournament among the members of the gang for the coming weekend. Micro being the word for the size of the tournament, not the bass we proposed to catch and release.

"If you would water your lawn a little less frequently and stop using so much fertilizer, you could have a normal lawn like the rest of us," Freddie commented as Jason stood to leave.

"You guys are just jealous of my lawn and if you would put a little effort into it, you could have decent lawns, too!"

"Well, for my part, I prefer a less luxurious lawn to polluting my yard with all those chemicals," Big Al said.

"I agree," I added. "All that crap you put on the grass just gets washed out by all the water you use. Furthermore, it ends up in our lakes. We like to blame golf courses for pollution but there is more acreage in lawns than golf courses."

"If it were only 'crap' it wouldn't be so bad," Pierre said. "A little real fertilizer, like Genuine Cow Manure or some Dehydrated Ram Crap or Organic Sheep Shit it would be a lot better for the yards and the ecosystem."

"All right," Jason said. "Fill up my glass. I can see you people need to be educated on the values of having a great lawn." Jason sat again as Alex refreshed our glasses and signalled to Sammy the waiter that we would likely take another half hour and a jug of draft to settle this latest problem. It is major concerns like this that keep us late at the Disraeli.

"First of all, let me say that none of you have what I would even call a lawn," Jason said by way of an opening salvo.

"Well just because I have a few weeds in my front yard, and by the way, those two dandelions were left for salad stock, and the little patch of clover is for the bees. I think that elevates my 'lawn' to something much more than your perfect green carpet of grass," Pierre said in defence of his grass scape that does need a little more attention by his lawn mower.

"I think a lawn should be more than just a perfectly preened green rectangle in front of your house. I like to see my kids out there, playing catch, throwing lawn darts, playing croquet, whatever. It's a good place for them to play," Freddie said. Freddie lives in the country and it is difficult at times to see where his lawn ends and the field begins. Especially around opening day for bass. Or during any extended period of high pressure when the fish are supposed to bite the best.

"What I like about my lawn," John said, "is the fact that I can go out any evening and catch night crawlers. Great big, fat worms, the kind you can't get in the bait shops. I'll bet you couldn't find enough healthy worms in your lawn to catch crappies!" he challenged Jason.

"I don't like picking worms anyway," Jason said.

"Is it the fertilizer that kills his dew worms?" Alex asked me.

"No, I don't think so. You'd have to use so much that it would 'burn' the grass before it would hurt the worms. No, I think it's the stuff that the "Mr. Grass" company sprays on Jason's lawn several times a year to kill the bugs that gets the worms," I said, *submissa voce* but Jason overheard me.

"That's not true. Mr. Grass is certified by the government as meeting all the guidelines for protecting the environment. They use only biodegradable organic chemicals that become harmless in a few days. The sunlight and the water break them down into inert components within two days." Jason had obviously read a label or a sales brochure on the pesticide.

"Sure, but in those two days the chemicals kill everything they touch. Worse still, little birds, like the traditional friendly robins and sparrows, ingest all that poison - they die too!" Alex said.

"Oh come on, you guys," Jason complained. "If the stuff they put on the grass was that bad, it would have been banned a long time ago, like DDT."

"That's a perfect example and I'm glad you brought it up," Freddie said. "Look how long it took them to realize that DDT was killing everything - it took them years and years. In fact, those chemical companies still argue that DDT isn't all that bad - not as bad as having mosquitoes and malaria. That's why they still sell the damn stuff in Third World countries."

"And that's exactly where all our summer birds go for their winter vacation - somewhere nice and warm that used to be free of all our pollutants," Pierre commented. "I read that we almost lost all of our Swainson Hawks because they ate poisoned grasshoppers in Argentina."

"Come to think of it, have you guys noticed how few robins there are this year? My wife mentioned it just the other day. I'll bet those pesticides are taking a toll on the robins."

"You're right, Bill," Alex said, "I haven't seen as many robins, or for that matter, any birds on the lawn or in my garden." The rest of the members of the Club agreed that there was a scarcity of ground-feeding birds this year, even Jason acknowledged he had not seen as many.

"But it can't be the stuff they put on the lawns," he continued, "there just isn't enough of that product used - Mr. Grass was telling me how many of his customers are turning to natural insect control, even though it is not as effective."

"I still think that poison is killing the birds," Freddie continued, as he motioned me to top up his glass, "Think of the amount of poison they use on golf courses! Seen any birdies there lately?"

John mentioned how had scored a birdie on number eleven but we ignored his attempt to draw the attention to his golf game. He had been hitting the ball better than any of us so far that season.

"But, you know something else," Pierre said, "I haven't seen nearly as many frogs or toads this year, either. I'll bet they are the first to feel the effect of grass poisons since they eat all those bugs that live in the grass."

"Come to think of it, the old toad that has lived in my garden for two or three years didn't show up this summer," Alex said.

The discussion degenerated down to blaming the loss of the little creatures on everything from increased road traffic to a natural cycle and the global warming that was changing the habitat. We finally got back to the bass tournament and picked teams for the Saturday trip into Little Loon Lake. I drew Pierre as my partner and knew I had a good chance to win the eighty dollars that was in the pool. Pierre would bring his fly casting gear and tease the bass into striking those colourful bits of yarn and feathers that he ties during the long, cold winter months. I told Pierre I would pick up a couple of new lures at *Bites and Bucks* that Amelia said were doing well this year and be well prepared for the tournament.

It was in the Canadian Tire store that I met Alex, the Friday before the fishing contest. He was rummaging through the spray paint display, looking for particular colours, a special shade of brown and 'grass' green he said. "What are making now," I asked, assuming Alex was working on another project in his workshop.

"Nothing, actually. Freddie and I are playing a little prank on Jason." He went to explain that he and Freddie had talked to the Mr. Grass man and found out that Jason was having trouble with that little cinch bug that dines on the tender grass roots, leaving small brown circles of dead grass on a lawn. Mr. Grass has sprayed for the bug and was certain that Jason's lawn was once again in perfect order. But Alex and Freddie were going to sneak over to Jason's later that night and spray-paint a number of small brown patches on the luscious green carpet that was Jason's pride and joy. They had let Mr. Grass in on their joke so he could stall

Jason and pretend that the whole lawn might have to be ripped up and replaced.

Personally I think they were just trying to put Jason off for the bass tournament. Anybody who is worrying about their lawn won't do well fishing bass. Smallmouth bass especially require your full attention. We had to wait twenty minutes for Jason and John to arrive at the lake Saturday morning. Jason was obviously upset.

"How come you guys are so late?" Pierre asked. "You know you two will need all the time you can get to catch even half as many bass as the rest of us."

"Aw, it's that damn lawn of Jason's," John complained.

"Don't tell you were cutting your lawn this morning?" Big Al asked.

"No, I wasn't cutting it. I just happened to look out the window this morning and I noticed a whole bunch of brown spots on the lawn. Something is eating all the grass roots. My lawn is a mess! We had to wait until Mr. Grass came. He's going to dig around today and let me know what has to be done when I get back. I may have to replace the whole lawn!"

"Gee, that's too bad, Jason," Freddie said. "Maybe you just have fertilizer-burn, or something like that."

"No, I'm pretty sure it's those damn cinch bugs. I've been having a real problem with them this year - there have been two or three spots on the lawn that they ruined before we sprayed. It is funny the spray didn't get them all," Jason said.

"Well, let's get fishing," Alex said. "We'll meet on that little grassy island for lunch at eleven thirty."

"Maybe we should pick another spot," Pierre suggested, "Jason might not like to be reminded of his lawn by eating there. How about that bald rock on the shore, over there?"

"Naw, the grass will be nicer," Alex said, giving me a wink. Pierre and John did not know about the joke perpetrated by Alex and Freddie but I knew the choice of that grassy island had something to do with the prank. The island used to have a cottage on it and the remains of the old lawn still afford a pleasant place to eat your lunch.

We fished until just before eleven thirty, when Pierre and I, with three large bass in the live well, headed to the island for lunch. Freddie and Alex were waiting for us. They had already spray-painted a large number of brown circles on the grass.

As Jerry and John motored up, a loud, animated discussion was underway on the shore. Alex was saying, "And I say it's the same thing that makes those strange marks in the wheat fields. They are just using smaller space ships here!"

"You're wrong. These look just like a wild version of the cinch bug to me. See how the grass has died, but is still standing? It's been cut off at the roots by that bug!" Freddie asserted.

"What's the problem?" John asked.

"Look at the grass - it's diseased or something. There are brown circles everywhere," I said.

"Let me see," Jason said, climbing out of the boat. "Gosh, it looks like - no, it can't be cinch bug out here." He bent over and pulled at a tuff of brown grass. The brown paint came off on his hands. Slowly, the light came on.

When Big Al shook the rattle in the spray can, and offered the can of green grass paint to him, Jason went off like a five cent firecracker.

When things had settled down and Alex and Freddie came back to shore to dry their clothes we had our lunch. I had always thought that anyone who had the patience to keep a lawn as nice as Jason's would be a little more tolerant, but I guess the tee shirt I awarded Jason for sportsmanship that day shouldn't have had "Mr. Grass" written on it. I thought it was a rather tasteful shade of brown.

GULLIBLE

(2016)

We were discussing the merits of using big lures to catch bigger fish when Jason and John challenged Pierre and me to a contest. The fact that we were on our second jug of Sleeman's had nothing to do with my ready acceptance of the rules for the event. The BSBGSC members will use any excuse to go fishing.

The rules, as laid down by Jason and John, were that each canoe could use one trolling lure and one casting lure at a time. Pierre and I would be using only smaller lures while the other two would use the larger lures that they were certain attracted bigger fish. We chose the lake where Pierre has his cottage as the testing grounds. The Owner's Association at the Lake did not permit gas motors on the lake, but electric trolling motors were allowed.

John had a trip to downtown Toronto early that week, supposedly on business, but I really think he just wanted to get some more special tackle at *Bites and Bucks*. What kind of business a real estate broker who specializes in residential homes has to do in the commercial core of big city, I did not ask, but when John dropped into my office Thursday afternoon, I could see that he had made the trip worthwhile. I could also see that he had invested heavily on winning the fish contest. All of the lures that he had purchased were well over eight inches long. Some were pointed, some had feathers. One even had an adjustable 'lip' for regulating the depth at which it would run when trolling. It had its own computer printout showing the running depth for various line weights and trolling speeds. It was, I thought, the ugliest lure I have ever seen. The $18.95 price tag was still dangling from one of its treble hooks.

"You didn't pay $18.95 for that?" I asked.

"Sure. It was on special, marked down from $22.49. Geraldine said they were having great luck with them in the Kawarthas."

"Yeah, but John, that looks like a piece of garbage more than something a pike would eat!"

"No, the yellow sides represent a perch's markings; the red, right here, could be blood or something the perch is eating; the black stripes are to give it a sense of motion as it goes through the water," he explained, carefully indicating all the salient features of the lure.

"I dunno," was my polite comment.

"And look at the one I got for Jason," he said, bringing out another monstrosity. "Geraldine said that she had heard that the muskies in the Thousand Islands area were really hitting hard on these. It should be an excellent casting bait!"

This one was green with black wiggly markings and large luminous eyes. I supposed it represented a frog but it could as easily have been a miniature from the set of Spielberg's latest science fiction story. Those Thousand Island muskies must have been attacking those lures out of concern that it would harm their kids - their minnows or whatever baby muskies are called. Muskettes, maybe?

John went on to explain that he had bought surface lures that would 'dive' when being trolled but that would float to the top of the water when the trolling line slacked. This would be handy in case the fellow who was casting managed to get snagged. Jason had the habit of over-casting and getting hung up on the shoreline and he was trying to make life easier on his fishing partner. It did seem like a good idea at the time.

Sometime during the visit I managed to say something uncomplimentary about his ugly lures and ended up betting a case of 24 beers that Pierre and I would win on Saturday. After John left I called Pierre.

"Pierre, are you all set for Saturday?"

"Yep. We said 8 a.m., didn't we?"

"Yes. I suppose you know where to catch the biggest fish in that lake?" I asked.

"Sure. At 5.30 p.m., right off my dock."

"Off your dock?"

"Yeah. You'll see." Pierre replied.

Saturday morning the two canoes departed Pierre's dock with the wager now up to two cases of 24. Pierre is usually pretty careful with his money, but he seemed very certain of the day's outcome. Jason and John had checked our tackle box to ensure that we did not have any big lures with us. They had their recently purchased contraptions along with some older pikies, flatfish, and Williams spoons.

By noon we had caught and released two largemouth bass and one 4 pound pike. Jason and John were working the area near the island where we had planned to meet for lunch. As we approached, John cast towards the shoreline and caught a small cedar tree. Jason shut off the electric motor and paddled into the shore to retrieve the lure.

"You guys catch anything?" I called.

"Kept one," Jason said, indicating his stringer. "Only about 4 pounds."

I cast an inquiring glance at Pierre as if to say maybe we should have kept the pike we had released, but Pierre just smiled.

"All those junky lures you two have, and that's all you caught?" Pierre kidded.

"I don't see even a small fish on your stringer," John replied as he was trying to get his lure out of the tree.

I was watching a sea gull that seemed to be interested in something just aft of their canoe, about 30 metres away. It was that floating thing that caught pike and muskies in the Kawarthas or was it the Thousand Islands?

"Hey, Jason . . . I think you had better retrieve your lure or that gull is going to eat it."

The gull was serious about what it thought was lunch. Maybe it thought that one of the men in the canoe had accidentally dropped a hot dog. Gulls, like, pike, will eat anything. Jason started to reel in the line but there was too much slack. The gull grabbed the lure, lifted off the water and then quickly ran out of slack line. The sudden tension on its lunch caused the gull to somersault back onto the water. It tried to shake off the lure but it was hooked. The squawking attracted two other gulls who tried to share the first's lunch.

We yelled and waved our paddles to try to keep the other two birds away but one was too greedy and got tangled in the fish line. We were all shouting advice to Jason about giving slack, keeping the line tight, reeling in, keeping his rod tip up or down.

The gulls finally calmed down enough to allow Pierre and me to get them netted and into our canoe. We took them ashore and began the task of freeing the two birds. The one that was only tangled in the line was soon set free but the other bird had the hook right through its beak. Pierre snipped off the barb and we worked the hook back through. The gull would have a bit of a sore beak for a few days but it flew off without any sign of discomfort, just a few words of embarrassment.

Naturally there was a lot of kidding over lunch but Jason took it all in good spirit. It was, after all, his first gull! Afterwards he would relate the tale saying it was this long - the wingspan of a gull being rather impressive in fish-story hand measurements.

We agreed to meet back at Pierre's dock at 6 p.m. when the contest would end. I caught another pike, about five pounds but Pierre insisted that I throw it back too. It looked like a case of 24 Sleemans as it swam away.

"Pierre, are you sure about catching something big?"

"Yep. It'll be about 10 or 12 pounds. At 5:30, right off my dock."

"How can you be so sure?"

"Trust me."

At 5:15 we were just off his dock.

"Put on a June bug spinner and a couple of these." he said, pulling a tub of worms out of the lunch cooler.

"Worms?"

"Yep. Every day for the last week I've been coming down here at 5:30 and throwing in a dozen dew worms. The last two nights there's been a big pike waiting."

I baited up as instructed and cast out the June bug spinner

with its two juicy worms.

I caught a 10-inch perch.

I rebaited and tried again. Another perch.

"Keep trying," Pierre said, looking at his watch and then down the lake to where Jason and John were slowly coming towards us.

I cast again. I felt a tug and set the hook, thinking I had another perch. Out of the water came a large northern pike. I set the fighting tension on the reel and began the ten minute contest that landed a 16-pound pike.

John and Jason were there to watch the netting. Pierre held up the pike and they conceded the contest. Pierre threw the fish back.

"What kind of lure did you catch it on?" asked John.

"A worm," I said, "A small, small worm . . ."

Buck Law

(2016)

It was the 15th Anniversary of the founding of the BSBSC (10 years since we changed to the BSBGSC) and we had decided to have a special dinner meeting. Pierre had already retired and within the next year Alex, Freddie and I would be retiring. Geraldine and Amelia had an offer to purchase their store, *Bites and Bucks*, and they were thinking of semi-retirement to join the Pro Bass Fishing tournaments in the States. Catherine was two years from retiring and Amanda's husband George had finally landed a seat in the Federal Government so she would be in Ottawa quite often. Of course, we all thought we would have more time to fish and hunt when we retired . . .

There is a banquet room upstairs at the Disraeli Club so we rented the hall and hired a caterer. Since it was my idea for the anniversary dinner, they elected me chairman so I could do all the work, selecting the menu, decorating the hall, hiring the caterer and the cleaners. It also behoved me (Freddie's words) to entertain the Club members with a story or two. My wife Martha suggested that I read one of my Grandfather's stories about hunting. Grandfather 'Dob' Haggarty was a raconteur and had a collection of unpublished short stories that I kept thinking I should do something with to preserve the history.

Herewith is the story that Martha chose - titled 'Buck Law' written by my Grandfather.

~/~

At five thirty old Mike O'Connor banged on a cake pan and sang out to the bunkhouse, "Breakfast in ten minutes for the guides. You dudes can eat in fifteen minutes. Everybody up!" The guides slept at the north end of the camp, separated from the hunters' comfortable bunks by a canvas curtain.

It was November, 1928 and the Caribou Lake Hunt Club was being called to the hunt. No fancy horns, just the raspy voice of Old Mike. The same ageless Mike had called the men back in 1913 when the camp was formed. Some of the same faces were there to greet him. Doc Ellerton, Jim Hardy (V. P. of US Steel), Fred Wilson (ACME Motor Sales), Judge Smith, all of them veteran hunters from Pittsburgh. They were all that remained of the original crew. The depression had taken its toll. But when the fall air gets crisp and the geese wing south, a true hunter knows he must get away to the woods regardless of the financial problems of the world.

We had all finished our bacon and flapjacks and were ready to set out when Doc Ellerton called us all together.

"Boys, we all know that the Department of Lands and Forests has declared this to be a 'buck only' year. It is the responsibility of the local guides to report any violation of this rule and I expect them to do just this. Anyone shooting a doe will have to go before a camp court and may be expelled from the Caribou Lake Hunt Club. Are there any questions about this before we start out this morning?"

"What if you shoot a doe by mistake?" asked John Percival van Horne, director of the Penn State Railroad, a new man in the club.

"In this camp we don't shoot anything by mistake, J. P." replied Doe. "Make sure what you shoot is a deer first of all and then make sure it is a buck."

"Okay, let's get out and at them." said Judge Smith. And the hunt of 1928 was underway.

The Buck Law was imposed because the deer herds in Parry Sound District had been hard pressed by two winters of exceptionally deep snow. The wolf population had been on the increase and the toll taken by wolves had added to the deer herds' problems. Bucks are generally pretty wily and it was felt by the Department that not too many would be shot and it was better to have a limited hunt than to close the season altogether.

The guides waited until the hunters were on their watches and then let the dogs loose and followed them through the woods, making all sorts of noise that was supposed to scare the deer and send them running past the watches, where they would be shot at and presumably turned into venison steaks. Jimmy Brooklyn, Stinky Smith and I were the guides that fall.

About five minutes after the run started we heard three rapid shots and then one shot.

"That sounded like a cannon," yelled Stinky.

"Must have been van Home's Two Forty Three," I called back.

"Yeah, sounded like it came from the pine ridge," replied Stinky.

We continued the chase and there were a few more shots but no yelling or cheering, so it appeared that the deer had made it safely through the lines. We all headed back to the camp.

"Who let go with the cannon?" I asked when we were all together.

"I got a few shots at a really big buck", said J.P. van Horne. "He came running through just after the dogs started to bay. There was a lot of brush, so I'm sure I missed him with all three shots. Man, that was the biggest deer I've ever seen!"

"If you would take them damn scopes off those guns you'd get more deer", said Mike as he dumped out the dishwater.

The hunters ribbed van Horne a little over coffee and fresh oatmeal cookies and then we went out again on a short run before lunch. When the hunters had left, I asked Stinky "Didn't you hear four shots?"

"Yes, I'm sure there were four," he replied.

"Jimmy, wasn't there four shots, not three like van Horne said?"

"Yes, I counted three and then one. Dob, you had better go up to the ridge and take a look around before supper tonight." Jimmy was the head guide and he didn't want any problems. We were all thinking that maybe van Horne had shot a doe and was trying to cover up the mistake.

The afternoon hunt was uneventful. The dogs wouldn't run, and there was some wolf sign around. We got back to camp about three o'clock and began the evening chores. As soon as I had my work done, I slipped off to the pine ridge to have a look around. I soon saw where van Horne had been standing when he shot that morning. I picked up the three brass shell cases and started to look for tracks. I found the fourth brass and pocketed it. Then, down the knoll to the left, I saw some white. A small doe lay dead, one shot through the chest section.

I cleaned the deer and slung it across my shoulders. Old Mike saw me coming.

"Hey, Dob has got himself a deer."

The camp emptied and everyone was asking where I shot it.

"I'm afraid it wasn't me," I said. "This deer was shot this morning up on the pine ridge."

Then, as I dropped the deer to the ground, Jimmy Brooklyn said, "That's a doe."

There was a silence. Everyone looked at J. P. van Horne.

"But I shot at a buck. It was twice as big as that deer. I swear I never shot that deer." claimed J. P.

Judge Smith cleared his throat, "I guess we'll be having a little trial after dinner. Dob, you'll be the prosecution; Hardy, you'll act as the defence lawyer; Jimmy, you take J. P. into custody until we eat."

It was a very quiet meal that night. There was none of the usual camp rowdiness and joking. Doc Ellerton tried to loosen things up by telling the story about how Judge Smith had been treed by a black bear the first year of the hunt, but even Doc's colourful descriptions of the Judge sitting in a maple tree swearing at the bear didn't dispel the seriousness of the upcoming trial.

The judge selected a jury of peers for the case and then gave the charges against J. P.

"You are charged with shooting a doe deer and withholding evidence of said misdemeanour. How do you plead?"

"Not guilty", said van Horne.

"Is the prosecution ready?"

"Yes, Judge," I said.

"Prosecution may proceed."

"I call on Jimmy to make a positive identification of the exhibit."

Jimmy carried the doe in and declared that there was no doubt that it was a doe.

"Were you not on the pine ridge, this morning?" I asked J. P.

"Yes I was."

"Was anyone else there with you?"

"No, I was alone."

"Do you own a .243 magnum rifle?"

"Yes, I do."

"Your honour, I have here four cartridges that were found on the pine ridge this afternoon. I suggest that these are the shell cases from Mister van Horne's gun."

"Objection, your honour," Hardy broke in. "That's circumstantial evidence. We can't prove that those came from J. P.'s gun."

"That's true. But this whole case is circumstantial by the fact that there were no eye witnesses. J. P., do you want to inspect the shell casings and then state whether they are from your gun?"

"Yes, your honour, they are from my gun."

"Proceed, prosecution."

"Well, Judge, all the evidence I have is the cases and the doe. To the charge of covering up the crime, I will call on Stinky." Stinky came up to the table. "Stinky, did you hear four shots fired from the general direction of the ridge this morning?"

"Yes, I did. About five minutes after the hunt began."

"And when we came back to camp, how many shots did Mr. van Horne say he had fired?"

"Three."

"Thank you. Judge, I rest my case."

"All right. Is the defence ready?"

"Yes, your honour," said Hardy.

"You may proceed."

"I call J. P. to the stand. J. P., did you shoot at a deer this morning?"

"Yes, I shot at a big buck and missed him."

"Did you check to see if there was any sign of blood?"

"Yes, but I didn't see any."

"Are you sure that it was a buck?"

"Yes. It was the biggest deer I've ever seen."

"As to the charge of not telling you had shot at a deer, I think this is reasonable, since you believed you had missed."

"How about the discrepancy in the number of shots?" asked Judge Smith.

"Well, your honour, where I hunted before, whenever we fired three shots we would always fire a fourth. This is so the three shots wouldn't seem like a distress signal," said J. P.

Doc Ellerton stood up. "Judge, could I beg the court's indulgence? I would like to ask the defendant a few questions that might help to decide this case."

"Any objection, Hardy?" asked the Judge. "No objections."

"J. P., would you tell the court how you can tell a doe from a buck deer."

"Well, a buck has horns, and a doe doesn't."

"Did you see the 'horns' as you call them?"

J. P. was silent. "Well, to tell the truth, I can't remember seeing any horns."

"Judge, this fellow didn't see any 'horns'! They are called antlers, for your enlightenment, Mister van Horne. Is there any other way that you could tell a buck from a doe?"

"Well, the buck is usually a brighter colour than the doe."

"That's true. But I doubt if you would have time to decide on that basis when a deer is running past you. Is there any other way?"

"Yes, the buck has a more rounded hoof than the doe."

"Again, that's true. But did you have time to check that before you shot this morning?"

"No, I guess not."

"Well, what else is there about a buck and doe that helped to tell them apart?"

"I don't know."

"Jimmy, would you tell J. P. here how you so easily knew that Exhibit A was a doe."

"Hell, all you got to do is look at its sex organs."

Everyone had a good laugh at J. P. who turned a bright red in the face.

Judge Smith broke up the laughter. "I think the jury should be able to come to a decision on the facts we now have before us. The jury may go out on the kitchen to take their vote."

The jury returned. Their verdict was 'guilty'. "Do you have anything to say before I pass sentence?" asked the Judge.

"Your honour, I honestly don't think I shot that deer. The one I saw was a real big one. If I've made a mistake then I'll beg the court's mercy."

"I find it hard to believe anyone could shoot at a buck and not remember if it had antlers so I am willing to accept the possibility that you hit a deer other than the one you aimed at. I fine you thirty dollars and four bottles of bourbon. I also sentence you to spend the next day of the hunt sitting on pine ridge, the scene of the crime, and I further order that you remove the scope and all sights from your gun so you look more closely at whatever may visit you on your hill of exile. Court is adjourned. Get that bourbon, I need a drink!"

The next day we left van Horne on the pine ridge again and set out to chase in the opposite direction. We had just started the chase when once more from the ridge came three shots and then another. There was no mistaking that .243 magnum of van Home's.

"Better go and see what he's done now," yelled Jimmy from the edge of the swamp we were entering.

"Okay, I'll go." I said. I figured it would be a waste of time since I didn't think van Home could hit anything without his sights on that cannon of his.

"J. P.," I yelled. "Where are you?"

"Over here." He was trying his best to clean out the biggest buck I had ever seen. He had hit it three times in the neck, without sights.

"Dob, come over here. We walked over to where the doe had been shot. J. P. pointed about three yards farther on. There were big buck tracks, about a day old.

"Well, J. P., I owe you an apology. I guess you never did see that doe. The buck must have been standing there and you shot low and hit the doe,"

J. P.'s buck was the biggest shot that year and he got the fifty dollar prize.

The funny thing was, that buck didn't have any antlers!

Goldfish
(2016)

I was exchanging a Christmas shirt that my Sister-in-Law had given me for one that did not have the horizontal stripes that accentuated my slight paunch, when I thought I would take a couple of minutes to visit my favourite store. Whenever I am shopping at the Yorkdale Mall, and have a few minutes to spare, I join the line of little people and wander through the Pet shop aquarium display. The regular sales clerks at Pets R Us recognize me and kindly refrain from asking if they can help me, knowing that no matter how long I stand in front of the fish tanks, I am 'just looking'.

The colours fascinate me. How could these brightly coloured little fellows hide from their predators? They seem to flaunt their brilliant blues, greens, yellows and reds. Colourful fish like that would never survive in our waters, I thought, thinking how the Oscars looked like a Mepps spinner.

Tropical fish are just more colourful than the local fish. Well, except maybe for our sunfish. Or a Bluegill. Or maybe a perch. Or a speckled trout. Perhaps our local fish were just as attractive. I was watching a swarm of Neons darting around the ceramic diver who was aerating the tank with his bubbles when I recognized a fellow fisherman making a purchase at the goldfish tank. He had the young clerk net six of the largest fish in the tank.

"Hi," I said, "I see you're into aquarium fish as well as pickerel."

"Uh, yeah. Just getting a few goldfish for a start," he said. "Have you been out on the Lake yet?"

"No, I'm not much for ice fishing, but a couple of fellows at work said the pickerel were hitting."

"Just small ones so far, down at the point."

I did not want to show my ignorance by asking which point but I thought he meant Deep Water Point. Or maybe it was Long Point. It could have even been Cross Point. We left the store together and as soon as we were outside, he said, in a voice that I could only describe as conspiratorial, "I don't really have an aquarium."

"Then what are you going to do with those goldfish?"

"Bait. I didn't want to upset the clerk, or any of those kids in there, but these big goldfish are great bait!"

"Really?" I asked. But then something about using minnows from lakes other than the one you are fishing in came to my mind. "Isn't it against the law to use them? I mean, you might be infecting the lake with some virus or disease . . ."

"Naw. We make sure they're well hooked. They die as soon as they hit that cold water anyway," he assured me. "Besides, whenever you buy minnows at a local bait shop, you can't tell if the minnows are from the same lake or even the same area. Nobody worries about that rule anymore."

"Well, I don't know about that. At least the minnows are from this general area - not the Caribbean." He did not seem impressed by my concern about spreading disease to our lakes.

It was about three weeks later, at *Bites and Bucks*, that I met him again. Even though Geraldine and Amelia are no longer at the store, it is still a good place to shop. I was shopping for some treble hooks to set up some plastic shads for lake trout fishing and had wandered off course to the shelves of colourful lures that were saying 'buy me, buy me'. This was almost as good as watching the tropical fish at the mall. The fisherman was asking the clerk for some gold sparkle flakes.

"Hi, how is the fishing?" I asked.

"Oh, hi. Not bad. We gave up at the Point and are just off the Reef now. We caught a couple of three pounders last weekend."

"Still using the, uh, special bait?"

"No!" he said and added a few expletives. "The damned Conservation Officer came around for a check on our hut and saw them. She fined us a hundred and sixty bucks each! Guess you were right. Goldfish are only for looking at!"

"Too bad," I lied, not feeling the least bit sorry for him. "Are you going to try the gold sparkle instead?"

"Yeah. I hope it works half as well as the goldfish!"

I could see the clerk hiding a smile. I too have tried that sparkle stuff. All that glitters is not gold.

The Enfield

(2016)

"The motion fails, five votes to one," acting Chairperson Alexander announced.

Every year, for the past four years I have presented a motion to the Club to allow me to use my old .303 British in the fall shooting contest, and so far my motion has failed by the same vote. It all started back one fall day five years ago when Pierre and I had accompanied John to the local Legion hall . . .

Pierre and I were guests of John at the local Branch of the Royal Canadian Legion a week before Remembrance Day. John, who is a member of the pipe band, served a short stint in the Militia when he was a young man, thus entitling him membership in the Legion. The band had just held their final rehearsal and as a reward for coming out and watching the drill, they invited us in for a refreshment. Not that either Pierre or I needed to be bribed with a drink to spend an hour enjoying the sounds of the pipes and drums. The skirl of a bagpipe has some magical hold over both of us, unless it is when John is struggling with a new piece of music and the haunting call of the pipes becomes the caterwauling of a couple of angry cats settling a domestic affair in the alley. Tonight's band music was excellent. The echoes of the Last Post were still in our minds as Pierre and I waited at the bar for John.

"It's good to see how these fellows remember their friends who are no longer with them," Pierre said.

"Yes," I agreed, "The Legion is very important to some of these people, according to John. Not only do they do Community work but I guess it is a place where former soldiers can talk about things in a way that we civilians might not understand."

"True. Even though some of these people have never been in a war, the military life leaves a lasting impression on most of them."

I saw John coming up the stairs and motioned to the bar attendant to bring us three glasses of beer. "That was a good rehearsal, John," I said. "You'll need a cool beer to whet your whistle after all that puffing and huffing into that sheep's belly!"

"I've told you a hundred times - it's not a sheep's stomach!" he laughed. "Com'on over here, there's someone you'd like to meet," he said, indicating a table where a couple of old fellows where having a drink.

"May we join you?" he asked. When they motioned us to the chairs John made the introductions, "Mister Johnston, Mister Fellows, these are my friends Bill and Pierre."

The older of the two and I would have guessed his age at about ninety-five, said, "That was good music, young John. Sounded the same as it did seventy years ago!"

"Thank you, Sergeant," John smiled.

"Seventy years ago?" Pierre asked before I could. "That had to be . . . that was 1941!"

"Mr. Johnston, you're not going to tell me you are old enough to remember . . ." I said.

"Yes, I was there in 1941. I was only seventeen, but I had spent two months at the front. I lied about my age, same as a lot of other young men did back then."

"How old are you now?" Pierre asked.

"Guess I'm eighty-eight. Be eight-nine in the spring, if I last that long," the old man replied.

"How about you, Mr. Fellows? How old are you?" I asked.

"Oh, I'm just a young fry. Never served in the Second War but I was lucky enough to make it into the Korean War. I was twenty-eight in '49 - they took me because I was a Reservist. They didn't want us older guys, but they needed somebody with a little experience, so they let us in. I made it all the way through without a scratch, too. Some of those younger men may have been quicker and smarter than me, but I made it through!"

I calculated his age at a respectable ninety years. "You two must be the oldest members at this Legion," I commented.

"Yep," Sergeant Johnston said. "I guess we are."

John knew that we all enjoyed hearing about the olden days so he prompted Mr. Johnston, "What was it like, when the Armistice finally came, back in '45, Sergeant?"

"Cold and wet, as I remember. And muddy. Seems there was always mud. The fighting had really not been too bad on our front from the time after we got ashore in Holland until it was all over. I missed out on the invasion. We did have one attack where we took about twenty miles in one day until we came to a bridge where the Germans stopped us for a couple of days. We lost about sixty men from the company - fifteen dead, I think. By the time they had declared the Armistice, I had seen enough."

We chatted on, hearing some interesting tales by Mr. Johnston about his exploits. It turned out that he was his company's marksman or sniper in today's jargon. "Which gun did you use when you had to do some sniping?" John asked.

"I used the Enfield, Mark IV, the same gun as the rest of the guys used at the start of the war," Sergeant Johnston replied.

"Yes, that's essentially the same gun we trained with," the Private said. "Ours was just the old standard Enfield. Good gun that. Never jammed, a little mud didn't bother it," he recalled. "We had the M1 Garand in Korea as well as the Enfield."

"Yes," agreed the Sergeant, "We found it pretty good. Of course, by the end of the war, there were a lot of semi-automatics and automatics around and the old bolt action was becoming a relic."

"I'm surprised you didn't have a special rifle for sniping," Pierre commented.

"Well, we did pick a gun that was the best in the company. There always seems to be a special in everything, whether it's guns, cars or even people," Sergeant Johnston said. "We found one and I worked on it a bit to meet my needs - I filed off the roughing on the trigger, used the emery on the action so it was really smooth. We used special cartridges, too - extra powder for more speed. Yes, that was a good gun. I even filed in a few small nicks on the top of the breech for each of the six Germans I shot."

"What happened to the gun? Did you keep it after the war?" Pierre asked.

"No, we had to turn them in. The army checked them over to see that they were safe and sold them as 'Army Surplus' after the new rifles were issued. Those new automatics are fancy, but I bet I could shoot straighter with that old Enfield than any of these modern-day soldiers and their fancy guns."

"You're right, Vic," the Private said, "All they do today is fill the air with lead and hope they hit something!"

"That's the same as some hunters," I said. "Some of those guys with semi-automatic rifles just point in the general direction of what they think is a deer and let fly with the whole clip! Darn near as stupid as those people who advocate the need of fully automatic rifles for game hunting!"

"Well, it seems to me," Private Fellows said, "That the young hunters today simply do not take any pride in being able to shoot accurately. Hell, I'll bet old Vic here could out-shoot most men a third his age!"

Old Sergeant Johnston nodded his agreement, "If I had my old gun!" he said.

The Private continued, "I was watching the telly just last night - showed some guerrilla firing an automatic rifle - he just pointed over a wall and pulled the trigger! Damn fool didn't even look where he was shooting. There could have been women and children in the street!"

"I guess things have really changed since World War II in that respect," Pierre said.

"Hell, yes! We had to conserve our bullets. Used the bayonet whenever we could," the old man replied. He went on to relate a rather detailed account of a gory attack they had made back in 1942 but I was thinking about what Mr. Johnston had said about his .303. The Ross Modified that I had purchased from a sporting goods store in Winnipeg many years ago had a smooth trigger. And it had a nicked breech block that I had attributed to rough handling during the war.

I caught the bartender's attention and signalled for another round of beer then asked Mr. Johnston "Sergeanrt, how many 'notches' did you say were on that sniping rifle?"

"Six."

"Hmm," I said. "You know, I bought one of those old .303s . . . and I think it has notches on the breech."

"Well lots of guys marked their guns. But it wouldn't be hard to tell if you had my old gun."

"How?" I asked.

"I remember the serial number," he replied.

"After all these years?" John asked.

"Sure. One thing you learned in the army was to remember numbers. 2214 W42714 0439," he said, calling off the numbers in rapid order.

I asked him to repeat the numbers and wrote them on a business card that Pierre supplied. "You don't think that's your gun, do you?" John asked.

"Well, it has a smooth trigger and you guys know how straight that gun shoots!"

"Yeah," Pierre admitted. As I stepped outside to use my cellphone Pierre was telling the old men about my winning the shooting contests that the Club held in the fall of each year. Over the phone, Martha did not sound too keen on getting the .303 out of the locked gun closet, but she finally agreed to co-operate when I gave her some of the details of the story I had just heard. After trying to explain what the breech block was, I finally told her to read off all the numbers she could see on the gun.

"It says, 'BAP 303 2.222 18.5 tons and there is a Crown stamped on it, under the Crown is 1941 and some numbers I can't make out," she said.

"No, that's not them. Turn it over. Do you see any on the other side?" I asked. I knew there were more numbers.

"Oh, here's some more. '2214' then a 'W' and '42714' and then it looks like '0739'."

I checked the numbers I had written on the card. "Are you sure about the last four numbers?" I asked.

"Well, it could be '0439'," my wife said.

"I'll be damned. It's his gun! Thanks, Hon, see you in about an hour," I said and headed back to the table with the exciting news.

"I'll be a son of a gun!" Mr. Johnston said. "I'd sure like to see that gun again. Maybe even fire a few rounds, if you wouldn't mind."

"Sure," I said, "We could go out the range this Saturday, if you want. Private Fellows, would you like to come along?" I asked.

"Yes, I would. I'd like to see if Vic here can really shoot as well as he's been bragging all these years!"

"Well, my eyes aren't what they used to be, but with that old gun, I'll bet I could still hit a target!" he said with a bit of challenge in his voice.

"Yes, you probably could," Pierre said. "But I know one guy who's going to miss a lot of targets from now on."

"You're not going to ban my gun under Rule Two!" I exclaimed.

"Yes," Pierre said and John nodded his agreement. "'No guns modified for target competition will be allowed'. Rule number Two!"

"Damn!" I muttered to myself and took a goodly gulp of brew to mask my disappointment.

Every year since then I have tried to invoke Rule Ten at the fall meeting. The Rule that allows antique rifles, but I guess the last war is still not that far removed from our memories.

Hot Pink Wipers

(2017)

Winter ice fishing was causing so many problems for us in the Club that we were about to pay off the mortgage on our fishing hut, sell this finely crafted building to the highest bidder, and then resign ourselves to the occasional fishing trip on rented snowmobiles. "My back is still sore from trying to lift that darn shack out of the slush last week," Amanda complained as we sat down for a mid-week meeting at the Watering Hole. Amanda is always complaining about her aching muscles so we ignored this latest announcement. My wife says she ought to take up Tai Chi.

"And the good news is that it is supposed to get warm again this weekend. We'll have to raise that hut again so it doesn't freeze into the slush," Alex said as he poured a round from the pitcher that Sammy had placed before us.

"There's only another three weeks before we have to take the fish hut off the lake anyway - why don't we just bring it in now?" Geraldine asked. Geraldine was home in Toronto, waiting for the Bass Tournament season to begin in Georgia. Her partner Amelia was up north visiting her uncle Tim. She was using a snowmobile to access Beaver Lodge.

"But this is the best part of the season," I replied. "It is just getting warm enough to sit outside, and the walleye are just starting to bite."

"Pickerel," Alex automatically corrected me and then continued, "Judging from the number of fish we have caught this season, I'm inclined to agree with Geraldine. It might be a lot easier to move that big hut now than wait until the last day. Like we did last year."

"That was a memorable day, wasn't it?" Freddie said. "I'm sure all that jerking and yanking in the slush destroyed the clutch in my truck."

"And I lost that good axe that Cindy gave me for Christmas," John complained.

"Well, if everybody agrees, we can take the hut off this weekend," I said. There was a murmur of consent around the table.

"The one good thing about this is that we might try fishing on some other lakes next winter," John said. "In fact, I was talking to a fellow at work who knows a couple of good lakes just north of here that you can drive to. It is about 4 hours from Toronto, but he said they were getting some large lake trout and a few pike."

"Maybe we should give it a try this year. Anyone interested in going the next weekend?" Geraldine asked. After a brief discussion Alex and I said we would join Geraldine and Amanda. John then went on to tell us about this friend of his who also had a unique way of jigging for fish through the ice. Using your warm vehicle for a fish hut did seem very practical. It appears that this fellow attaches his line to the windshield wipers on his truck, turns on the intermittent wipers and waits for the fish to bite. Not only does the movement of the wipers attract the fish but it keeps the hole free of ice. I could see that Alex was paying close attention and would no doubt be using his mechanical genius to improve on this novel way of fishing.

We managed to remove our fish hut from the lake without any major disasters that weekend. It had been a poor year for us, catching a few walleye, a couple of pike and quite a few jumbo perch. There was a growing consensus in the Club that ice fishing was generally not all that much fun. And we agreed that it was not in the best interest of conserving enough fish to enjoy the summer fishing that we all looked forward to at this time of year. The biggest problem we had was that we could not release the fish caught through the ice. Any decent sized fish seemed to get itself into the snow before we could remove the hook and we all agreed that frost bite on a fish most likely spelled its demise. Everywhere one looked, people were keeping smaller fish than they would in the summer when they throw the little guys back with words of encouragement to grow, grow, grow.

The following week the four of us, Alex and me in his truck, and Geraldine and Amanda in Geraldine's recently purchased Toyota RAV 4, drove to the lake that John had heard about from his friends. The Ministry person we contacted said there was 18 to 22 inches of ice on the lake, so we could drive to the fishing spot without any danger, although we all wound the windows fully down just in case. If the truck did fall through the ice one did not want to be rolling down a window to escape. The water pressure is too much for a person to open a door as an escape hatch.

The snow cover was light and we had little problem driving the vehicles out onto the lake. The power augers were soon buzzing and the lines set. There was a light wind blowing from the north, making it just too cool to stand outside and tend the lines so we quickly adapted to the intermittent windshield wiper technology of fishing. Alex had brought some low test monofilament that he attached to the line at the end of our rods. This line was then connected to a small coil spring and then to the wiper arm. The effect was that line with the bait attached to it would move quickly up with the action of the spring and then smoothly lower it into the depths. Geraldine and Amanda had their lines tied directly to the wiper arms on Amanda's still new Toyota truck.

"What gave you the idea of using a coil spring on the line, Alex?" I asked as we poured some more hot coffee into our thermos cups.

"Well, I think that the fish are most likely to hit the minnow as it starts on its way up. By the time it starts to swim away, the wiper would be letting out slack, giving the fish a chance to spit out the hook. By using the compression factor in the spring, I have calculated that the exactly 16 cm. that the wiper arm travels will be extended to 2.5 seconds instead of the 1.75 seconds that General Motors has used in their intermittent wiper cycle. This significantly increases the time that there is tension on the line since the spring stretches more slowly than it will contract to its normal state of rest."

"Oh," I said.

"If, on the other hand, the fish takes the bait on the down cycle, the line has a shorter time of being in the slack mode."

"Do you want another donut?" I asked.

"Sure. Are there any more chocolate ones?" Alex asked. He then went on to explain that he did not want to tie the heavier fishing line directly to the wiper arm in case there were some larger fish. I think he even had the breaking strength of GM wiper arms figured into his calculations. Just as the wiper went through its cycle, Alex's rod tip went down. For a large man, he sure is quick. In a matter of seconds he had a two pound walleye on the ice. Just as I went to look at the first fish of the day, down went my rod tip. My fish was just slightly smaller than the one Alex had pulled in. Geraldine and Amanda were outside their truck in anticipation of getting a strike. The brief flurry of activity was over and we all were soon back inside the warm comfort of the truck cabs. "There must have been more than just two fish down there," Big Al commented.

"Yes, they usually school at this time of year. Maybe something chased them away, or maybe they heard us running on the ice," I said.

We spent the next two hours just keeping the ice from forming on the holes and visiting the other truck. We were about to move to another spot when we saw Geraldine jump from her truck and run towards her rod. She lost her footing and then began scrambling in the snow, trying to catch something. Amanda joined in, making a dive for Geraldine's rod just as it was about to disappear down the hole in the ice.

"Pike," Alex said as we got out of the truck and trotted over to watch the excitement.

Just as Amanda handed the rod to Geraldine, the line broke with a high-pitched 'ping'.

"Dammit!" Amanda said.

Geraldine added a string of oaths of her own (which we had not heard before from her). When she had slowed down a little, Alex said, "Too bad to lose that one, Gerri. It must have been a dandy."

"Probably just a big pike," I said by way of offering my consolation.

"Maybe if you hadn't stopped to roll in the snow, you might have reached the rod in time," Alex joked. "Were you trying to make snow angel?"

"Yeah, Geraldine, just what were you trying to do - sneak up on the hole so the fish couldn't see you coming?" I asked.

"Very funny, guys. I was trying to catch the windshield wiper."

"You don't mean . . . ?"

"Yes, that fish tore it right out of the clips. I just bought the new colour-coordinated set last week."

The one remaining wiper was one of those neon-coloured wipers that seem to be the rage for people who are not very discriminating on what they put on their vehicles.

"I think I have a spare blade in the truck," Alex said. "It may not fit exactly but it'll keep the arm from scratching your window on the way back into town."

He walked over to the truck and came back with the wiper blade and his tackle box. He opened the box and set it on Geraldine's truck hood. We all watched in silence as he pulled out a couple of plastic neon worms and tried to match the colour with the remaining wiper. "Yep, Bill," he said, holding up the bait we commonly call the pink wiggler, "This should do it. We had better change our bait. Seems like they are hitting 'hot pink' today!"

Amanda threw a snowball at Alex and we ran to our truck.

Water, Water Everywhere
(2017)

The past weekend was one of those treasured times we call 'Indian Summer' - a few brief days when summer returns after the leaves have fallen and nature is almost ready for the long winter rest. I had spent Saturday finishing off most of my winterizing chores; tidying up the woodpile, raking the maple leaves from the lawn one last time and securing the tarpaulin on my boat. Sunday morning I cleaned up the lawn mower, adding some gasoline stabilizer to the tank, removed the sparks plugs, and just as the instruction manual said, put a generous squirt of oil into the cylinders, knowing full well that next spring I would have a devil of a time getting it started with all that oil fouling the plugs. I had just settled into my favourite chair to watch a little CFL football when the telephone rang. My wife answered the call and before I could offer any contrary advice, we were invited out to Freddie and Thelma's for an afternoon walk, then dinner.

Freddie retired a couple of years ago after he had a session with prostate cancer. He seems to be all right now but he and Thelma decided it was time to get in a little travel during the winter while they could still enjoy it. Freddie still fishes and will attend the meetings of the Club at the Disraeli if he just happens to be downtown.

Freddie and Thelma have a country place, about 30 hectares of what used to be an old farm, some twenty kilometres from the city. There are kilometres of old bush roads leading into the semi-wilderness, excellent trails for walking and, in the winter, ideal cross country skiing. Thelma and my wife are keen walkers. While Freddie and I have often discussed the merits of a good brisk four mile hike followed by a refreshing glass of ale, we both offered to stay behind and tend to the small 6 kg turkey that was cooking in the oven. And to watch the game just in case Toronto Argonauts might pull an upset and beat those pesky Edmonton Eskimos.

"The girls are very capable of looking after that turkey," Thelma said, referring to their teenage granddaughters who were both writing essays at the kitchen table on their laptop computers, and were paying little attention to either us or the rock music emanating from the radio beside them, or the turkey roasting in the oven. "Besides, you two both look like you need some fresh air."

So Freddie and I decided to inhale a little fresh air with the ladies.

I noticed some recent tractor tracks and fresh earth leading away from the house. "Have you been having water problems again, Freddie?" I asked.

"No, but we decided to dig a well and install a back-up system before winter. Last year the spring ran very low and we had to ration the water in the middle of winter."

"And winter is no time to run out of water," Thelma added. "In the summer we can always carry laundry or washing water from the creek if we have to, but there's no way I'm going to trudge through the snow carrying two pails of water!"

"I don't blame you," my wife sympathized with her. "I can't imagine what we would do in the city if the water suddenly stopped flowing."

While the ladies continued their discussion about the domestic water supply, Freddie noted that the annual draw-down of the local lakes, the fall activity that lowers the water level, had begun. “I have often wondered what effect the dropping of the water level has on the marine life,” he said.

“Well, I guess the fish just go out a little farther and deeper for the winter.”

“No, I wasn’t referring to the fish. I mean things like clams, crayfish, snails - all those little beasties that are near the bottom of the food chain - the ones that live in the mud. Any larvae that thought to spend a comfortable winter in the shoreline mud may find themselves frozen solid when the water level recedes.”

“Yes, I suppose you’re right. That could eventually have some effect on the fish population. I guess nobody ever thinks about the damage we are doing to the ecology by artificially changing the water levels in the lakes,” I said.

“Well, when we insist on building cottages and homes right on the water, we can’t have spring flooding. It seems that we have to try to control every aspect of nature - rather than adapting to it,” Freddie said, repeating a phrase he often uses when The Club gets into one of our frequent environmental discussions at the Disraeli.

I nodded in agreement. “I understand the Ministry is putting in more dams up north to control water levels. The engineers say it will protect water levels against flooding and supply reservoirs for forest fire fighting.”

“Yeah, I heard that too. Those damn engineers are worse than beavers,” Freddie said.

“I never knew an engineer that didn’t want to build something,” I agreed. Engineers and accountants frequently are at odds over building and financing things.

We had arrived at the first rest stop on the hike, a beaver pond, where the old beaver that Freddie calls ‘George’ in honour of his buck-toothed boss at work, was in the process of adding a few more inches to his dam. “That’s interesting,” I said, as we sat and watched George pulling some more alder sticks onto his dam. “The Department of Public Works is lowering their water levels and here is dumb George, raising his!”

“What are you talking about?” my wife asked.

"We were commenting on how our Public Works and Ministry of Natural Resources engineers lower the water level on the lakes to stop spring flooding, while the beaver is making his dam higher. It seems that man is at odds with nature again," I said.

"Why does the beaver make his dam higher?" Thelma asked.

"Well, I think he knows that the water level is going to go down naturally during the winter when the precipitation falls as snow. So he wants to make certain that he has enough water in his pond to cover his house and his food supply," Freddie answered.

"Evidently he doesn't care if he causes a little flooding in the spring," my wife noted.

"Actually," I said, "I think that is all part of the grand scheme. If there is flooding in the spring, water overflows into areas that normally do not hold water, forming little reservoirs to help maintain the water table throughout the long, dry summers."

"Those little ponds become breeding grounds for insects, frogs, even waterfowl, in the case of marshes and swamps," Freddie added.

As we stood to continue our walk, George gave a half-hearted slap on the water with his tail as if to say that he had been watching us and would we please get out of there so he could continue with his engineering of the dam. "So I gather that you two do not agree with the water controls on the lakes," my wife said over her shoulder as we walked.

"Well, no, not really," Freddie answered. "I think we have to have controls because we've disrupted the natural flow of water so much. We dam rivers to produce hydro-electricity, but that's not all: Look at you city folk, and how you are pumping millions of litres of water every day from one water sources to another. That definitely has to disrupt the ecology of the whole area."

"Millions?" my wife asked and then seemed to remember that I had been grumbling when reading about the 30 million gallons per day that Vaughan had pumped during the summer. I could see my wife doing the metric conversion for Freddie and me, but she stalled and said, "Well, there are a lot of people . . ."

"Sure, I know," Freddie interrupted her, "But you city people waste too much water. If you had to pay more for it, you'd be much more conservative with your water use." Before my wife could get in a word in defence, Freddie continued, "I read recently that the average Canadian home uses more fresh water in the first few hours of a day than a family in Bangladesh uses in a month!" I knew we wasted some water but this seemed a little extreme, however, before I could say so, Thelma joined in.

"I'll bet that you people don't even have the 'lo-flo' type of toilets - the ones that use about four litres of water per flush!" I figured that was less than a gallon and that didn't seem like much water to me – considering the important flushing of waste function of a toilet.

"Well, I did see a report about that somewhere . . ." I said, thinking about how that recent recommendation to City council had floundered in red tape. Something about the summer students not having the right to install these water savers in people's homes unless the students had a plumber's permit.

"And I'll bet if the City had water meters in every house, you'd see a lot less lawn watering in the middle of the day when most of the water just evaporates!"

"But it would cost too much to put meters in every house," my wife said, thinking I'm sure about how she likes to water her lawn and flowers.

"No, the cost would be recovered very quickly," Freddie assured her. "The reduction in water pumped would be part of it, but the saving in high costs of sewage processing would pay for the meters in no time at all!"

My wife was losing ground in this discussion so she changed tack. "Freddie, you're just trying to make us feel bad because you have to pump your water and pay for that sewage disposal truck to pump out your septic tank! Besides, Freddie, it would cost a fortune to hire people to read water meters and process the bills."

"Not necessarily," I said, forgetting myself and taking Freddie and Thelma's side of the discussion, "We could read the meters remotely, by computers and . . ."

My wife let go of a hazel branch on the side of the trail that smartly whacked me across the shin.

"Ow. Gee, it sure is a pleasant day for a walk, isn't it?" I said.

The Double Bass

(2017: This is my remembrance of a story that Pierre told me about a distant cousin of his who lived in Louisiana – a result of the Acadian expulsion from Nova Scotia in the 1760s. Pierre's ancestors had been expelled from Nova Scotia along with the rest of the Poligrew family, however Pierre's great, great grandfather had surreptitiously returned to Upper Canada from Louisiana at the first opportunity. Pierre's cousin Bert visited him in June . . .)

~/~

By the time Bert Poligrew was thirty-five his voice had deepened to sound like distant thunder. He had been able to sing a passable double-bass but now the choir director assured him he was a true Basso Profundo. Bert was a large man, standing 6'4" in his bare feet and passing 250 pounds. His chest size, when he could afford a new suit coat, was a 50 which sent him shopping in the Big and Tall shops. Hardly ever could he find a coat or even a shirt to fit him at the Goodwill.

Bert lived with his father, Ephraim Poligrew, in a small wood frame house across the train tracks, but in the good part of the city. Bert earned his living by playing a big bass fiddle at the Chanticleer Lounge or other gigs around the city with two or three bands, depending on who needed the bass fiddle that night. Bertram was a devout Baptist, sang in the choir very Sunday, but was not above taking a sip of the spirits when the occasion arose. He did not have a car and took a taxi to the gigs, his big bass requiring a van or an older large car, being a requirement for the ride. The taxi dispatchers all knew Bert and would order up a cab saying they needed room for a Double Bass.

Eula Kessel lived at 2471 Clover Lane, two doors down from Ephraim's house. Eula had two teenage daughters who were of a lighter skin colour than their mother, the result of a gene they had picked up from the departed Thomas Kessler, a successful insurance salesman. Kessler paid a regular monthly allowance for the girls and for their mother through an agreement that did not have a court order to enforce it. Thomas had visiting privileges but he had not been to Clover Lane in five years. He had liked Eula well enough and it had seemed like a plan to marry a Negro woman, for business purposes. However with his success in commercial insurance underwriting, Thomas moved up the corporate ladder. The promotional move to Denver, and Eula's desire to stay in the warmer south, ended in an amiable divorce with support payments for the girls and their mother.

Bert thought he loved Eula and she seemed quite happy to have him around. But she would not marry him until the girls left home. It just wouldn't look right for two dark-skinned adults such as Bert and Eula to have two half-tone beautiful young girls. Bert had Cajun blood and he thought that ought to answer any questions or gossip about the girls colouring but Eula was not convinced. Bert said he could handle any snide comments, and with his size and booming bass voice, no doubt he could. It simply wasn't fair to the girls. So they bided their time.

Eula worked in the Westside Mall as manager for Frontier Jewellery, a local company that had several branches throughout the South. She drew a fair salary and loved her job. Sparkling diamonds, set or unset, were beautiful. Set in gold or platinum, they lit up the eyes of brides to be or older ladies who needed a sparkling distraction from wrinkles and age spots.

Financially, Bert got by but some weeks it was touch and go for a coffee at the Dunkin Donuts with his chums. He always had a five spot for the collection plate on Sunday. Each Tuesday, the payday at the Chanticleer, he would fold a five dollar bill and tuck it down into a corner of his wallet where it would stay until Sunday. He shared the food and utility costs with his father who still worked as a night watchman / floor sweeper at the Ford transmission parts plant. Bert looked after cleaning the house and doing the laundry on Saturday morning.

Bert loved singing and playing his big double bass fiddle. He had a good ear and could substitute in any jazz band in the city. The conductor of the City symphony said he could sit in anytime but their practices were in the evening when Bert was working the lounges.

On the odd occasion when Bert pondered his future he saw himself playing and singing as a grey-haired old man. It was future he did not fear but he did realize that if he lost his voice or got arthritis in his fingers he would be a candidate for Welfare.

Try as he did, he could not seem to get much money ahead in his savings account let alone a 301k plan.

The problem was partly June 1st. That's when bass (the fish) season opened up north in Wisconsin. Bert loved to fish for smallmouth bass. And every year the lure manufacturers came out with better reels, more flexible rods, and new lures. And every year it seemed to cost a little more to rent a row boat up on Red Cedar Lake, his favourite bass fishing lake. Ephraim also loved to fish bass, so they would pool their money and once a month, from June to October, rent a car for a weekend and drive to Red Cedar Lake. A twelve pack of Yuengling lager beer would last them the two nights spent under the stars.

It was a July Sunday morning at the Lake that a man walked into their campsite just before they were ready to leave for a day of fishing.

"Good morning, gentlemen."

"Good morning to you, sir," Ephraim said.

"I see you are about to head out for fishing so I won't delay you. Was it you I hear singing *Old Man River* last night?"

"Yes, sir it likely was me. Sorry if we disturbed you," Bert said.

"Oh, not at all, not at all. I quite enjoyed hearing it sung so well. Are you a professional singer?"

Bert laughed. "No sir, they haven't started paying the church choir yet."

"Have you had any professional training in voice?"

"Uh, not really. I sing from music and play my double bass fiddle from sheet music sometimes, but mostly by ear and memory."

"Would you be interested in doing some recording work?"

Before Bert could think and reply, the man continued, "I record and promote a number of singers and we often need background singers. It's hard to find a good bass singer - even harder to find a good double bass."

"Bert is a true basso profundo, Mister . . .?" Ephraim said.

"Sorry - Eggers is my name. Alfred Eggers - from Cincinnati. Listen, I'm over at campsite 5B. You better get out while the bass are hitting - come and see me if you want to talk more about this. By the way, I was using a spotted green Bagley yesterday - worked really well."

Bert and Ephraim discussed the possibilities of a full-time job. If Bert could get regular work, and Alfred assured him he could - there were not that many basso profundos in the business - Bert could put some money aside for his retirement. Retirement might not be for another 35 years but Eula said her former husband had always turned to his actuarial tables and showed her how money could grow.

Back on Clover Lane, Bert talked this over with Eula. It would be a few more years before the girls finished university. It would be time enough then for Eula and Bert to get married. Eula would keep an eye out for Ephraim; Bert would come home as often as he could. Cincinnati was not that far north.

Bert and Alfred Eggers became good friends over the next two years. True to his word, he found recording work for Bert singing back-up for different artists. That Bert could play the big double bass got him a touring gig with Amanda White that lasted two summer months. Alf and Bert always carried their fishing tackle boxes and a collapsible rod with them in case they could find a spot to wet a line. Bert did get a weekend off towards the end of August and he and his dad did a little bass fishing. Eula was real happy to see him whenever Bert came back to Clover Lane.

Alfred Eggers was always open to a 'deal' or any opportunity to turn one dollar into two. That things sometimes strayed over the line of the law did not bother him. He could always put his fingers on a little cocaine if one of his clients needed it to boost their on-stage performance. Bert made it clear from the beginning that he wanted nothing to do with drugs. He might take a few beers, but even then he watched his diet: a basso profundo needed to be physically fit to exhale those low notes.

Bert was playing bass fiddle and singing for Travis and the Sweetwater Boys in Buffalo when things went wrong. Alfred got mixed up with a local promoter who was arranging for more than musical gigs. The drugs were bad enough but he was also into stolen goods of the jewellery variety. The payment for Travis and his crew got lost in the mix and Alfred ended up holding a small plastic bag of uncut diamonds as collateral until the promoter could raise the hard cash for payment due in two days. Travis and his business manager were not about to leave Buffalo for a three night gig in Canada without their money.

Arrangements were being made to exchange the diamonds for cash when the police, following a lead concerning a diamond heist the past week, showed up at the hotel. Alfred knocked on Bert's door, slid inside and said, "Bert, you gotta hide these rocks. The cops will be searching my room any minute now!"

"No way, Alf. What if they look in my room?"

"They won't check you - you had nothing to do with this. You're just the bass player." They could hear the police banging on Alfred's door down the hall.

"Aw shit, Alf," Bert said and took the small bag of diamonds. Alfred thanked him and left, greeting the cops with innocence as he opened the door for them.

Bert looked at the diamonds. There were not many - maybe 15 or 20 - of them in the little cloth bag. Where could he put them that the cops wouldn't look? He stood his bass fiddle upright and slid the package through the carved sounding hole. The precious rocks hit the bottom of the instrument with a soft clunk.

The detectives knocked on his door a few minutes later as he was doing chords on the double bass. They asked what Alfred was doing in his room a few minutes ago and Bert said he was checking on the arrangements to go to Toronto. He needed to have his bags and the bass fiddle down at the front lobby by 6:30 a.m. The cops asked if they might take a look around, Bert told them to go ahead. One of the detectives recognized Bert and chatted about music while the other detective snooped through his dresser drawer, his suitcase and shaving kit. He looked in the fiddle case but never touched the over-sized violin, as he called it.

There was a shooting at the hotel late that night. Alfred Eggers took two in the chest. His room was tossed by the perpetrators, but they left the crime scene at the sound of sirens. Travis and the Sweetwater Boys decided they should continue with the Canadian tour as the penalty clauses for non-performance were very onerous. They would observe a minute's silence for Alf before the performance. They would seek out the Buffalo promoter on their return the following Monday to collect their fees.

Bert played the three nights in Toronto with what the police said were two million dollars value of uncut diamonds in the Double Bass. The little cloth bag did not rattle or affect the tone of the big instrument. Bert did not know what to do. He now had transported stolen goods over an international border. He couldn't turn the diamonds in until he returned to the States and even then he thought he should talk to a lawyer first.

In the office turmoil following Alfred's sudden death, Bert found himself out of work for a few days. He attended Alf's funeral in Cincinnati and even sang *Amazing Grace* at the graveside service. A week later, the estate lawyer called to say that Alfred had left specific instructions that all his fishing gear should go to Bertram Poligrew. Where should they ship the large box? Clover Lane, Bert Poligrew said.

Travis called and offered him a permanent spot in the Sweetwater Band and as back-up singer. Bert's bass voice harmonized very well with the tenor/baritone notes coming from Travis's throat. Bert was a good looking, if somewhat imposing figure and his stage presence added some much-needed racial colour to the band. They would start a new seven-week tour the following week.

Bert told Eula about the diamond caper. The diamonds were still side the bass fiddle.

"Uncut diamonds are not that hard to fence," Eula said. She knew all about the diamond trade and what buyers needed to watch for. Blood diamonds were a no-no but there were ways around that if the diamonds were of a goodly size and could be cut into a carat or larger size. Smaller diamonds might just be good for industrial use and were not worth the risk of fencing them. "How big are your diamonds, Bert?"

"Truth to be told, I don't really know. Alf just handed me a bag and I hid them as quick as I could before the cops came a-knockin'," Bert said.

"Well, let's look at them and decide what to do. Maybe we'll just throw them away if they are industrial quality."

It took a lot of shaking the bass fiddle to get the bag into the sound hole. The sparklers looked quite large and Eula got her magnifying loop out to inspect them. A smile broke out on her face and then she began to laugh. Bert had been hiding a handful of broken glass in his bass fiddle all this time.

"But surely the police were after the real thing," Bert said.

"Oh, I don't doubt that. But somewhere along the line somebody switched the diamonds for glass. Probably the guy in Buffalo that owed Alf money. He gave him a handful of glass as security."

"Jeez, Eula, somehow I don't think Alf was that gullible," Bert said as he tossed the glass into the garbage bin under the counter.

An entire year passed before Bert looked into the cardboard box of Alf's fishing gear. Ephraim was with him as they sorted through the lures, each commenting on the possibilities of the coloured plastic and wood with their little treble hooks. Alf had liked deer-hair flies for his fly rod, sometimes adding a small spinner for effect. Bert and Ephraim stuck with their spinning rods and larger baits.

Ephraim picked up a large green frog-like plug and shook it. "I never held much faith in these rattling plugs. Might fool a pike, but not a bass," he said, rattling the lure from side to side.

"Let me see that, Dad," Bert said. "I don't remember this being a rattling plug when Alf used it." He shook the plug and then inspected it more closely. "Dad, this has been cut and glued. Give me your fish knife."

Bert pushed the sharp knife tip into a barely visible crack and the wood split. Three white stones fell out. They sparkled like blue fire on the table cloth. These were cut and polished, not industrial diamonds.

Seven more lures rattled, were opened and disgorged their contents onto the table. Bert called Eula to come and bring her loop. Even to his untrained eye, these stones looked really, really nice.

Bert was singing Leonard Cohen's *Hallelujah* and accompanying himself on the double bass when Eula knocked on their door.

Pierre said his cousin Bert had invited him to their fishing lodge over in Wisconsin. The bass there were hitting on artificial frogs. Pierre suggested that we might slip over to Minnesota for a long weekend. The Mall of America is a shopping mall located in Bloomington, Minnesota, Irene reminded Martha.

Fat Choy

(2017)

Last year was the Chinese Year of the Rooster and it was also the year that Pierre (1) decided to specialize in Chinese cooking, and (2), to get his body into better physical shape. Pierre and Irene are friends of ours, part of a group of fellows who enjoy fishing and whose wives allow us to pursue that sport without too much complaining or uncomplimentary remarks about our mixed success at bringing home something to eat. Pierre is an excellent cook and Irene a gracious hostess. They like having a few of us over for special dinners that Pierre enjoys cooking, and unfortunately for our waistlines, eating. Pierre had gained about five kilos since he retired.

Over the years, Pierre has mastered the French, Italian, German and Mexican culinary arts and we have all been treated to feasts on occasions of those particular nations' holidays. Talk at the Disraeli informed us that Pierre was into the Chinese recipes so it was not surprising when we received a special written invitation to dinner to celebrate the Chinese New Year with Pierre and Irene. Alex and Claire were to join us. We had not had a chance to visit during the busy holiday season and we were all looking forward to the evening.

Dining with Pierre and Irene is never simply sitting down to a gourmet meal after a few appetizers and a welcoming cocktail. There is always a theme to Pierre's dinners and Irene does her part by studying both the food for the dinner and something about the culture of the country whose delights we were about to eat.

2017 was the Year of the Rooster and Alex made the mistake of inquiring as to why the Rooster. Irene then gave us the twelve Chinese signs of the Zodiac and we all found our sign on a chart that appeared as if by magic from under the coffee-table book on Early Civilizations. It was no surprise to me that I was a tiger but it gave me pause to think that my wife was a rabbit. Alex turned out to be an Ox and Claire was a Rat but we all agreed just to call her a mouse that evening. Pierre was a Fire Pig while Irene admitted to being a Water Dragon.

After I asked why the Chinese did not celebrate their New Year on the same day as we did, I learned that they follow the lunar calendar. I have enough trouble keeping track of when the next full moon is due (poor time to fish) so I did not ask what the number was of the year the Chinese were celebrating. It turned out that we were dining on the evening of the Lantern Festival. According to Irene this was the fifteenth day after the first new moon of the lunar New Year and we believed her. Pierre disappeared into the kitchen while we all had another drink and sampled a spring roll. Alex and I had two.

The cooking smells were appetizing and we all were ready and primed for a feast by the time Pierre called us to table. As is his fashion, Pierre makes a printed menu for each of us so we know what we are eating and can take it home as a souvenir, or if we like, get the recipe to try on our own. It was just as we were being seated that my wife mentioned that she thought Pierre had lost a few pounds from his more than ample girth. Not only had Pierre been on a diet, tonight being an exception, he noted, but he was also doing exercises at his new class. Pierre had taken up Tai Chi.

Alex, putting his foot into his mouth again, asked what that was and throughout the dinner we got detailed explanations about several of the moves and were promised a complete demonstration after dinner. My wife was taking notes on the back of the dinner menu, writing down the unusual names of the moves so I could remember them and later use them at the Club to describe Pierre's new regimen. Martha teaches the Taoist Tai Chi and diplomatically allowed Pierre give his version of the moves taught by the club he attended without comment.

The menu began with what I thought was a traditional egg roll but these were filled, the notes said, with pork belly and Chinese olives. Alex had three because the olives had been marinated in anise. There was steamed rice for a side dish and Singapore noodles with just the right amount of curry. The roasted beet slices daubed with tofu were a favourite of my wife so I gave her my share. Next to be served was sweet and sour pork followed by a few dates stuffed with duck. This was followed by some walnut shrimp, which was my favourite of the evening although I did enjoy the Kung Pao chicken. For dessert Pierre had some egg tarts and for the women, some sweet red bean tofu pudding. We all drank green tea.

We retired to the recreation room downstairs where true to his promise, Pierre gave us a demonstration of his Tai Chi. Pierre invited us to try a few of the moves. We did 'Brush knees'; 'strum the banjo' (I think it was a banjo); 'ward off a monkey'; 'fist under elbow' (that one I could do); 'wave hands like clouds'; and 'ride a tiger'. Pierre admitted that the Tai Chi was not really part of the martial arts but that it was very good exercise for both the body and the mind.

Later, as we were all leaving, Irene gave us each a small red envelope that contained a toonie and a loonie. Pierre explained that we could not receive two toonies because 4 was an unlucky number. Coming away with a full tummy and three dollars made it a very enjoyable evening. We wished each other 'Kung Hei Fat Choy' saying we would all meet again soon.

All this is by way of telling you about the subsequent fishing trip that Pierre, Alex and I made some three months later. Pierre is a boat fisherman. His ample weight and circumference, although reduced by his diet and Tai Chi, did not make it easy for Pierre to manoeuver along creek beds full of tangled alders and willows in search of the elusive speckled brook trout. There is no finer eating fish than a fresh 20 centimeter brook trout fried in a pan of sizzling butter. Pierre knows and appreciates this fact so he agreed to join Alex and me one Saturday morning for a try at trout along Beaudry Creek. The creek is fairly open due to the diligent work of a family of beavers and not that far from the road.

Pierre was leading the way down the trail to the creek, Big Al and I tagging along behind. We normally just use worms for trout, perhaps attaching them to a very small spinner if it is a cloudy day. Pierre was not having any problems walking along the trail, carrying his collapsible rod, his wicker creel that contained both his lunch and a box of worms, so when Alex called for me to help him roll over an old rotting tree trunk to search for grubs, I did as he wished.

Alex's theory is that a trout will grab a grub before a worm, thinking that some bird with a too-full beak has dropped this manna from above while flying over the beaver pond. He usually catches more trout than I, so I agreed to help if I could use one of the grubs. We had found three white grubs when we heard a yell from down the trail. We looked up to see Pierre bounding up the trail towards us.

"What the heck is he doing?" Alex asked.

I recognized some of the moves from our evening at Pierre's house some months before. "Tai Chi," I said.

"Are you sure that's Tai Chi?"

"Yes," I replied. "You remember Pierre giving us the demonstration at the Chinese dinner. That leap over the log looks like 'Ride the Tiger', and those arm movements must be 'Stork Cools Wings'." Pierre was making the moves rather more quickly than my wife does but still with a great deal of gracefulness. There seemed to be many more hand movements than I remembered but I knew that I had not been introduced to all the finer points of this Oriental art form.

"Ah - so very interesting," Alex commented as Pierre approached us.

It appeared that Pierre was going to continue this high-speed practice session all the way up the trail. "What's that," I asked as he sped towards us, "'Wave Hands as Clouds'?"

"No!" he gasped as he went by, "Stepped on Hornet's Nest!"

We ran.

The Roadblock

(2017)

Amanda Young has a younger brother who is a Conservation Officer who works out of the North Bay, Ontario office. Billy Danlo is ex-army (military police) who applied for the Conservation Officer position because he loved the outdoors and still believed in Law and Order even though he had some trying experiences in Afghanistan. Billy readily admits that his sister's husband, George Young, helped him get the position. George is involved in the Conservative politics at the Federal and Provincial level.

Billy was in Toronto that December and Amanda invited him to meet the Club at the Disraeli. We all appreciate the work the Conservation Officers do and Amanda thought we might enjoy hearing some of Billy's stories. Herewith is my recalling of his story about the roadblock he encountered when he first started his job.

~/~

Conservation Officer Billy Danlo had been on the job only three weeks when the Manager of Operations sent him to check on the Turtle Lake Preserve. The office had recorded a voice mail message on the *Catch-A-Poacher* hot line, a message that said someone had seen a green truck and red fishing boat going into Turtle Lake on Friday evening. The Manager, who was at least twenty years his junior, thought it would be a good experience for Billy to work some unpaid overtime on Saturday. She did not like having this fifty-year old man foisted onto her staff. No matter that he was a veteran and some politician had pulled some strings to get him the job, she expected him to pull his weight with the younger people on her staff, and she told him this to his face. What she did not tell him was that everyone in the office knew who owned that green truck and red fishing boat – the troublesome McConnelly brothers.

Billy Danlo had simply snapped to a military attention and "Yes sir, Ma'am!" a knowing grin creeping across his lips. Master

Sergeant Billy Danlo (retired Princess Patricia's Light Infantry) knew how to handle young green commissioned officers. A military policeman, he had recently finished his twenty-five year career with a tour in Afghanistan and he had had enough of police work. However, all his working skills were in law enforcement and this job seemed to be the furthest away from actual policing. Besides, he loved the bush.

Turtle Lake was twenty miles north of the city and about seven miles off the main highway. A forest road, maintained only for fire crew access, led to the 100-hectare lake. The Ministry biologists flew into the lake to monitor the population of the Green Spotted Forest Turtle and the abundant pike and walleye who made this lake home. The fishery had been closed for seven years now and the only fish removed from the lake were breeding stock that the Ministry collected once a year for their restocking program. Billy was not sure why they had closed the lake, for no one was interested in catching the turtles. From his reading, Billy knew that the turtles spent most of their time foraging in the forest, not in the lake. He supposed the biologists were more worried about forest fires set by careless anglers than by people catching the turtles for soup.

The keys for the old Dodge truck were on his desk, along with the signed authorization for him to draw his sidearm. Conservation Officers seldom needed a sidearm, but they always wore them when working alone. The gun felt comfortable on his hip, a sensation of which he had mixed feelings. The Dodge growled itself to life in whining Chrysler fashion; Billy checked the gauges and radio; turned on his personal GPS and headed for Turtle Lake. A quick stop at the Tim Horton's coffee shop was mandatory but he was still at the forest access turnoff by 0900 hours. The tire prints were fresh, indicating that someone had been into the lake very recently. He slipped the transmission into four-wheel drive and began the long, bumpy ride.

The topographic map showed the myriad of trails into the bush but most of them stopped in the middle of nowhere or at a small-unnamed lake. Google and Garmin had never ventured into Turtle Lake but they did indicate a blue blotch that did appear in the shape of a turtle – the chocolate treat, not the green spotted variety. Billy was used to navigating with inaccurate maps, often following nothing more than cart paths into hostile territory as he investigated complaints against the Canadian Armed Forces. All too often these cart paths simply disappeared in Afghanistan and his patrol would come to a dead end, exposed to ambush. Today, he was looking for poachers, a far less dangerous mission.

His GPS showed that he was almost at the lake when he came to the creek. Heavy rains had washed out the steel culvert and a makeshift crossing of recently cut poles filled the depression made by months of running creek water. Billy stopped and tested the depth of water even though the vehicle ahead had apparently made the crossing without trouble. It looked passable.

The Dodge was halfway across the creek when the bottom gave way and he felt the front wheels drop. His reaction was to floor the accelerator pedal and hope to bounce out of the creek bed. Billy had not refastened his seat belt and when the Dodge bucked, he hit his head on the roof.

Billy Danlo regained consciousness when the cold water seeped through door and over his shoes. He did not know where he was.

Billy listened for any sound of the Taliban who had ambushed him, but heard nothing. There was no sign of the rest of his patrol. He exited the vehicle, his gun in hand and did a quick recon of the area. No sign of anyone. The old green truck did not seem to be damaged – no holes from gunfire, no blast damage. It must have been an anti-personnel mine that he had driven over. The Taliban often put them in creek beds. He tried the starter but the engine would not fire. The radio still buzzed with static so he pushed the send button, "Base, this is Triangle One. Come in." He tried several times, but got nothing in reply. "I must be in a dead zone, down here in this valley," he thought. He tried the starter once more. Nothing. The water was now flowing across the carpet in the cab, in one door, out the other. He tried his cell phone but he knew the chances of getting a transmission in the backcountry of Afghanistan were slim. The screen showed one tower – no signal. Maybe the cell phone would work from the top of the hill.

He checked his pistol, jacking a round into the chamber of the Sig Sauer 9mm. He glanced in the side mirror and saw the dried blood. The bleeding from his scalp had stopped so he wiped away some of the caked blood from his face. He probably looked a mess, but his head was not hurting that much. He tried to remember why he was wearing his green uniform, not the dessert tans. Maybe because he was in the hills where there was actually some greenery in this god-forsaken country. His truck, number 01-749, completely blocked the road. There was no way around it, so if anyone were going to get past him, they would have to help him move the truck first. He hoped it would be some friendlies – not the Taliban who found him. Billy wondered where the rest of the patrol had gone. Maybe they thought he was dead – all the blood might have fooled them. Maybe they had been taken prisoner and the Taliban left him, also thinking he was dead. He started walking up the hill.

He was only a few metres from the creek when he heard the approaching vehicle. He found some cover and watched as an old green truck crested the hill. It was towing a red boat. "What the hell are they doing with a boat?" he asked himself. He could see three men in the truck. All three had the usual Taliban beards. The boat had a cheap lawn chair strapped to the foredeck, two leather fishing stools were near the back of the boat. Billy could see a large insulated box in the back of the truck. "They must have opium in the box," Billy thought. The truck stopped in front of his disabled vehicle and the three men got out, looking around for him. They were dressed in a mixture of camouflage greens and tans. Probably clothing they had taken from dead Afghan army soldiers. They seemed to be under the influence of drugs or booze. All three had cans of American beer in their hands. Some Yank must have traded them the beer for drugs. He did not see any guns, however all three men were wearing knives. He would have to arrest them, commandeer their vehicle, and follow the road back to base.

Billy stepped from behind his tree, and using his best Farsi, said, "You are under arrest. Raise your hands!" When they greeted his order with blank looks, he repeated it, motioning with his gun for them to raise their hands. "Hands on the car, spread your feet," Billy said in Farsi, trying a different dialect that the some hill people used. It took the waving of the gun to make them comply. "What is in the box?" he asked. Blank looks.

"Jesus Christ, the fucking Ministry has hired a Paki Conservation Officer!" the fat one said in English.

Billy tried again, using Farsi and some English, asking if the box contained contraband. They caught the word for contraband for they all shook their heads. The Taliban with the Blue Jays ball cap said, very slowly, "No contrabandi. Justa fishies."

They spoke some English! Billy relaxed a little and speaking very carefully asked, "What do you have in the box?"

"Is justa few fish, officer," the fat fellow said trying carefully to enunciate his words.

Billy climbed into the back of the truck and lifted the lid. The box was full of fish fillets. "These guys might be commercial fisherman," he thought. He should ask for their permits to make sure. "Do you have fish license? Permit?" he asked.

"Uh, no, we do not have them with us," the fat one said very slowly so Billy could understand him.

The one who had been quiet until now took a sip from his can of beer and said to the others, "Maybe we should offer him some money to let us past the roadblock. I heard these Paki guys always take a bribe."

Billy jumped down from the truck but the sudden movement made him dizzy. He felt very lightheaded. He put out a hand to steady himself and passed out.

The sun was getting low in the sky when Billy Danlo regained consciousness. He was lying beside the road in the bush. He raised himself on one elbow, feeling his aching head. He had an old rag wrapped around his head. His truck was sitting off to one side of the road. He got to his feet and carefully walked to the truck. The keys were in the ignition. He looked in the mirror and saw that he had bled a little though the rag. He checked for his gun – it was in its holster. He could not find his cell phone or his GPS. He checked his wallet. No money but his credit cards were all there. It was coming back to him now – he had been stuck in the creek – the truck would not start – he was following some poachers. Obviously someone had come along and pulled his truck out of the creek, bandaged his head, taken his phone and money and left him there.

He turned the ignition key and the old truck coughed several times before finally running on all six cylinders. He drove to the top of the hill and found a place to turn around. He tried the radio. "Base this is 01-749. Come in."

"01-749, this is base. Are you okay?"

"Roger that. I was stuck but am now on my way back. I banged my head but I am okay."

"Billy, did you try to radio us earlier?" his boss came on the radio.

"Uh, no ma'am. I tried it but I was down in a valley and could not get through."

"Funny, we got a signal from somebody saying they were a Triangle or something."

"No Ma'am, not me."

"Any sign of those poachers?"

"Tracks going in and out – I must have missed them," Billy lied. He did remember seeing three men, but it was a little foggy to him. Sometimes it was like that with a head wound. However, he would definitely remember those faces. One day, he would recover his cell phone, GPS, and cash.

Billy put the Dodge in low gear and carefully crawled through the creek bed. As he wound his was along the forest access road he remembered how some of the roads in Afghanistan were like this – narrow tracks through the countryside. There were plenty of good place to set up a roadblock – or an ambush. Nevertheless, that was a lifetime ago.

Freddie asked Bill if he caught up to the Connelly boys yet. Billy said no, but he smiled.

Rx

(2017)

"By God, am I steamed!" Amanda announced as she pulled up a chair at our table at the Disraeli last Friday night. I took this as a signal to fill an empty glass to the top with the bubbling brew that Sammy the waiter had placed on the table just moments before Amanda arrived.

"What's the problem?" Pierre asked. "Still upset about losing your World Series bet?"

"No." Amanda lifted her glass and took a calming sip of the cool amber liquid. "I've just been down to the drugstore to get a prescription filled for George."

"I know how you feel," Alex said. "I had to get some pills last week and the cost almost floored me. It was a good thing we have a drug plan at work!"

"Hell, it's not the price of the pills that's bothering me," Amanda replied. I was a little surprised at her language that evening because normally she is very careful unless she has just missed a nice bass. "It's that charge they have for filling the prescription. It was almost thirteen dollars just to count out fifteen pills!"

I guess John had not been to a drugstore in a while either because he was scandalized. "You've got to be kidding! How can they charge that much? It couldn't take more than a couple of minutes to count out fifteen pills. Less than that." John went through the motion of sorting and counting out fifteen imaginary pills.

"Twenty seconds," Alex said. "Let's see, Pierre, you're the accountant - how much is that an hour?"

"Well, given that John is a pretty slow counter and has a touch of arthritis in his hand, but still allowing for time to find the pills, package them, print a label and look up the cost, I'd guess that it would take about three minutes to fill a prescription. At $25.00 dollars per hour for a clerk, that would work out to about five hundred dollars profit per hour." Pierre took a sip of his beer.

I could tell he was on a roll. "If you allow that the pharmacy is open for business about nine hours, or let's says it was in a mall, make that thirteen hours a day. That's about $6,500 a day, if they were busy all the time. Say they were busy only half the time. That gives them $3,250 a day. Let's say they pay the pharmacist $500, the cashier or helper about a $250 . . . store rent, utilities, that sort of thing, probably runs them about a $400 a day. Add in administrative costs of a couple of hundred a day, maybe three hundred, that should leave them with about $1,850 per day per person clear profit."

"There were four clerks working when I was there," Amanda said.

John was marking these figures down with a finger wetted on the condensation of our beer jug. "Yeah, that's about right. How about their franchise cost? Most of these drug stores are part of a chain, aren't they?"

"You're right," Pierre said. "Take off at least thirty percent for the franchise and advertising costs. That brings it down to about twelve hundred bucks a day. And that is only on prescriptions. I hate to think what the mark-up is on Band-Aids or cough drops! Add another couple of hundred clear - make that seventeen hundred a day clear. And that's for only one drug filler. They usually have two or three of them behind the counter! Not too bad for the owner - especially if he's a pharmacist too!"

There was a general grumbling around the table and Sammy took this as a signal that we needed our second jug of draft. The conversation drifted around to somebody that knew a drugstore owner and what kind of lifestyle the rich pill merchants enjoyed.

"You guys are forgetting about the high cost of the drugs themselves, though," I said. "Just think of the money that they have to have to carry their inventory. The interest rates being what they are . . ."

"You're right, Bill," Pierre said, "I forgot about the pills! They have to be making a mark-up of at least 40% on the pills! What did the pills cost you, Amanda?"

Amanda pulled the package out of her jacket pocket. "Let's see - the dispensing charge was $11.97 - subtract that from $29.30 - that's about $17 bucks for 15 pills."

"Okay, that sounds about an average of what I pay; no I think that includes the fee. Let's say the average is about half that - at 40% that still leaves a profit of a couple of bucks per prescription. Hell, that's got to be another thousand bucks a day!"

We all lifted our glasses.

"We have to be missing something," Big Al said. "These guys would be making more than the doctors. They must have more overhead than we are figuring."

"It seems to me that I read somewhere that the pharmacist could not mark up the cost of prescription drugs beyond 30%, something about how the Government protects us against the drug manufacturing companies and unfair pricing," I said.

"You're right, Bill that does sound familiar. Furthermore, we were likely a little light on the costs. Probably too high on the number of orders they fill each day, too."

"It still looks like a darn good business to be in," John said. "You always have to wait, so they must be busy."

"Well, we sure wouldn't want to do without them, though," I said. "The doctors prescribe pills for everything from sore backs to running noses. We take too darn many pills, if you ask me."

"I agree," Alex said. "If we ate properly, got more exercise and relaxed a little, we wouldn't need all those drugs." Alex's wife, Claire, has him on a nutrition routine that does everything except cut out his beer. Or so he says.

"I'm glad you mentioned that," John said, "because we are supposed to be planning our annual turkey shoot, aren't we?"

Every year we have a target shooting contest where both the champion and the loser win a turkey. The loser also gets to host a dinner for everyone the following Sunday, which if we have planned things correctly, coincides with the Grey Cup game. Pierre has lost the last couple of years but some of us have a suspicion that he only shoots to get a lower score than Amanda since the year Amanda cooked the turkey and it was less than memorable. A good turkey dinner is worth more to Pierre than being dubbed the poorest shot in the Gang.

Big Al drained his glass and stood to leave. "I have to get going guys. I have to stop off at the drugstore and pick up a prescription. Maybe I'll see if the druggist will fill all three repeats for one dispensing charge. I could save about thirty bucks that way."

"Ha!" Amanda said. "I already tried that one. No way will they do that. 'Too dangerous to have all those pills at once' they said. As if George were going to take try to overdose on gout pills!"

"I suppose that is a valid point," John agreed.

"Come on! If the thirty pills they give aren't enough to hurt you, ninety of the same wouldn't harm you either. They have no control over those pills once they give them to you anyway. That's just a scam to make more money!" Amanda was still a little hot under the collar. "And don't give me the story that the drug plan is paying for it anyway! I darn near chewed the guys' head off when he laid that line on me. Who does he think is paying for the drug plan? Santa Claus? Bah!"

"Gee, Amanda, you should calm down," I said. I pretended to reach inside my jacket for something, "Are you sure you wouldn't like a tranquillizer? I could give you one for about $8.97." All I had was my roll of Tums, but she didn't know that . . .

Finis

(2018)

In February of 2018 we called a General Meeting of the Bay Street Boys and Girls Sporting Club. It was time to disband the Club.

Alex had been retired for a number of years and now he was about to end his consulting work for the government. Claire wanted to move to Vancouver Island where her sister lived. The winters in Ontario were no longer enjoyable for either of them. Alex was having a hip problem and could no longer sit for hours in a boat while fishing without the hip bothering him.

Pierre was also retired and according to Irene his wife, they had a comfortable portfolio for their retirement years. Pierre was ready to liquidate our Investment Fund and was open to ideas as to how we should use the funds. He had sent us all a statement of the account prior to the meeting so we could make suggestions. I think we were all surprised at the amount of money we had accumulated since 2001. We also owned the Little Loon Lake camp, which John, our real estate expert, said we could sell in the spring when the camp-buyers' market heated up. He thought we could get 14 or 15 thousand dollars for the camp (after real estate fees).

John and Cindy had finally married in 2017. They were thinking of fleeing to British Columbia as well. John was 64 and wanted to work for another few years to pad his wallet. He jokingly said that if he had stopped buying lures and new rods he could have retired a year sooner.

Amelia and Geraldine had sold *Bites and Bucks* a number of years ago and they were doing fairly well on the Bass Tournament circuit. They were home in Toronto for February and part of March but then would be on the road again as the Tournament season started in the southern States. They agreed that it was time to close the Club, since they were seldom available in the summer for our little fishing expeditions.

Jason, still single and unattached as far as we knew, had retired from TV and was now working as a media consultant for a retirement home organization. Truthfully, he had seemed a little less excited about fishing and hunting the past two years as he was focusing on his new hobby, photography.

Katherine was in her last year as Catering Manager at the Royal York. She was thinking of moving back to Parry Sound for the summers and spending her winters in Arizona. She offered to take any of us fishing when she was at her cottage/home on Georgian Bay – an offer I intended to accept. There is some great bass fishing around those rocky islands.

Amanda and George spend time in Ottawa when the House is in Session and she is busy helping George with the riding work. She promised to be at the general meeting.

A week before the meeting Freddie received some very bad news: He had a stomach cancer that needed immediate attention. He would be at the meeting but thought his surgery was sometime in the next two weeks. Freddie had retired from being Sales Manager at York Fine Cars but he still worked as a greeter in the sales office on Mondays and Tuesdays. He was spending more and more time trying to keep his 'farm' under control and had missed a number of our short fishing trips last summer.

Both Martha and I had retired in 2016. We spent 4 weeks in Mexico the first winter and had just returned from a 10-day cruise in the Caribbean that was supposed to break up the winter into livable portions. Martha was making noises about British Columbia and I was thinking there might be enough of the old Club out there to start anew. The British Columbia Boys and Girls Sporting Club had a nice ring to it, I thought.

I had checked with the owner of the Disraeli Tavern concerning getting a private room for our meeting. There was an area that had just been renovated and he thought that it would accommodate us quite comfortably. The manager said they were changing the décor of the old tavern and would be reopening with a new name. Apparently Benjamin Disraeli had some political baggage that upset some people although most of the patrons had no idea who or what Disraeli was. The manager said they thought about The White Owl Tavern as being innocuous but attractive to the conservationists; however the word 'white' was verboten according to the publicist who was consulting on the name. Loon had connotations, as did any name to do with cats and dogs. The consultant was wary of any name that connected to a country or a person. The manager said they were at an impasse. I told him they should just call it 'The Tavern on Bay Street' and he said he would run that by the others on the committee.

Pierre was in charge of ordering some snacks for the meeting as it might take us an hour or two to do our business and drink some ale. The snacks turned out to be heure d'oeuvres and they must have been okay as none remained on the platters when we adjourned.

We were all rightly concerned about Freddie but he assured us his doctor and the surgeon said the operation to remove part of his small intestine was not that difficult and they expected him to recover completely in a month. He would be ready for fishing in June.

I had polled most of the members before the meeting as to any ideas of what we should do with the $37,382.75 that Pierre had in the Investment Fund plus the $12,000.00 we expected to clear on the Camp. There were suggestions to just divide the money equally; donate some to charities; set up a scholarship, and Katherine's idea. Katherine asked me to allow her to give her presentation first, and when I had a hint of what she had in mind, I concurred.

At precisely 3:30, when everyone had their first glass of beer and eaten some tasty tidbits, I called the meeting to order. "Members, pleased be seated. This meeting of the Bay Street Boys and Girls Sporting Club is now in session. Our first order of business is the financial report by Pierre. All in favour of accepting the report as circulated? Good. Carried. Now, I pass the floor to Katherine Westcott who has a presentation regarding the disposition of assets of the Club."

"Fellow members," Katherine began, "As much as we might not like to admit it, time and health has caught us up in the landing net of life. Most of us are retired and some are considering moving away to warmer climes. Freddie's health scare reminds us that our time here is coming to an end. However, we are not finished yet. There is time for one more cast."

"Hear, hear," Jason, the youngest member of the Club said.

"If we had one last wish for the Club, what would it be?" And before we could answer, she continued, "To catch a trophy fish; to have one last excellent week of fishing, to fly into one of those legendary 'Outposts' and fish in that heaven on earth." Katherine took a sip of her beer. "I have found the answer to your dreams. There is a 5 Star fishing lodge northeast of Flin Flon Manitoba that is the answer to our dreams." Katherine took her cell phone from her pocket and tapped the screen. "I have just sent you all an email with pictures of the lodge and the fishing."

Everyone dug out their cell phones and read the email. There were comments that befitted the size of the fish – walleye and pike and trout; the lodge dining room; the bedrooms; the floatplanes, and happy customers. The web address of the lodge was at the end of Katherine's message.

When the room had quieted, Pierre asked the questions we were all thinking, "When can we go and how much will it cost?"

"I have tentatively booked for 10 people for the first week of August. It is a 4-day fishing trip with four nights at the Lodge. We will need a day to travel to and from Flin Flon via Winnipeg so we need a week for the whole experience."

"What is the cost?" John asked.

"The flights, the Lodge with meals, guides – everything included - is about $6,200.00 each. That means, if we use the funds we will have, each person should only have to kick in about $800."

"I'm in," Freddie said. "If I ever really needed a reason to feel confident about my surgery, this is it! Trophy pike - look out!"

We all needed to consult our significant others but everyone received clearance for August 3 to 10.

Amelia caught the longest pike – 47 inches; Pierre landed the longest walleye – 21inches and John (he and Jason opted for a day of lake trout fishing at a one-day fly-in trip) caught a lake trout that weighed 28 pounds.

I won $16.25 playing Liar's Dice.

We had enough money left in the kitty to buy each member a lined windbreaker and ball cap with the BSBGSC logo. If you see one of us, say 'Hi' and ask how the fishing is . . .

Bill with the Powassan Players

Bill Walton - Biography

William Warren Walton CPA (Ret'd)
Born December 14, 1938 in Port Loring, Ontario
Bill has 6 publications; 35 self-published books; and 800 + articles (opinion / columns) with Baytoday.ca online news service. Hobbies, besides writing, include photography, golfing, motorcycling, bird watching, fishing, gardening, Tai Chi, and dragon boating with the Warriors of Hope Breast Cancer Survivors Dragon Boat Racing team. Bill has recently appeared in stage productions with the Powassan Players.

Appendix of Characters

(Sketches by Claire Henderson)

Alexander Henderson was a lawyer for Provincial Government (he retired in 2015). His friends in the Club call him Al, Alex, or Big Al, however his wife Claire insists on calling him Alexander. (Claire provided the sketches of the members.) Alex was 68 on his last birthday. The couple have two children, both married and living outside the Greater Toronto Area. In 2001 when the Club was formed, Alex worked at Queen's Park but now works from a satellite office in Markham, nearer the suburban home they bought in 2012, north of Markham. Alex will call and let the Club members know if he can happen, by coincidence, to be in in the City on a Friday for a meeting at the Disraeli Club. An excellent organizer, Alex quite often books Friday afternoon client meetings in downtown Toronto. I met Alex in the late 1990s when the Bank was lobbying the provincial government over service fees. We talked fishing.

Pierre Poligrew toils daily as an investment consultant for Mercury Investments. His wife, Irene, works for the University of Toronto at an office in North York, close by the office of Mercury Investments. They have no children but are both involved in different community clubs. Pierre is a Big Brother and assistant Scout Master; Irene is a Big Sister. Pierre is bilingual and will often use his mother tongue to express fishing disasters. Other members of the Club have adopted a few of his lost-fish exclamations such as *sacrament, merde, and câline de bine.* Pierre will retire in 2018. Pierre and I met through our wives at a Tai Chi Christmas luncheon. I mentioned I had met Alexander Henderson and he too, was interested in going fishing sometime.

Frederick Smith, or Freddie, works at York Fine Cars where he is the Used Car Sales Manager. He and his wife Thelma bought acreage just south of the Holland Marsh, near Bradford, where Freddie pretends to be a gentleman farmer. Freddie is the oldest member of the Club, having passed the 70-year mark last year. They had adopted two young girls in 1999 – both girls are now studying at the University of Toronto. Freddie retired in 2016. Freddie came into our Bay Street office in 1997, looking for loan financing not only for the business but also for their customers. Freddie sold Fine Cars that came at considerable cost even when they were used – his customers needed loans. Somehow fishing and hunting came up in the conversation and I invited him for a beer after his four o'clock appointment. The Disraeli Tavern is just down the street from my office.

Jonathon 'John' Lucenti is a very successful salesperson. He makes a comfortable living with ReMax; indeed during the early 2000s he managed to earn enough to buy a very nice home in a posh area just off Avenue Road where he keeps his 'toys'. John is a confirmed bachelor although Cindy has been living with him for the past 12 years. John became a member of the Club when he was helping Alex find his new home and the conversation drifted to fishing. John may never retire but Cindy will have her pension due in 2020. John sold Freddie the Gentleman's Farm and Freddie set up a meeting of the five acquaintances to spend a day at the Sportsman's Show that spring.

Geraldine Scott became a member in 2005. She and her fishing partner, Amelia, own *Bites & Bucks* the tackle shop that the Club members frequent. 'Gerri' is about 50 years old; however your scribe will never try for an exact age. Geraldine is single and in conversations, one soon gets the idea that she will remain that way. She is an expert with a casting rod and knows how to sell a lure for any freshwater fish.

Amelia 'White Star' Restoule is the other partner in *Bites and Bucks*. She is a divorced single Mom with a twenty-two year old daughter, Karin, who has just finished Law School and is working downtown in an office on Dundas Street. Amelia is of Algonquin heritage and has a great background of native lore. As well as being an excellent fisher, she hunts and knows the business end of all the rifles and bows in the store. The two partners sold the store in 2013 so they could join the Bass Tournament Association fulltime.

Jason Garcia works as an MCTV news host. He has filmed a couple of documentaries of the BSBGSC that TV World nominated for awards. There is always one member of any organization who we can describe as 'inept' and Jason is our man. His antics will often bring a smile while we are on the water or even having a cool drink on a Friday evening at the Disraeli. Jason is single; unable it seems to 'hook' a permanent mate. He most often fishes with John but lately Amanda has taken him under her wing. Jason is 61 going on 16. We met Jason at the Sportsman's Show where he was doing a TV series on The Great Outdoors. He was practicing casting a dummy plug and Pierre offered to show him how to do it properly. He joined us at the Disraeli, which was only a block away from their offices.

Katherine Westcott is the Catering Manager at the prestigious Royal York Hotel. She is a widow whose wealthy husband (part of the Davies family) loved to fish from their cottage on Georgian Bay at Parry Sound. She dropped by the Disraeli one evening ten years ago, heard us talking about bass fishing, and sat down for a beer. Kate is of indeterminate age (my guess is 64 however I hope she doesn't see this). She wears her grey hair in a short cut that likely does not require those hairnets one sees on people working near food in the catering business. The wives of the men in the Club have all met Kate and have no reservations about any of us taking Kate as a fishing partner for a day on the water.

Amanda Young works as a Fashion Consultant for the Hudson's **Bay Company. Her husband George is not a sports person, being** more involved in local politics in Halton Hills where they live. For the past ten years we expected George to announce his candidacy for the Liberals – or the Conservatives. Amanda grew up in the country and she loves the outdoors; she especially likes camping, canoeing, photography, and fishing. She met Jason when he was doing a documentary on Ducks Unlimited and he invited her to a Club meeting. Duck hunters apparently love the HBC jackets. Amanda and Kate often fish as partners when we venture out in two or three boats. George will come to the Disraeli once in a while and join us in a beer before he and Amanda take the Go Train home to Halton Hills. Amanda is about 60???

Nickolas 'Nick' Papadopoulos is the part owner of the Disraeli Club tavern. The Disraeli Public House has been in existence since 1875 when Benjamin Disraeli held sway in the British Empire. The Disraeli's décor is rustic 19th century and a most inviting atmosphere for the Club. The ownership has passed through many hands, but the location of the pub in the downtown business section of Toronto assures it of steady patronage. Nick loves to work as a waiter while keeping his eye on the till. If we give him a call on a Friday afternoon, he will reserve seating for the BSBGSC. The same courtesy extends to other days of the week if we have an emergency meeting. Nick retired to Greece in 2015 – his nephew Sammy has filled in for him since.

Bill Haggarty, your scribe and original recording secretary for the BSBSC, worked in Client Services for the Royal Bank on Bay Street. My wife, Martha, was a Classics professor at U of T. We have home in Vaughan Township where our son and daughter occasionally visit when they are back in the country. I grew up near North Bay, a town about 320 kilometres north of Toronto, so they members often defer to me on woods lore and even fishing. I bluff a lot. Martha and I both retired last year.